THE DEVIL'S CHAMBER

NEIL COCKER

CLOUDBURN BOOKS

First published in 2021 by Cloudburn Books

Front cover design by Ivan Cakamura Cakic
(http://www.cakamuradesigns.com/)

ISBN 978-0-9928329-1-9

For Anna

Neil Cocker was born in Scotland in 1972 and lives in Luxembourg with his wife and two rescue dogs. His short stories have won prizes (Canongate 2001), been shortlisted for prizes (Bridport 2010), published in print (New Writing Scotland 21 & 23), and taught on a Scottish Literature course at Oldenburg University. His first novel Amsterdam Rampant was shortlisted for the Dundee International Book Prize.

Singapore
January 2019

PROLOGUE

The fire alarm wails – its pulsing siren is a needle in my brain.

Around me in the open-plan office, colleagues stand up, grumbling and stretching, grabbing their wallets and phones. This will mean all of us trooping down twelve flights of stairs and stepping out into the courtyard in the blistering Singapore sun, waiting while the appointed ones with clipboards tick us off their lists. But just as abruptly as it began, the alarm shuts off, and for a second I still hear its echo, feel that spike pushing through my eardrum.

"Just a test," someone says. The Singaporeans return to their desks quietly but from a few of the foreigners muttered swearwords are audible.

When I turn back to my screen, I see the email drop into my inbox. I only see the sender name and title but it's enough.

I vomit chilli crab onto my desk.

A hubbub explodes around me: shocked cries, a gasp, and a hooting laugh that can only be the Aussie IT guy. I feel another heave building in my guts so I run to the bathroom.

I get in a cubicle just in time to throw up second helpings. After a few more retches I spit out the last strands and slowly get my breath back, forearms resting on the toilet seat, staring down at the puddle of pink soup.

A knock on the door. "Miro? Are you OK?"

The voice sounds like Warren Chang, one of the data analysts.

"Miro? Do you need help?"

"It's OK, I just need a few minutes."

"I already called the cleaner, Miro. We are worried about you."

The big boss puking on his desk. This is great for my career, if I still have a career or any kind of future on this planet.

The bathroom door flops shut and I listen for any other signs of life. None.

I unlock the cubicle door and at the sink I wash my face and my forearms and hands. In the mirror my eyes are red. I don't want to read this email on my iPhone cowering in a toilet cubicle. I want to read it in the open, with a coffee and a view. Die with my boots on. I scrape a fleck of sick off my shirt collar with my fingernail, check again for any other spray-back, and then head out into the office.

The cleaner's trolley is parked by my desk and a few heads turn in my direction. I walk past reception to the other side of the office, see that the coffee area is mercifully empty, and grab an espresso and a bottle of water. The boardroom was booked for my meeting with the CEO of Malaysia's second largest snack company but he cancelled this morning so this is someplace I can go to be alone. I step into its air-conditioned silence and drag one of the chairs over to the window.

Twelve floors below, Singapore bustles. In the business district the skyscrapers wall the streets in, snaring the traffic in one-way loops. Pedestrians move in shoals along the narrow pavements, clutching umbrellas and takeaway lattes.

I down the espresso. Combined with adrenaline, the caffeine glow amps up my heart and I feel its techno-beat high in my chest. I take a slug of water, and another, washing away the puke taste. It is time to read the email.

I take out my iPhone, and there it is at the top of my inbox.

The sender: Neve Pinkerton

And the title, neatly summarising the thing that has kept me awake on hundreds of nights and kept me running around the world, always one step ahead of my biggest fear.

The title.

They Found Us

Edinburgh

1999-2000

CHAPTER 1

The alleyway was easy to miss: from a distance it looked like a disjointed gap between buildings, an architectural flaw in the grandeur of Charlotte Square. When I got closer, I saw it was wide enough to back a car into; perhaps in its eighteenth-century heyday it had been a servants' entrance, its slight curve keeping it out of the sightline of the gentlemen and ladies of the city. I stopped at the mouth of the alley, my new life within touching distance. *Here goes.* A deep breath and then I walked down past a row of dirty wheelie bins and stopped at the frosted glass door of City Archive 17.

The sweet stink of the rubbish hung heavy around me when I pushed the buzzer. I straightened my shoulders and tried to smile. I was dressed in my new navy-blue suit and carried the stiff leather briefcase that Auntie Sarah had insisted on buying for me.

The door opened and a stern middle-aged woman looked out at me. "You must be the new boy. How do you pronounce your name? My-ro or Mee-ro?"

"Mee-ro," I confirmed.

"It's a Polish name, correct?"

I nodded and opened my mouth to speak, but she had already turned and walked back into the building. I followed her along a corridor deep into the interior, until she stopped at the top of a stairway. "I'm Mary Cullen. I am in charge of Overspill. Were you given any information by Head Office regarding this placement?"

"No, they just told me to come here for nine o'clock."

She pursed her lips. "Three minutes late. Not the best of starts, Miro. Regarding your duties, you will be based at the office here to help us categorise records at Overspill. Any questions?" Her accent was Highland – soft but clipped, gentle but abrupt.

"What's Overspill?"

"Overspill is our name for City Archive 17. We temporarily store materials which cannot be housed elsewhere in the city – the overspill, so to speak. We ensure these materials are looked after properly until such a time when we can relocate them. Any other questions?"

Her severe expression suggested that I had used up my quota for the week, but I pushed on. "Where is the office you mentioned?"

She tilted her head. "It is at the bottom of the stairs. You will share it with Robert. He will keep you informed with regards to the way we do things."

She turned and clopped off down the beige corridor, made a military turn to the right and disappeared.

The stairs had once been a bright blue colour but time had worn the linoleum down, and in places chipboard peeked through. As I descended, each step thunked out a hollow drumbeat, so no doubt Robert would be aware of my impending arrival. At the bottom of the stairs a smell of damp paper hit me.

"Hi lad, come away in."

I followed the voice through the open door. Sitting at a large desk was a chubby man with fingerprint-smeared glasses. His hair was thin on top but long at the nape, greased back not with gel but, I suspected, his own natural oils. He was wearing an off-white shirt and a maroon Heart of Midlothian tie. "I'm Bob Hamilton, that's your new home over there."

On the other side of the room, situated between two shelves, was a smaller desk with a PC and monitor. The vast room stretched out for maybe thirty metres, a jumble of rolling stacks, boxes, shelving, filing cabinets, tea-chests, cardboard folders, stacked ring-binders, and metal cylinders.

"Welcome to hell," said Bob.

On my desk was a folder. Inside were two sheets of A4 paper – one had my log-in details and some notes on how to use the database, the other was headed 'City Archive 17 – Rules.' Twenty-three rules instructed me on my working hours, my lunch break, dress code, etiquette when dealing with members of the public, and other minor pedantry.

"That's Scary Mary's rules," said Bob. "Stick to them and you'll get on just fine."

I logged in to the computer. On the home page there was a list of the categories of records and artefacts. I clicked around for a couple of minutes – architect's plans, antique books, items of historical interest in the field of industry, public transport schedules 1965-84, development records for public parks…

I clicked around some more until I had explored each function. Compared to the university library database this was old school. The flashing green cursor was already burning my eyes.

"Bob?"

"Aye, son?"

"Do we not have any internet?"

"Any what?"

"Never mind. Listen, Bob. What am I supposed to do in this job?"

"Not sure," he said. "I've been trying to work it out for eighteen years. If you find out, do you promise to tell me?"

I sat there for an agonising few minutes, sweat trickling down my sides. I reorganised my desk, explored the drawers, and moved my pen, pencil, and notebook from the left corner of my desk over to the right. During this time Bob was reading his newspaper. I took off my suit jacket and hung it on a protruding nail.

Up above, the buzzer rang.

"Showtime!" said Bob. "Come on lad, what you waiting for?"

I followed him upstairs. At the front door stood a small bespectacled man in a green raincoat. "Good morning, sir," said Bob, his voice suddenly plummier.

"Aye hello there, I'm looking for the compendium of Edinburgh bridges. I was told it might be here."

"Certainly sir, why don't you come in. My colleague here will get you comfortable while I go and locate the record."

Bob led us through to a small waiting room with a kitchenette. I made a cup of tea for the visitor, who fumbled nervously with the pockets of his raincoat, then

I headed back downstairs. Bob was clattering around at the back of the room, working the rolling stacks back and forward. "Bridges, bridges, bridges…"

"How does it work? We just give him the book?"

"If we can find it. Take a note of his name, address and library card number. Update the database. He's got it for four weeks. Ah, here it is!"

Raincoat-man hadn't touched his tea when I got back upstairs with the compendium. His face lit up when I showed it to him. We completed a photocopied form and I walked him to the door.

Back downstairs, Bob was on his crossword.

"How often do we get visitors?"

"Oh, maybe three or four times per week. You're lucky to have so much excitement on your first day."

It was a quarter past ten. More than two hours until my lunch break. I stared at the wood grain on the desk and the familiar sensation of light-headedness rushed in on me – a feeling of teetering on the brink of an abyss, of peering into bottomless darkness. A void waiting for me.

I got up and walked through the rolling stacks and found a dead-end aisle cluttered on all sides with box-files and encyclopaedias, walling me in with paper and words. It would do. I gripped the metal shelf and rested my forehead on its hard ridge. Closed my eyes. Tried to wish the bad feelings away.

"You alright, lad?"

I let go of the shelf and raised my forehead. Composed myself. "I'm fine, thank you."

Bob had already gone.

Over that first week, I developed a survival strategy. In my briefcase I smuggled in a newspaper and a book, and would read whenever Bob did, which was most of the day. At lunchtime I walked, and sometimes I'd go for a pub lunch. Unlike Bob, I wouldn't have any alcohol. By the end of the first week I had worked out his schedule. I'd spotted him going into a pub round the corner, where I estimated by the pickled smell and frequency of post-lunch toilet trips that he had drunk perhaps three pints and a whisky, and then he would disappear for half an hour on his afternoon break and come back bright-eyed and in good humour. Scary Mary would only venture downstairs once a day, mainly to check her twenty-three rules were being adhered to. I always looked busy on the keyboard when she appeared, which seemed to please her. I suspected she found the computer terrifyingly modern.

Bob's prediction of four visitors per week was spot on in that first week. For the other three visitors, I was able to locate two of the requested records. Bob shrugged off the other one – "you win some, you lose some" – and apart from this, I probably worked for about two hours out of my contracted forty.

The light-headedness hadn't come back since that first day. The books and newspapers helped. It was all about keeping my mind busy, always skating around that terrible fact, never addressing it head on, staying a few steps ahead. It was more difficult in the evenings – I had bought a flat with the inheritance money, my own place at age twenty-two, but I had never lived on my own before. Closing the door on the world in the evening was something of a relief but watching videos or listening to music brought little solace. Instead I found myself in the same place every evening, sitting by the window looking down on the traffic on Lothian Road, the upper decks of double-decker buses illuminated and allowing me a brief view into other lives – families, lovers, solitary individuals just like me. By ten o'clock the traffic calmed down and the drunks took over – the yells of students, the raised voices of middle-aged couples, the occasional scuffle between the local homeless with dogs barking. I watched it all, invisible from my perch on the third floor of the building. There were rarely any signs of life in the buildings opposite, just lights going on and off, and on the rare clear nights if there was nothing happening on the street I would look up at the stars. Eventually by midnight the street was empty save for the occasional taxi, or lone drinker staggering along with a pizza or kebab.

That first weekend, I went out two nights in a row with my cousin Fergus. I knew other people in the city but meeting them would inevitably mean talking about the events of the summer. With Fergus, everything had already been said. The first night was a boozy blur, pub-hopping along the Cowgate and Grassmarket, and ended with me spilling chilli sauce down my navy-blue suit. On the Saturday I met Fergus and some of his colleagues in the Hebrides Bar, where a complicated drinking game involving a matchbox accelerated our drunkenness and at some point we crossed the road to the Mercado nightclub where I lost myself in dry ice and techno. I woke in shock on the Sunday morning with hazy memories and the sudden realisation that my mother was dead and I would never see her again. That Sunday I was crippled with grief for the umpteenth time and walked the city for several hours until I had tired myself out.

The weeks passed in a similar cycle, the routine never changing – Monday to Friday in the stifling boredom of Overspill, watching life go by in the evenings from my tenement window, Friday through Sunday in pubs and chip shops and walking the streets with a deadly hangover, followed by my loneliness, always a few steps behind.

Things changed one October Friday morning when the Overspill buzzer rang and Neve Pinkerton walked into my life.

CHAPTER 2

When the buzzer sounded Bob didn't even look up from his crossword. It was clear that all buzzer-answering activities had been delegated to the junior. I didn't mind, to be honest; anything that speeded up the time paralysis of Overspill was welcome.

Rain rattled the glass as I opened the door to find a young woman around my age standing with her jacket pulled up over her head. She bustled past, thanking me as she went. At first my eyes were drawn to the halo of raindrops she'd trailed on the floor, then to her cherry-red Doc Marten's, thrashed blue jeans, and donkey jacket. Her red hair was bedraggled, darkened in places by the rain, and she smoothed it back, as if preparing for a performance.

"Some weather. This is Overspill, right?" A soft Northern Irish accent.

"Yep. Do you want some paper towels?"

She tilted one arm towards the floor and more water dribbled onto the linoleum. "That might be an idea."

I brought her to the kitchenette and gave her a handful of the paper towels. She took off her jacket. I watched as she used the wad of paper to dry the worst of her soaking. She smoothed back her hair again, and caught me staring.

"So what are you after?" I smiled and hoped it came across as friendly.

"A cup of tea would be grand for starters."

I made two and we sat down around the ancient coffee table.

She leaned closer to me when she spoke. “I’m looking for materials on The Devil’s Chamber. Have you heard of it?”

“Nope. I’ll need to search our database. What is it? Mythology?”

She smiled at me, not breaking eye contact. “It’s an old Edinburgh legend. Might be in your folktales section. I’m doing research into it as part of my English literature degree.”

“Do you know the author, or any more info? It’ll help my search.”

She shook her head. “It’s all very obscure. I was told there was something here, that’s all.”

“Who told you, out of interest? They’re always keen to know how people find out about City Archive 17.”

She smiled. “This individual would not appreciate the attention.”

That killed the conversation. I abandoned my tea and told her I’d go see what I could find.

I went downstairs and found Bob asleep in his chair. His morning nap was vital training for his lunchtime drinking. I keyed “Devil’s Chamber” into the database and got no hits. I browsed through the rolling stack where we held a collection of legends and folktales, but there was nothing. For the first time in my brief Overspill career I was motivated to find something. Going back upstairs empty-handed would mean failure. At a loss, I shook Bob awake.

“The fuck?” he said.

"Bob, I need your help. Your sage advice."

I told him about the request. He harrumphed. "The Devil's Chamber. What rubbish. Never heard of it. Now leave me be."

I returned upstairs. She was standing by the window, peering up at the heavy skies.

"I'm sorry, we've been unable to find anything based on the search criteria. If you like, I can take your details and give you a call if something shows up?"

She rummaged in her bag and took out a pen and a scrap of paper. She wrote her name – NEVE – and a number underneath. "Call me as soon as you find anything. OK?"

"I will do. I'm Miro, by the way."

She gave me an impatient smile as if to underline that my name was irrelevant. "Thanks for the tea, and the paper towels."

I walked her to the door.

"Remember – as soon as you find anything, call me. Got it?"

"Got it."

She left, and the brief flare-up of interest faded back to familiar, endless, stultifying boredom.

For the remainder of the week I couldn't focus on anything. Neve's appearance had disturbed the stagnant waters of Overspill, reminding me how isolated I was from any source of excitement in my day job. To make matters worse, I'd formed a habit of dropping in to a nearby internet café after work, and there was an email string in my inbox from old university friends and friends of friends that seemed to have been designed specifically to fuck with my head. There were eighteen email addresses in the string, including my two closest friends and a former girlfriend. Needless to say, they were having the times of their lives. My two mates had flown to Sydney for a working holiday, and were pulling pints in dive bars, bed-hopping backpackers, and sleeping off hangovers on the beach. My ex had started an entry level lawyer's job in London and was in love with a semi-professional cyclist. One of the group wrote that "our real lives have now begun" and even Calamity Ken, the group's comedy punchbag, had just published a feature in a lads' magazine and was sleeping with the bassist from a minor Britpop band.

I imagined them as I stared at the Overspill clock, seeing their lives grow and expand in time-lapse, speeding along busy streets and blue skies as I sat motionless in my chair. Opposite me, Bob slept at his desk. *This is who you will become.*

One evening, hunched over the keyboard in the internet café, it clicked with me that only a select number of the eighteen email addresses had replied. I counted – seven in total, meaning that eleven on the mailing list, including me, were not perhaps having an amazing time of it. I still had twenty minutes of internet access left but logged off and went home. *Enough.*

I lay awake that night thinking about the future. Losing my mother had closed down one of my lives, but many surely lay ahead. As I dipped in and out of half-sleep, I understood that the future was not a series of straight highways, clearly signposted, accelerating towards glittering buildings on the horizon. No, the future was like a tumbledown port city, modern grid layout intersecting with a warren of backstreets and blind alleys, a city you had to get lost in first before you knew your way out of it.

I woke strangely refreshed the next day. When I turned up at work there was a stapled print-out on my keyboard. Mary had written on it in sharp pencil – *Please prioritise this activity above all others*. It was a memo from head office, explaining a new project to combine all the existing databases onto one platform. There were twenty-eight archives in the city and twenty-eight unconnected databases and centralisation was critical. It was especially necessary given the arrival of the Millennium and the possible impact of the Y2K bug – the new database would protect city archives from these potentially disastrous consequences. Each archive would have an appointed project manager and their duty was to ensure that any records not already in the system would need to be logged by 8th November in advance of data transfer to the new consolidated database.

Bob had made vague references to the records that had not yet been captured in the system – this scientific assessment involved him gesturing like a traffic policeman at an area of the back of the room he referred to as 'The Jungle' – and from my brief time at Overspill I feared that the records there were already a lost cause, an untamed slagheap of boxes and books.

But something in this sequence of events – Neve's visit, the email string, my weird half-sleep revelations, and now the project – woke the archivist in me. I read through the print-out again, feeling the gentle buzz of a puzzle to be solved, of uncharted territory needing to be mapped and perhaps hiding something precious. I remembered the scrap of paper in my desk drawer with Neve's phone number on it and smiled.

I'd first felt this buzz at age seventeen when I had gone through an obsessive phase of tracing my family history. There was not much to trace, with my grandfather's side disappearing into pre-war Poland and my mother's side mainly slipping out of sight into Northern Ireland, but nevertheless I got hooked on climbing the few branches I could find.

It was before my mother got sick, back when I was still at school, and she encouraged me to find out what I could and gave me some names and dates to get me started. So one November morning I got on the train to Edinburgh, nervous about going to the city, unsure what secrets I would uncover. New Register House was easy enough to find – hidden in plain sight just behind a burger joint on Princes Street, a proud Victorian building caged in by spiked railings. Once through the main door and past security, into that sanctum of quiet punctuated by the sound of rolling trolleys, the building had a feeling of mystery and magic that was instantly addictive. I took my allocated desk and looked up past row upon row of stacked records towards the skylight dome high above. Knowing that on those shelves, where porters shuffled around retrieving leather-bound books, the secrets of my family history were carefully stored – the scrawled signatures of my ancestors inked onto birth and marriage records, the only evidence they had once lived.

After three visits I had traced my paternal grandmother's side back to the mining villages of Fife, reams of documents which told of their one-room houses and early deaths, a black underground hell that had lasted at least a hundred and fifty years – or as far back into their misery as I could go. My mother's side was equally bleak – four generations in Dundee's jute mills, Highland and Irish names hinting at their even poorer origins. Those long, lunchless days in that library of life and death were the start of my love of archives. It felt like I had only discovered one tiny scrap of land in the continent of who I was – my father remained unknown, and the oppressive silence would yield no more. But the weight of knowledge locked up in this building, the hidden stories coded into dusty books, the dishevelled porters with their quiet nods and air of members of a secret society; all of this nudged me towards my calling in archives. My degree in library and information studies, which for long spells bored and frustrated me, was one step; Overspill would be another. I remembered last night's epiphany – I would need to get lost in the city before I knew the way out – and the buzz built up into elation. I hadn't felt such a wild happiness for years and hid behind a rolling stack until I got my composure back.

I spent the morning triangulating between shelves at the back of the room and returning to the computer to key in entries and see if they produced a result. By lunchtime I worked out that the uncharted zone of Overspill comprised the back left corner, some eight wobbly racks and approximately forty percent of the overall archive.

Energised, I worked out a system. I stuck numbered scraps of paper on each shelf, and started work on the first, lugging as many files as I could carry over to my desk and then logging their details. Eight fields of data to be filled for every record, always starting with location code – CA-17. City Archive 17. After the first hour I found myself slipping into a trance-like state, fingers rattling on the keyboard. The lunch break surprised me, and I ran out to grab a macaroni pie and ate it at my desk. I dived back into my work, Bob complaining that the noise of me typing was distracting him from his crossword. Compared to the normal glacial pace of the day at Overspill, I lost all sense of time and was surprised to find it was already five o'clock. By the end of the following day I had completed the first shelf – the outer rim of the Jungle. Nothing on the Devil's Chamber, but I took pleasure from knowing that the contents of this rack were captured for the first time ever. I refiled each record carefully, dusted the shelves, and enjoyed looking at the orderliness of the records. Bob seemed to be enjoying my new industriousness and was showing his appreciation by extending his lunch breaks by half an hour. Three days later, Mary came downstairs for an inspection, pressed her lips together to prevent a smile, and marched off again.

This sudden eruption of energy took over my waking hours and spilled out into my life outside of work. I couldn't sit still, attention jumping from one topic to another. It occurred to me that this restlessness could be symptomatic of a new stage in my grieving process. I had moved out of numbing shock and into a phase of physical chaos. I would find myself ravenously hungry at strange times of the day or night – sometimes only an hour after eating dinner I would leave the flat to pick up a takeaway curry or pizza, which I would then wolf down like a street urchin; I had also eaten my way through the massive tin of Overspill guest biscuits, which saw me on the sharp end of a rebuke from Scary Mary.

I was also unstoppably and embarrassingly horny. I was twenty-two years old and it felt like I had reverted to the throbbing seediness of a fifteen-year-old, constantly in heat but woefully short of any outlet. This was accompanied by a yearning for female contact that was becoming overwhelming. My weekend nights out had so far failed to expand my social circle beyond Fergus and his friends and acquaintances, and I was only really on drunken small-talk terms with them. On the walk to and from work I would watch couples pass and feel a stab of loneliness between my ribs.

The fantasy came to me one night in a dream. Neve. Rain-soaked, bustling into Overspill. The duffel coat. Telling me she needed to warm up. Opening the coat, naked underneath. Cold skin, beaded with raindrops, her pulling me close. And me, lying there, heart beating crazy fast, done in seconds.

One morning I woke and recreated this scenario for the umpteenth time, and knew I had to find a solution soon or I would go crazy.

After two weeks working on the project, I had catalogued and reorganised around a quarter of The Jungle. When he was awake, Bob reprimanded me for making too much noise when rolling the stacks back and forward, or rearranging boxes. I kept the scrap of paper with Neve's scrawled number in my desk drawer, but the truth was I had already written it down in three other places just in case I lost the original. I had thought about phoning her despite my lack of success with the Devil's Chamber search but remembered her withering look when I'd told her my name.

When Bob got back from the pub one afternoon, even later than usual, I asked him again if he'd ever heard of the Devil's Chamber.

"Nah." He had a cheeky grin and his face was flushed bright red. I realised that his advanced state of inebriation was because Scary Mary had taken a day of holiday to visit her sister in Inverness, and he had been having a few extra drinks to wish her well on her journey.

"Miro, do you want to see something special?" He stood over me, grinning. Mixed in to his cheap aftershave smell was the sharp waft of whisky fumes.

"Not really."

"Watch this," he said, and wandered over to the shelves behind his desk. I heard him clattering around with the stepladder and then the creak of him climbing one step at a time. His raised voice bellowed out from behind a high shelf. "I shall delve into the secrets of Overspill… to reveal… illicit photographs taken backstage… at the 1977 Portobello theatre production… of Fiddler on the Roof…"

There was a strange pause, then a single, yelled word – "fuck!" – followed by a splintering crash. I ran across the room to find Bob crumpled on the ground with the stepladder on top of him, his leg bent sideways underneath him. For a moment a wave of nausea made my eyes prickle with dark spots, then Bob's moaning brought me back to earth.

I dialled 999, and within fifteen minutes I was escorting the paramedics down the Overspill stairs to where Bob lay waiting, by now mournfully silent. They strapped him into the stretcher and as they hoisted him up his eyes met mine. For the first time I saw loneliness and fear looking back at me, instead of the usual world-weary amusement.

"Is there someone I should phone?"

He shook his head.

The paramedics told me they were going to the Royal Infirmary, and I watched as they loaded Bob into the ambulance. The blue lights flickered on and they slowly pulled away.

I was alone. In charge of Overspill.

I closed the door behind me and listened to the silence. I walked past the stairs to Overspill and continued along the corridor, past the toilet to Scary Mary's office. I tried the door, but it was locked. I had never been upstairs, so I climbed the creaking steps and wandered the upper corridor, which had several doors on either side – all locked. A sudden noise startled me, but it was only rain pounding on the skylight window overhead. I returned downstairs to the basement and back to my desk. A lingering whiff of Bob's aftershave still tainted the air.

I locked up Overspill at 5pm and headed straight to Waterstone's, where I bought a crossword book. On my walk across the city I stopped at a confectioner's in the

Cowgate to pick up some kola kubes, and an off-licence on Forrest Road for a half bottle of Johnnie Black. Before getting to the hospital I organised my carrier bag so that the whisky was hidden between the sweets and the book.

Bob was in a shared room with four others, his left leg encased in plaster. When he saw me he struggled to sit upright. “Alright, lad.”

I always suspected he called me lad because he couldn’t remember my name.

“Bad break?”

He nodded for me to sit down by the bed. “Broken in two places. Out of action for four to six weeks.”

“Do you mean I’ll need to cope with the crowds at Overspill on my own?”

He almost smiled but seemed to decide against it. “Afraid so. What’s in the bag?”

I showed him.

His voice dropped to a whisper. “Pull the curtain.”

He asked me to help him rearrange his pillows, and soon he was all set up. Crossword book in front of him, sweets next to his left hand and whisky his right. He put a kola kube in his mouth and unscrewed the whisky. “You’re a lifesaver, lad.”

“Is there anything I can do, Bob? You need me to tell anyone?” I winced, realising it was the second time I’d asked that question, and I already knew the answer.

Bob took a mouthful of the Johnnie Black. “Nah. I lost touch with my family. Wife left me ten years ago. There’s a spider plant in my living-room but I’ve not watered it for a few weeks so I suppose it won’t miss me much.”

"What about at the pub?"

His face brightened. "Aye, good point. Maybe if you just drop in and let them know I won't be around for a few weeks."

We sat there for a couple of minutes in silence. He flicked through the crossword book and the only noise was the clack of the hard-boiled sweets on his teeth and the glug of the whisky.

"Well Bob, I think I'll head off if that's OK."

"Aye, lad." His eyes were fixed on a jumbo crossword.

I got up to leave, and just as I was parting the blue curtain I heard a word that surprised me.

"Miro."

I froze.

"Come back here a sec."

I sat down on the chair again. He leaned across, so close I saw for the first time the pinhole in his left ear, a relic of an earring in a past life.

"The Devil's Chamber. The girl was right. We have materials."

"Really?"

He nodded. "Your predecessor was a nice guy. Auld Harry Robertson. He warned me off it when I found the box, said there was nothing but bad luck ever came from the file."

"Aye? What did he mean by that?"

"Ach... old wives' tales. But archivist's code of honour and all that, you know? I respected his opinion."

"Where are the materials?"

Bob sighed. "Promise me you won't get into trouble?"

"Promise."

"So, you know the shelf in the Jungle that touches the back wall? Better men than you and I have entered its dark heart and failed to return. Anyway, on the third or fourth rack there's a shelf with golf archives – landscape plans for the development of courses, all the planning approvals, reams and stacks of the stuff. In the middle shelf, look behind all the golf shite – you'll find a boxfile. Beige cardboard, a number scribbled on it. 467, or 476, I forget. It's all in there. I only looked once. Photocopies of pages from books, handwritten notes."

"What is it, though? The Devil's Chamber?"

Bob screwed the cap back on his whisky. "Don't really know. I heard a story about it once, claiming it was some sort of secret underground room. There would have been hundreds of those in Edinburgh, that's the thing – easy to build up a legend out of something like that. Look at Mary King's Close and all those ghost tours, all you need is something underground and you can create a nice wee business."

"Thanks Bob, I'll check it out."

I got back to the flat just as Thursday night was warming up, squads of students barrelling along Lothian Road with cheap drink in their crosshairs. I took my jacket off, made myself a cup of tea, and got comfortable on the sofa. Neve would probably be out, but I was ready to make the call.

I counted eight rings and was ready to hang up when a female voice answered. "Hello?"

"Hi, I'm looking for Neve."

There was an agonising pause, and I had the feeling that she was composing herself, as if she'd just run up the stairs or out of the shower. "Speaking."

"Hi, Neve. It's Miro." I let the name hang there, see if she remembered.

"From Overspill?"

She could probably hear me grinning. "Yep."

"Did you find something?"

This time I let her wait. After a few seconds: "Yep."

"Cool! When can I have it?"

"Well, it's not actually at Overspill but at another location. Maybe we can get together on Saturday and I'll bring it with me?"

"OK. Where shall we meet?"

I needed somewhere quiet, but not my flat. "You know the Holyrood Tavern? See you there at three o'clock?"

"Fine."

"See you then!"

She hung up. I hoped I hadn't sounded over-enthusiastic with my sign-off. But this was a great development, so I opened the fridge and took out a can of Stella. Things were looking up. I imagined myself on Saturday, turning up with the bundle of papers and spending three hours with Neve, going through the archive page by page and impressing her with what I'd found. Her asking me to help her carry the papers back to her place. A small room with a double mattress on the floor and a single lamp casting shadows. A bottle of wine opened, sitting on the mattress because there were no chairs, an admission of loneliness…

There was a quiet knock at the door. I thought I'd imagined it, then the knock came again, a little louder.

I'd lived there for eight weeks and nobody had ever knocked on my door except for food delivery drivers.

In the corridor stood a female slightly older than me. Curly brown hair, short, plump, and kind of pretty.

"Hi, I'm your neighbour. Kim!" She announced. She almost bounced when she said her name and I tried my hardest to smile. I introduced myself and we shook hands. Her hand was small, limp, and warm.

"I need your help if that's OK!" Again, the almost-bounce. She beckoned me towards her door and I followed. In the middle of her living-room was a half-assembled IKEA bookcase. "I'm too small to do this properly!"

For the next hour I worked through the instructions step by step. She talked throughout, at me and over me. I learned that she was from Dingwall, had studied Accountancy in Newcastle, now worked in financial services, had been in the flat for two years already, missed having a cat, didn't like pizza or any type of Italian food, had one brother and one sister who she liked equally, went to kick-boxing on a Tuesday, was going to New York next spring, had been to Paris once but thought it was over-rated, and liked to read the works of Armistead Maupin. To her credit, she also asked me more questions about my life than Mary and Bob had in six weeks at Overspill, so in the end I was grateful for the contact. As I moved the bookcase into position against the far wall, she asked me what I was doing for Christmas.

It hit me at that exact moment that I wouldn't be in my childhood home for Christmas. And that my mother wouldn't be there. To my shock and embarrassment, I started crying.

Kim switched immediately into crisis management mode, leading me by the hand to the sofa, making me tea, asking me to talk about it, to please just talk about it. I sat there, frozen.

"What's wrong?" she said.

"My mother." I shrugged. It was the first time I had mentioned her to anyone in Edinburgh.

"What happened?"

"She died in the summer."

"Do you have anyone else?"

I spoke in staccato sentences. "Yes. I have an aunt and uncle, grandparents, two cousins. They all live in my hometown. They are my family."

"What about your dad?" Kim's eyes were full of tears.

"I don't know. Left when I was a baby. The only thing he gave me was my name. I'm named after my grandfather. A Polish paratrooper."

"What's your full name?"

"Miroslaw Kubik."

She laughed. "Sorry. It's a cool name."

I drank my tea, and we both sat in silence for the first time since I'd been kidnapped from my flat. My compulsion to talk had faded, and already I had the uncomfortable feeling that I'd revealed too much.

"So what will you do for Christmas?"

Back to the question that triggered it all.

"I'll go up the coast, up to Fife. Big family Christmas. After five days with that mob I'll be ready for some peace and quiet again."

Kim smiled.

I apologised and said I'd better get back. She offered me more tea, or a beer or wine, but I declined, told her I'd had enough excitement for one evening. This made her laugh a bit too much. She asked if I'd like to do something again sometime, maybe come around for dinner or something, and I said sure, I'd like that. It was only when she gave me a farewell hug, squashing me tight against her breasts, that I realised that maybe I now had two dates in my immediate future rather than just one.

CHAPTER 3

The next morning I got into Overspill at eight-thirty, half an hour earlier than normal. The building was utterly still, all mine for another day. Scary Mary would be back on Monday so this was my best chance to get to work.

I located the golf archives without any problems and hauled out stacks of paper, hardback journals, and magazines. Just as Bob had promised, nestled snugly in the alcove between two adjoining shelves sat a beige boxfile. I lifted it out carefully, arms straining from the weight. Bob had a good memory, despite the booze – scrawled on the front was the number 467. I took it over to my desk and untied the knot of coarse string looped through the eyelets on the side, loosened the reinforced cardboard cover, and flipped it open.

Inside, reams of loose-leaf paper, jumbled together in one hefty block. I lifted the whole stack out and broke it down into blocks of paper, lining them up in a row across the desk. I wanted to first see if there was any particular order to the records, or if it was a jumble of non-related paperwork. Some of the paper was browned and hand-written, other sheaves were photocopied from books. It occurred to me for the first time that Neve had never once indicated what exactly she was looking for. The photocopier would surely chew up all these mismatched pieces of paper if I put them in the feeder tray, so I would need to copy in small batches, or one page at a time. I'd be here all weekend. I realised there was nothing else for it but to browse through the pile, speed-read sections, and try to locate juicy bits.

I worked all morning, right through lunch, and on into the afternoon. It was only the hunger pangs at around three o'clock that interrupted me from my reverie. I grabbed my jacket, locked up Overspill and headed out into the city to pick up a bite to eat. As I walked through the rain I recapped what I knew so far from my reading.

Despite the many sources and conflicting accounts, one thing seemed to be agreed on: the Devil's Chamber was an elaborate underground room in central Edinburgh that was built sometime in the early 1800s. Beyond this, opinions varied wildly. Photocopies from a nineteenth-century book called 'Edinburgh Folk Tales' claimed that the chamber hosted a Hellfire Club, a gathering of gentlemen 'intent on misdeeds.' Reading between the lines these gatherings seemed to involve debauched drinking, gambling, pagan fancy dress, and fornication with 'procured street-walkers.' The photocopies ran out just as things were getting interesting.

Next up, another ream of photocopies, this time from a pot-boiler novel which I guessed had been written in the 1930s. Three and a half chapters starting at page 84, starring a young gentleman by the name of Larius Carruthers who is invited by his university professor to a secret society gathering. He is led by the prof to a townhouse in Edinburgh's new town, and after quaffing a mysterious spiced liquid follows the prof to a cupboard and a staircase which takes them deep underground to a vault where a crowd of shadowy individuals in Nazi-esque uniforms are sacrificing a deer on an altar. Larius gets his forehead daubed with blood from the sacrifice and takes part in a rambling conversation about the supremacy of the northern European race. At this point a ghost or hologram appears in the chamber causing the crowd to break into song, and then thankfully the photocopies ran out.

There were two more sets of photocopies, jumbled out of order, both from folk histories. The first claimed the chamber was a naturally formed cave under Edinburgh Castle in which the Stuart kings were taken to drink from an ancient spring said to have strength-giving properties; the second claimed the chamber had been built under Edinburgh old town as a tomb for witches, and had then later become a meeting place for a secret masonic fraternity.

The most difficult to decipher was a thick sheaf of yellowed paper, written on in a tiny, spidery scrawl. It seemed to be somewhere between a letter and a confession, lamenting some sort of loss in quasi-religious language, and then halfway through seemed to change again into a poem. My eyes tired of its scribble and I gave up halfway through.

The rest of the material that I managed to work through was loose scraps which offered glimpses but little else – a photocopy of a newspaper article from 1923, claiming 'trolls and bogles' hid in the chamber beneath 'the unwitting footfall of pedestrians' on Princes Street; a sketch of the chamber, looking not unlike an Edwardian public toilet with black and white tiling and strange troughs; cuttings from newspapers, letters, pages torn from books. It was overwhelming, and I had little idea of what to take to Neve.

I bought fish and chips drenched in brown sauce at the Rose Street Fry and ate them huddled in a doorway. The answer would come to me – I was still only halfway through the boxfile. Rain leaked onto the greaseproof paper of my chip poke, and by the time I reached the final scraps it had disintegrated into an oily rag. I licked the salt and sauce off my fingers, flipped my jacket collar up, and plunged back out into the cloudburst.

I worked for another four hours straight through, long past Overspill's traditional closing time, oblivious to anything except for the stack of paper in front of me. In those dreamlike hours I forgot that my mother was gone; I forgot that I was doing this to get closer to a girl, I forgot that I was in Edinburgh, I forgot that I lived in the flat in Lothian House. All of that had gone.

And by eight o'clock, just as tiredness was creeping in and reminding me of the world outside my basement walls, I photocopied the pages that most quickened my heart, replaced everything into the boxfile as I had found it, and secreted it back on the shelf behind the golf records. Tomorrow I would show my treasure to Neve.

CHAPTER 4

On the walk across Edinburgh I was already starting to regret my choice of venue for the big date. The Holyrood Tavern was a pub I liked very much but it would certainly send out mixed messages. Not far off the tourist trek of the Royal Mile, it was popular with a diverse range of drinkers – real ale aficionados, goths, career alcoholics, and transvestites. This eclectic mix was enabled by the landlord, who dressed in a kilt, sported painted nails and eye shadow, and would upbraid any misbehavers with the industrial language of a bricklayer. The jukebox hosted an epic mix of alternative and classic rock, everything from the Rolling Stones through to The Pogues and Dinosaur Jr. The pub was spacious, with plenty of room for standing at the bar, but also had tables pushed into nooks and crannies, some of them with ancient sofas burst at the seams, the kind that looked like they had been dragged into the bar under cover of darkness on bin day. The whole ensemble was supported by an excellent range of ales and whiskies, and I'd spent a few happy evenings here with Fergus, chatting to each other and random punters (sometimes in drag). Somehow the pub's ramshackle craziness worked, but it was a far cry from the city's more sophisticated drinking holes.

I pushed my way in through the heavy doors, five minutes to three, and there she was, standing at the bar.

"Miro," she said, and smiled.

My heart flipped.

"Neve," I said, my voice cracking halfway through. Her eye contact slipped away to my shoulder bag. "What are you drinking?"

"Oh, I just ordered. Let me get this."

The kilted landlord nodded at me, long grey hair and eyeliner. I asked for a pint of Deuchars and he yanked the pump, hairy wrist and bangle and purple nail polish.

"So you have something impressive for me?" Her fingers brushed my upper arm, and a charge of excitement bristled from my head to my stomach and back again.

"Let's get a seat and I'll show you."

She led the way, and chose the window table in the alcove. I tried to engage her in some pleasantries but she interrupted. "So what have you got, Miro?"

I took a mouthful of pale ale and unclipped my bag. I had hoped for a bit more time before the big reveal, but now we were already rushing to the finishing line. As I slid out the ream of photocopies I had the feeling of losing control, of giving away too much.

"Cool." She snatched up the papers and began reading. I drank more of my pint. A punter wandered over to the jukebox, and a moment later Portishead seeped out the speakers, warbling their uneasiness around the pub. Neve shook her head impatiently and flicked forward through the pile, then resumed reading on the first page. By the time I was halfway through my pint she made a little noise of approval, then a few seconds later, gasped a little.

"What is it?"

She didn't hear me – or ignored me.

I finished my pint and asked her if she wanted another. Without lifting her eyes from the documents she nodded and pointed at her empty wine glass.

At the bar I took some time to compose myself. Clearly I was just the messenger at the moment. I had to do something to get her attention. Thankfully I hadn't given her the whole boxfile, but I'd probably handed over all the best cards. She didn't know that though. I could reveal this later – the fact that I still had at my disposal twenty times the documents I had given her. I was not just the messenger – I was the message. I smiled at myself in the bar mirror.

When I turned the corner back into the alcove someone was sitting in my seat.

He was hunched over the table, whispering to her. I could already see from the angle he was leaning in that he knew her well; she was laughing. He wore an army surplus jacket, and as I got nearer, I could see it was faded and threadbare in places, the garb of a street-sleeper, but this was offset by his nape-length brown hair, curly and tousled and held in place with a smear of gel. Neve broke off their conversation when she sensed me approaching and he stopped talking and turned around.

He stood up and shook my hand too firmly, squeezing my fingers together. "Miro, right? I'm Danny Gunn. It's great you found this stuff about the Chamber."

Neve passed Danny a few sheets of paper and he started reading too. I sat there in silence, watching the pair of them. Danny had brought a smell into the pub with him; of tents, of dampness and woodsmoke, underlaid with tobacco. He still hadn't removed his army surplus jacket, and up close I could see patches of dark green, outlines of removed badges. I continued my analysis of the newcomer while they read and occasionally pointed to areas of text. His jeans were ripped at the knee and he wore lightweight hiking boots; his fingernails were bitten, and a ragged scar disfigured the back of his right hand. He caught me staring at the scar and winked at me.

"This isn't all the papers you have, right? There are more, aren't there?"

I paused for a second too long and he smiled. "Thought so. Let me get this round."

I still had half a pint but I didn't object. I needed some time to work this all out. When he was at the bar I nodded to the photocopies stacked on the pub table.

"So you lied to me?"

"What's that?" Neve's face was colouring a darker shade of pink.

"When you came to Overspill you said you were researching the Devil's Chamber as part of your English degree."

Neve wiped the condensation off her wine glass. "Ah, you got me there, sure." Her accent now more Northern Irish, like she'd held that back too.

"So what's it all about, Neve?"

She smiled. "It's a long story. Another time, maybe."

Danny returned with the drinks and derailed the conversation with talk of his climbing exploits. He finally took off the army surplus jacket and was only wearing a washed-out black t-shirt underneath, revealing the corded and rippled muscle of his arms. As he talked he bobbed on his chair like a boxer, unable to stay still, sparring at the table to ensure the conversation never strayed outside of reaching distance.

As he came to the end of a rambling story about being stuck in a snowstorm on Ben Vorlich, I jumped in. "So how do you two know each other?"

"Death," said Neve.

Danny laughed. "Aye, that's true."

Neve leaned across the table towards me. "We're both temps at Scottish Standard. Settling claims when the policy owner passes on to the big tenement in the sky."

"Boring as fuck," said Danny.

"Every day is just a stack of letters and then making phone-calls to the next of kin. Doing the paperwork of the reaper. *I'm so sorry for your loss Mrs McCallum, now if you could just fill in the form that we sent you…*"

Scottish Standard was one of the massive pension firms headquartered in Edinburgh. Fergus worked there, but this was no co-incidence. About ten thousand people in Edinburgh worked for Scottish Standard across its multiple offices. I'd heard dozens of stories from Fergus and his colleagues on those drunken nights out. The blandness of the work, the heavy drinking culture, the departments where nothing got done, the whispers about who was shagging who.

"We both started on the same day," said Neve. "Shoved in a corner next to a stack of filing cabinets.

Four years of university for a job I could have done aged seventeen."

Danny got up to pee, and I waited until he was out of earshot before speaking.

"I'm tired of this. It wasn't easy to get all this fucking stuff on the Devil's Chamber. I'm heading off." I got to my feet.

She reached over and placed her hand on my wrist. "Stay. It's my round. We've not been straight with you. I'll tell you a bit more."

Danny returned from the toilet and began an elaborate cigarette rolling procedure: deftly pinching the rolling paper, flattening it, sprinkling tobacco with a chef's finesse, wetting the paper edges with a sliver of tongue and crimping the cylinder between fingers and thumbs, all the time ensuring that his hands and elbows were in the centre of the table just a little too close to everyone's drinks, a couple of centimetres into everyone's personal space, the whole process just a smidgeon too theatrical. Neve came back from the bar with a tray – another round of drinks, plus glasses of scotch.

"I got some Oban chasers," she said.

"Niiiice," said Danny. He sparked up his skinny cigarette and blew a puff of smoke away from us.

We clinked glasses.

"To Miro," said Neve. "For being patient with us."

"Miro," said Danny, swallowing his whisky in one gulp. "What kind of name is that anyway?"

"Polish. My grandpa was Polish."

"Polish Free Army?"

"Aye, he was a paratrooper. Stayed on after the war ended. He died before I was born."

Neve was looking at me, a curious light in her eyes. "Miroslaw Kubik," she said.

I was taken aback – at no time had I given her my full name.

"I know lots about you," she said, raising her glass.

I sipped the Oban and let its spicy fire leak over my tongue. I made eye contact with Neve and held it until she looked away.

"The Devil's Chamber?" I said.

Danny grinned. Drunkenness glinted in his eyes. "Boring as fuck, working in an office. We need to do something for kicks, right?"

Neve tilted her whisky glass, examining the golden liquid. "The thing is, Miro, there is so much in the world that we don't know about. We all live the nine-to-five, we're spoon-fed news and popular culture, encouraged to ignore all the sketchy things that have no answers. That's the life the establishment wants us to lead. But there's so much we don't know about. All around us."

"Meaning…?"

She looked at me, this time holding eye contact unwaveringly. "Normal life is like tunnel vision. You only see what you're instructed to see. We explore the blind spots."

"This is starting to sound a bit X-Files."

"Sometimes folktales and legends are simply just that – old wives' tales. But sometimes they grow out of some other truth, spin off in different directions. We're just trying to get to the truth, that's all."

Danny cut in. "It's like pub stories. Chinese whispers. Stories grow arms and legs, go down rabbit holes."

"What you gave us, these papers..." Neve patted the photocopies. "They're really important. They may not seem to mean much on a first read, but maybe once we've gone through them a few times we'll find what we're looking for."

"From what I read it's very contradictory. A legend that nobody can agree on."

Neve nodded. "That's the problem – it's slippery. It's not like other legends, where eighty percent of the story remains the same and twenty percent shape-shifts. The Devil's Chamber is like the hydra – chop off one head and two grow back in its place."

"So what exactly are you looking for?"

Neve took a drink of the whisky. I sensed that Danny was staring at her, warning her off saying any more. "The truth."

I tipped back my whisky and waited for the glow. Rain hammered the pub window. I took a mouthful of pale ale. This had been an unusual afternoon. The booze buzz was building momentum and I didn't want to go home just yet, but there was a feeling of a moment passing.

Danny picked up his cigarette papers. "Okay dudes. I got to scoot. Need to see a man about a dog."

He slung his jacket on and rubbed a porthole in the steamed-up window. "Christ, it's chucking it down. Wish me luck." He walked off without saying goodbye – we heard the door open and flop shut, and there he was outside, walking past the rain-blurred window.

"Want another one?" I tapped my empty glass.

"I'd better not," said Neve. "Got a date."

Those words – a knife to the guts. "What is it you're really looking for?"

She was putting her jacket on, and I started doing the same, ready to follow her until I got an answer. "It's complicated," she said. "I'll borrow the papers if that's okay."

I followed her out into the rain. The Edinburgh afternoon was darkening, rainclouds pressing down on the city. The streetlights clicked on as we reached the junction and the pedestrian crossing. Her hair was already wet. Traffic rumbled past, and she said something to me, but it was lost in the noise and splash.

"What?"

She leaned in close until her damp cheek touched mine, her voice loud in my ear. "A map. We're looking for a map."

CHAPTER 5

I watched Neve cross the road, stooping into the heavy rain. The pedestrian crossing changed back to red, and I remained where I was, gazing at her as she disappeared from sight. When the crossing beeped again I walked towards the Cowgate.

I didn't mind the rain – it was a reason to tilt my head downwards, to scowl at passers-by, a shield from the world. I took the long way home, cutting up George IV Bridge, then up the Royal Mile and over the crest of the city. My jeans were soaked and my hair a tangled mess. I reached Lothian House and just as I ducked into the lobby I heard a voice behind me.

"Miro!" It was Kim, holding a transparent umbrella beaded in raindrops.

"How's it going?"

She nodded towards outside. "Shit day. Just split up with my boyfriend. You?"

I rubbed a hand back over my hair, squeezing out a trickle of rain. "Oh, a weird day for me too."

"Fancy a drink?"

"I already had a few."

"Oh me too, but I've got room for a few more."

We went to the nearest pub to the flats, a tacky joint with flashing fruit machines and blaring music.

"Darren's such a dick." She stirred her G&T violently with the swizzle-stick. "Out with his rugby pals, drinking and puking, oh they're all the life and soul of the party but you can't get any meaningful conversation out of them, not one word. So he's out with them most nights, and then just turns up at my place expecting sex and a sandwich. Do I look like a hooker to you?"

I assured her that she did not.

It all came out, how she'd been with Darren for two years on and off, squabbling all the time but there was something comfortable about it, like shoes that didn't originally fit but after months of blisters they had stretched into a shape that was sort of workable. But she wasn't going to put up with it anymore, life now wasn't like being at university where you could just go drinking all weekend every weekend, there came a time when everybody had to grow up and act their age, Darren had to realise that he couldn't rely on his private school network for career progress.

She stopped, breathless. "Let's do shots."

I got two cherry vodkas, another G&T, and a pint of Caley.

We downed the shots and she re-launched her monologue. "I'm twenty-six, Miro. No spring chicken. He has to fucking realise that a woman needs more than nights out with his moronic friends, more than CDs for my birthday presents, more than date nights at the cinema watching his fucking car chase and explosion films, more than his two-minute wonder missionary position idea of hot loving…"

From where I was sitting I could see out onto the street, the taxis swishing by in the rain, the buses grinding past with their dirty maroon livery, the city's young walking along with smiling faces, waking up to Saturday night and its endless possibilities. I thought about Neve, probably heading out for her date now. Maybe it was the cherry vodka but I didn't feel so heart-sore about it. Today had been a riot. I had a gut feeling that I would be together with Neve. There was just a feeling, a kernel of something inside, that destiny would intervene.

"God, I'm talking so much, it's just so rude of me. What about you, Miro? Do you have a girlfriend?"

I laughed. Female intuition. "Nope."

"What about in the past? Come on, tell me all your secrets…"

She leaned in close, arcing her eyebrows theatrically, and I laughed again.

"Nobody at the moment."

"But you have some good stories, right?"

I was in a good mood. Like the world had been corrected somehow, however temporarily, and the pieces were falling into place. So I told her about Hannah.

When I was a teenager I grew tall early, and managed to avoid most of the awkwardness that goes with it. My pale skin combined with a shaggy crow-black hairstyle gave me a moody indie guitarist look. There was a girl I'd known since I was six years old – Hannah Haldane – who throughout my childhood had alternately been a Sunday school annoyance, a bossy Mary in the nativity play, a buddy in the evenings at the local library, the tomboy who had all the football stickers I was missing, someone to hunt crabs with in rockpools in the endless grey summers, someone to ignore aged eleven through to fifteen, and then suddenly, explosively, the most desirable girl I had ever encountered.

"She sounds cool," said Kim, slurping her G&T up through a pink straw.

We were a good match at age sixteen – both tall, quiet, a bit geeky, obsessed with the same music and movies, mirror images of each other. Together we ticked off the rites of passage. Alcohol: smuggled out of the parental home and consumed in smuggler's coves, rainspray and waves thundering on the beach. Dope: smoked at the park bandstand, stars sprinkled above us on the black sky. Sex: graduating fumble-by-fumble until we were unbelievably entwined in her family's abandoned spare room, wrapped in a sheet behind a bookcase, knocking over lamps and sport trophies and magazine stacks with flailing limbs, like drunken snow angels creating a space in the debris that we would use umpteen times until one grim afternoon when Hannah's mother went on a cleaning binge and found a dried-out condom.

School ended with a party on the beach, the summer sea-fog obscuring the view onto the horizon. Over the summer I worked in a local hotel kitchen and broke up messily with Hannah – a misinterpreted comment from me about the prettiness of one of her friends led to a heated argument about what would happen when we went away to university – *was this really love or just some temporary madness?* – the sudden pressure causing a hairline crack that splintered into others until the thin ice under our feet gave way. Weeks of heartache, underlaid with the stink of dishwasher disinfectant and the swill bin.

"Oh, that's so tragic. Where is she now?"

I shrugged. "Last I heard she was in London."

"That was a long time ago, Miro. How about your more recent romances?"

I shifted in my seat. "Not much to talk about." My mother's illness had dominated the last three years. I'd had the occasional entanglement at university and gave Kim a brief rundown. A four-month understanding with a German exchange student – every time we met when we were out drinking, we would go home together. Sweet girl, good fun, no future. A startling flare of a relationship with a Glaswegian called Suzie Kay – love declared after three weeks, retracted soon after, four months of fucking and fighting, and after we split and the lava hardened, a friendship developing that saw us hang around platonically for two years (she was the one now in love with the semi-professional cyclist in London). And finally, in the interests of full disclosure, a one-night stand with a primary school teacher as my mother's illness accelerated, an urgent and dislocating night in a flat on Rose Street with no curtains, screwing three times in different positions in full view of the brightly-lit windows opposite, a hunger in each other that was not discussed but only acted on, a few hours where our bodies fitted perfectly but when the perfect storm was over I snuck out of her place and took the short walk home to shower off our mingled sweat and collapse into my own bed and wake up four hours later as if nothing had ever happened.

"It's strange to meet a guy who's actually honest," said Kim.

The fruit machines seemed to be flashing more frantically and the passing headlights were searching the corners of my vision. Ah, I thought; I'm drunk. Kim lurched over and kissed me. Our tongues battled. We left the pub in a rush – the rain had stopped and the fresh air injected energy; I grabbed her hand and tugged her across the road, and within two minutes we were in my flat, performing a clumsy waltz towards the bedroom.

Naked, our images reflected in the wall-length wardrobe mirror, we fucked in a hurry, her legs tight around me. She bit my lip, clawed at the back of my head, dragged her sharp nails up my back. I came, and lay there trapped in her embrace.

I must have fallen asleep, because when I opened my eyes again she was gone.

CHAPTER 6

When I left to go to work on Monday morning, the door to Kim's flat opened and a short, burly man stepped out. Darren. I turned my key slower than usual, hoping that he would head off down the corridor, but instead he fumbled with his jacket zip, and I had no option but to walk past him.

He looked at me with expressionless eyes and nodded. "Alright."

"Alright."

I walked on ahead and could hear his footsteps close behind.

I had spent Sunday morning jittery with dread, aware of vague noises next door – voices, furniture moving, a hairdryer. To intensify my anxiety, my grandparents and aunt and uncle were due at noon, the first time I'd seen them since moving to Edinburgh more than two months ago. They arrived in a clamour of noise and back-slapping and I hoped they couldn't smell the booze off me. I gave them a tour of my hastily vacuumed flat and we headed out into the city for lunch.

Fergus met us at the Italian restaurant on Leith Walk and I was relieved to see he looked even more hungover than me, bleary-eyed and shirt untucked. We took our seats by the window and the questions came thick and fast. How was work? Had I met a girl? Did I know my neighbours? Was I eating properly? I could see in their searching eyes and over-eager smiles that they wanted to know if I was coping, if I was moving on. I ate my tortellini slowly, each mouthful a chore, until the red wine took over and I got a second wind. They bid their farewells with crushing hugs and a stray tear or two and within minutes I was sitting with Fergus at the Theatre Royal bar halfway down a pint of Czech pilsner, and I turned to him and said: "You won't believe what happened last night. I banged my neighbour."

And now, as I headed past the elevator and took the stairs, lingering at the bottom for an extra minute to give Darren the time to leave, it wasn't so funny anymore. The six pints with Fergus yesterday had encouraged me to think it was all a bit of fun, a good story, but today's hangover was hammering home what a mistake it was. My flat had recently started to feel like home, a sanctuary of sorts, and now my drunken fuck with Kim was going to forever cloud this corridor walk. By the time I got out into the damp morning air I could see Darren on the other side of the road bundling along with the violent energy of a scrumhalf.

My day didn't improve at Overspill. Scary Mary parked herself at Bob's desk for the morning. I got to work on Jungle Shelf 5, but my hangover worsened and grew corrosive. The memory of seeing my family yesterday looped back to other memories, of my mother and my teenage years, of things that were in the past and gone forever. My hope for Neve had faded too. The dread accelerated, staining my mind dark, blotting out all that was good.

I lost myself in the blinking screen and the stack of records. My fingers clattered on the keyboard and eventually my mind emptied of the grey acidic thoughts. Mary got bored and headed back upstairs to her office. I got up from my desk and wandered to the back of the room between two shelves, made a mattress out of some old phonebooks, and using my jacket as a blanket, settled down for a snooze.

I woke re-energised and returned to the back shelf with the golf records. I had reorganised the files so that I could lift out two blocks and easily access Boxfile 467, and sat on the floor with my back against a bookshelf and the file on my lap. For the next three hours I sifted through the documents looking for the map, thinking that perhaps it was scrawled in a margin or hidden in some code. Nothing. When Mary shouted her goodnight from the top of the stairs I also called it a day.

For the next week little changed. Rack by rack, shelf by shelf, I mapped out the lost records, sorting and cataloguing Edinburgh's abandoned local history. The Zen state of higher consciousness I'd achieved from keying in all the records in the first couple of weeks had faded. Sometimes while I inputted the data into the system I could transport myself to another dimension for an hour or two, lose myself down a wormhole of memory, reconstruct long-lost nights out in Aberdeen or nights with Hannah, rebuild the visual picture detail by detail, until I was completely unaware of my hands moving on the keyboard and was instead back in those moments, dizzy with sensory awareness, recalling with full clarity the taste of a pint of Export in the Blue Lamp in Aberdeen, Hannah's perfume as I kissed her neck, the salt-shock of swimming in the North Sea on a moon-bright summer night. But most of the time it wasn't like this anymore – I typed in the data and saw every pixel on the screen, was aware that I was sitting in a basement doing work that was utterly futile.

Worryingly, a certain thought spiral had started to dominate my blank moments – my father. I had barely thought of him during my childhood but now his absence had started to haunt me. I didn't know if I was an orphan now, because I had no idea if he was dead or alive. Uncle Donnie told me he'd heard he was down in Birmingham, but that was maybe five years ago.

I bumped into Kim one evening at the nearby corner shop and we chatted as if nothing had happened, and she touched my arm with sisterly affection as we said farewell, which simultaneously made me feel better about the boyfriend thing but disappointed by her lack of interest in bedding me again. I thought about calling Neve, but the lack of a reason made me stop. I met up with Fergus and his drinking buddies a couple of times, but their work-related chat and office boy cockiness was tiring, and those nights always ended messily with fallouts or minor streetfights. I was slowly but steadily sliding towards a black pit of depression and I didn't know how to get out of it.

A few days into this gloom, a soft knock on my door startled me. It was late, and I had just brushed my teeth on the way to bed. Dressed in jogging bottoms and a t-shirt, I opened the door to see Kim standing there still in her work clothes. "Can we talk?" she asked.

I made some tea and we sat on the high stools next to the kitchen worktop.

"Are you avoiding me?" she said.

"Of course not. We talked in the shop, right?"

"But you've never once looked me up."

I gestured through the wall. "What about Darren?"

She tilted her head and looked at me with a slight smile. "What about him?"

I shrugged.

From my position on the stool I could see the blue trim of her bra through a gap between the buttons of her blouse. She saw me looking. For the first time I picked up the smell of wine on her breath. She hopped off the stool and took my hand. "Come on. Let's have a special arrangement. The rule is we only do it at your place."

Lust shut down my common sense. We stumbled into the bedroom and I tried to get her clothes off but struggled with the fastening on her skirt and she laughed and obliged. She sat on the bed and tugged down my trousers.

"Fuck me from behind," she said.

This time, completely sober, I took my time, speeding up and slowing it down again, paying close attention to her muttered guidance until she screamed into the pillow. She told me to lie on the bed, then climbed on top of me. When I came it felt like the toxic waste of the last two weeks was being released – I laughed until she clamped a hand on my mouth.

At some point during the night she left, and I woke to an empty bed. But this time felt different – I had a *special arrangement* with my neighbour. This could work in the short-term, help me get my life back, and nobody would find out. I went to work with a smile on my face and the feeling that somehow I'd tapped into a seam of good fortune that had been missing for a long time.

My luck continued that day, because when I took boxfile 467 off the shelf for another look, I noticed for the first time that the box was assembled by folding together one large piece of reinforced card. I took all the documents out and disassembled the box, untucking the folds one by one. As I pulled the final fold free, a single piece of paper fluttered to the ground. I snatched it up – a few lines written in blue ballpoint pen.

There it was – exactly what they'd been looking for.

I headed over to the photocopier, ran off two copies, then returned to the high shelf. Methodically I reassembled the boxfile, replacing the precious piece of paper in the first fold, returned the documents, and replaced the box in its niche. Back at my desk, I dug out Neve's work number. She answered on the second ring.

"Neve. It's Miro."

"Long time no hear, cowboy."

"I found it. The map. I found it. I know how to get into the Devil's Chamber."

CHAPTER 7

This time the pub was Neve's choice – the Cumberland Bar, in the New Town. It was a Thursday night and the place was over-busy with students and a few disgruntled locals. I sat through the back wearing old clothes as instructed. Danny came in first, carrying a bulky rucksack, looking pissed off. He dumped the rucksack next to me and without saying a word turned around to go to the bar. I saw Neve arrive and go up to him as he was ordering drinks. They stayed there for a couple of minutes, talking. Probably discussing again how much they would reveal.

They sat down opposite me, interview style.

"So you found the map?" said Danny, again not making eye contact.

"Yep. Very clear directions."

"Where is it?"

"The map? Or the Chamber?"

Danny's eyes hard and emotionless. "Both."

I took a leisurely drink of my pint. "As I explained to Neve, that knowledge stays with me – until you tell me more."

Neve had a smirk on her face.

Danny took out his tobacco. There was something different about him tonight and I realised he had washed his hair – it was fluffier than last time and made him look like a seventies rock star. Nobody spoke. He sprinkled fronds of tobacco onto the Rizla, crimped it, licked it, rolled it tight. He placed the ciggy in his mouth so that it dangled from his lip. "Okay, but here's the deal. First you come with us and take part in what we do."

I looked at the heavy rucksack. Were they thieves?

"What exactly is it that you do?"

Danny sparked his lighter and dipped his head towards the flame. He took a moment to inhale and look at the ceiling. I was getting used to his amateur dramatics.

"You're either in or you're out," he said. "So if you give us the map, you're coming with us to the Devil's Chamber."

"And if I don't give you the map?"

He looked at the glowing tip of his roll-up. "We'll get there one way or another. Just faster with you."

"What are you looking for?"

"We don't know yet. That's part of the fun."

I decided to play his game. I took a mouthful of Deuchars and slumped back in my chair. At the bar, a pretty female student was telling a story to her drinking buddies, and I feigned interest, watching as she sketched shapes in the air and touched her hair.

"Hey," said Neve. "Focus."

The edge in her voice pleased me. "Maybe I'll just go to the Devil's Chamber on my own," I said.

Danny fidgeted in his seat and ran his hand through his fluffy hair. I rotated my pint glass as if tightening a screw.

"Fine," said Danny. "We'll show you what we do. After you finish your drink. Then you decide what to do with the map."

Danny extended a hand across the table and I shook it. Neve did the same.

"You're in the club now," Danny said. "No turning back."

We knocked back our drinks, and they got to their feet.

"It's not far," said Neve.

We walked along the darkened streets, the grand cliff-faces of eighteenth-century townhouses looming above us. Danny and Neve speeded up as we crossed the road over the misshapen cobbles, and we cut down one alleyway, then another.

"No talking," said Danny. "Just follow us and do what we tell you to."

We stopped at a gap between two tenement buildings. Nestled in the space, hidden behind railings, was a graveyard and compact church. The gates were padlocked and a faded Church of Scotland sign declared the church as St. Magnus's. Two overgrown yew trees hung over the railings, partially obscuring us from the upper floors of the tenement buildings around us. I glanced up at one to see movement behind a frosted glass bathroom window.

"Quick," said Danny. He extricated a rolled-up carpet from behind a grit bin, flopped it over the railing spikes, then presented his cupped hands to Neve. She stepped into his grip and he boosted her up onto the fence, and she scrambled over and down to the other side. I followed – hands on the frayed carpet, the hardness of the spikes underneath, Danny's clasp bouncing me up, a worrying moment as the cuff of my jeans snagged on one lumpy railing spike but then momentum carried me over and down. I lost my balance on the other side and stumbled backwards onto smooth stone. A tumbledown gravestone caught in a beam of streetlight, the carved lettering faded beyond recognition.

The slap of Danny's feet as he landed near me. "Move," he whispered.

We wriggled through a tangle of tree branches and bramble bushes to the church door. Danny produced a bulky key from his backpack and slid it into the lock. He jiggled it back and forth, metal scratching on metal, until something clicked. He turned it with a rusty thunk and the door squeaked open. We followed him into darkness and damp.

Somewhere ahead Danny stopped, and Neve walked into him, and I into her. Pitch darkness, my mouth in her hair, Danny muttering at us to back up. Then a rush of light, a glaring white eye. It took me a couple of seconds to realise Danny had put a headlamp on. He gave another one to Neve. "Only got two," he said. "So stay close."

The interior of the church was coated in thick dust, and the beams from their headlamps splashed light across the stark brickwork, and at the back of the church, some kind of mural on the wall, spooky long-limbed people painted in block colours. I walked down the aisle to the altar, which had been used years ago as a table for workmen – a torn and paint-stained sheet had transformed it into a makeshift table littered with empty drinks cans and crisp wrappers. I picked up these artefacts reverently, marvelling at the ancient faded packaging designs for Golden Wonder crisps and Irn-Bru, the remnants of a twenty-year-old lunch. Neve appeared at my shoulder and I passed her the brittle can.

A little streetlight leaked in through the stained-glass windows, enough to show me more of the church's hidden treasure. Lined up on the pews, as if waiting for the next service, were hymn books – mildewed and rotten, when I picked one up it collapsed in my hand into fragments. On the walls, memorial plaques for the church's notable benefactors, inlaid with gold lettering. A black marble slab commemorated the fallen of the parish from the Great War – fifteen names, including three MacDougalls.

"Pssst." Danny's sharp hiss made me jump. He waved over and tilted his lamp beam to a doorway in the wall. Neve moved towards him and I reached the doorway at the same time. Stairs to a crypt.

We descended in single file, Danny in the lead. A choking smell of mustiness and damp crept up towards us, and my heart pounded crazily as we walked towards death. In the tiny chamber three stone sarcophagi were lined up side by side, carvings at their foot naming the inhabitants as belonging to the Kilgarry-Stewart family, the patrons of the church, the most recent of whom had died in 1812. The middle sarcophagus had partially collapsed, and the headlamp beams revealed a ribcage the colour of granite and the rags of Margaret Kilgarry-Stewart's burial gown. I stared at the bones until Danny's light moved closer, and he blocked my view, peering directly into the crumbled coffin, leaning in up close. When I blinked I could still see the ribcage imprinted on my retina.

Neve traced a finger over the engraving on the plinth. I looked up at the low ceiling above us, stained with spores of damp.

Danny and Neve turned back towards the steps and for a moment the electric light swept up and away, leaving me alone in the dark. I made a noise involuntarily and the light dipped back downwards, showing me the steps. I scrambled upwards, back into the church.

The clouds had parted and the moon now blazed through the stained glass, casting a dappled light onto the church's interior. Danny pointed towards the street and we walked in single file back up the aisle until we reached the door and the headlamps clicked off – first Danny, then Neve.

The door screeched as Danny edged it open and we slid back out into the night. He nudged the door shut until it clicked into place and was about to step forward when I grabbed his arm and pointed. At the railings: a Golden Labrador watching us curiously. The scuff of footsteps, and a dog-walker edging into sight, whistling, only his body and arms visible, swinging a dog-lead like a nunchuk. "Come on, Stookie boy," he said.

Stookie the dog looked at us vacantly, a line of slobber dangling from his mouth, then turned on his heel and trotted off, belly swinging from side to side. Danny glanced at me and nodded – a small gesture of thanks. We waited for a full three minutes – Danny showed us his watch – before moving swiftly back over to the railings, flopping the carpet over the spikes, and up and over one-by-one, landing onto the empty street, unseen and back into the real world.

Within ten minutes we were back sitting in the Cumberland, not speaking, just looking at each other in wonder.

Eventually I couldn't contain myself anymore. "What… the fuck… was that?"

"Welcome to the club," said Neve.

"Not bad for your first time," said Danny.

"But what? Why?"

"We," said Danny. "Are urban explorers."

For the first time I saw a vulnerability in Danny's eyes. Like he'd given too much of himself away.

I had a vague memory of reading a feature in the Guardian about urban explorers – anonymous adventurers, faces swathed in scarves, scurrying about in abandoned London Underground stations and disused sewers.

"I read something about this. I think."

Neve nudged Danny. "Explain to him. You're good at explaining it."

Danny sparked up another skinny roll-up. "It's pretty simple. There I was, twenty years old, already a university drop-out with no impulse or inclination for any sort of career. No connection with my parents – both doctors, both spent their entire lives accumulating stuff. House, cars, clothes, jewellery, art. No connection with my brother and sister – she's a doctor, he's a sponger living off our parents' gullibility. It doesn't feel like I've got much to live for. Except climbing. It's the only thing that gives me the buzz. And a feeling of peace. Those moments when you're up a ridge, wind buffeting you, certain death below and probable death with the next move above. And yet you make it. It's like you grow a little every time you brush up against mortality. And this is my life for five years, doing shitty temp jobs to scrape by and live for the buzz at the weekends."

He's shaking a little, agitated.

"And then it's not enough anymore, the climbing. I need other stuff. I'm driving my shitty Fiat Panda at a hundred and twenty on the M8 at two a.m. Surfing in Thurso in December, so cold I'm crying, getting smashed up by icy waves. Ticking off Class A drugs one by one every weekend until I'm fucking bug-eyed with boredom. Searching for the next big thing. Then I transfer into Deaths at Scottish Standard and meet…"

He points at Neve. She does a pretend curtsey.

"And she keeps going on about how fucking boring office life is and how she wants to explore the hidden other. I'm thinking she's mad then I realise… I've been going up all the time, climbing shit for thrills… how about if I go down?"

Neve took over. "It's simple, Miro. We walk past and over things every day that deserve to be explored. Buildings, tunnels, whatever – the architecture and infrastructure of our cities, of our pasts, stories that have been tucked away into storage. The establishment wants us to forget, doesn't want us to always be poking around in the corners where they conveniently swept up the things they don't want us to see."

"Like what?"

"We've been to a disused mental hospital, an abandoned whisky bond, a Victorian sewer, a theatre slated for demolition…"

"Eight trips, in total," said Danny. "Nine including St Magnus's."

"What about tonight? St Magnus's? Will you go back there?"

Danny sipped his pint. "I doubt it. Saw the place, had an experience. Got a souvenir." He reached into his jacket pocket and pulled out a gold ring with a green stone.

"Fuck. Where did you get that?"

He shrugged. "Mary Kilgarry-Stewart's not going to need it, is she?"

"From the coffin?" I couldn't believe it.

"Always take a souvenir. That's one of my rules." Danny winked at me.

Neve was quiet. Judging by the way she fidgeted with her drink, she was not comfortable with Danny's choice of souvenir either.

"That's grave-robbing," I said. "That's a pretty serious crime."

"And you were fucking complicit in it," said Danny. "Now, where's this map?"

CHAPTER 8

We entered the Guildford Arms. The walk had taken us fifteen minutes, Danny grumbling all the way about going to a new pub instead of staying put in the Cumberland. The rush was still lingering after our illicit visit to St Magnus's, and all I could think of was the gold ring burning a hole in Danny's pocket. We got drinks and found a table in the corner.

The Guildford was a pub I'd fallen in love with at first sight on a night out with Fergus – the grand old corniced ceilings, the beer-stained carpet, the snugs through the back, the absence of music, the draught ales, the feeling that at every table stories were being told that unfolded the secrets of life. I looked above and saw our reflections in a crescent-shaped ceiling mirror – the three of us and the discs of our drinks.

"Hey Miro! Back in the room. Come on, the map."

"Well?" Neve hit me on the arm. She was smiling too, and I felt a tingle of pleasure.

"Let me have a couple of pints first."

They both groaned.

"Okay, okay. Just give me a second to get settled."

I sipped my Caley 80, enjoying the anticipation. All around, the pleasant hubbub of the pub gave the feeling of a stage, and I was the lead actor about to deliver my soliloquy.

Danny puffed on his roll-up, frowning.

"Guess," I said.

Neve grabbed my arm and tugged, and I laughed, mainly at the pleasure of feeling her fingers tight against my skin. "Miro, tell us!"

I reached into the back pocket of my jeans and removed the photocopy. Danny made to grab it but I handed it to Neve. She unfolded it flat on the table.

<u>ACCESS POINT 3</u>
Cellar of Guildford Arms
Back of storage room through ventilation shaft
Enters onto stairwell
Return access not easy
BE CAREFUL

Neve looked up. "Here?"

Danny pointed at the floor. "Under us," he said, in a voice softer than I had ever heard him use.

Neve reached over and hugged me and Danny gave me a grudging pat on the shoulder. "Where was it?"

"Hidden in the inlay of the boxfile."

"So there are at least two other access points," said Neve.

We were quiet for a moment. Neve looked at me again – she had been looking at me a lot in the last couple of minutes. "There's something different about you, Miro."

I'm having sex, I wanted to say. *The glacier has melted.*

"So how do we get downstairs?" Danny was scanning the bar.

"Easy tiger," said Neve. "Let's think this through."

Danny tapped his lighter on the table. "Need to scout this place out. Find the storage room."

"Come on, be serious about this." Neve was now also scanning the bar, as if looking for a weak spot in a barricade. "I've got an idea." She loosened her hair and let it fall on her shoulders. "Back soon."

We watched her go up to the bar and speak first to the bearded barman, who pointed at the other barman, who wore his dark ginger hair in a rockabilly quiff. Neve's body language changed – both hands resting on the bar, shoulders back, head tilted a little. I remembered the first time I'd seen her, wet hair and raindrops on her skin. The shy Ulster princess. Rockabilly had a serious face, but then it softened, and he smiled. He said something and Neve laughed.

Next to me, Danny spoke. "Do you fancy her?"

I reacted instantly, but with a flinch. "No. Not my type."

"Out of your league mate, anyway."

I gripped my pint glass. "So what are you expecting to find down there?"

"In Neve's trousers?" He chuckled.

"Under the fucking pub."

"You know, I have been there. In Neve's trousers."

I could feel my cheeks burn. "Under here. What are we going to find."

"Absolutely no idea. That's the thrill of it."

"What have you found on your other *adventures*?"

He acknowledged my sarcasm and his face changed, as if backing down. "OK, so the mental hospital. A total ruin, but easy to access. The padlock fell apart in my hands, just crumbled into fragments. Everything was as they left it – bedframes and rotten mattresses, the straps to tie down patients still dangling from the sides of the beds."

Danny grinned and supped from his pint. "We went down into the basement and found a room with sheets of paper scattered all over the floor, records of patients from the forties and fifties, all these bleached photographs and psychiatric reports. We headed further along the corridor. There was a sign for the morgue. Then we heard a noise."

Danny laughed. "A voice, we think. Maybe we're mistaken. Could have been a startled animal. We both ran for it. When we got back to the car, Neve grabbed me. Like an elemental force needing release. And we fucked on the back seat of my Fiat Panda."

I stared at the wood grain on the table.

"But you know what, mate? I thought this might be part of the package, like every time we did a trip and she got a buzz she would want to top it off with sex. But it never happened again."

I looked over to the bar where Neve was chatting and laughing too loudly with the barman.

"You're not her type at all, Miro. She likes rough sex with bastards. Not cuddly stuff with baby-faced dudes like you."

I clenched my fists under the table.

Neve returned to us, smiling. "I got a job. They'll try me out starting Sunday. My name is Fiona, by the way."

"Fucking great," said Danny. "It's my round, same again?"

Neve gave a thumbs-up and Danny swaggered off to the bar.

The anger still simmered in me, but Neve slung an arm around my neck and rubbed my head with her knuckles. Her closeness calmed me. Danny came back with the drinks, and soon I was anaesthetised. On a trip to the toilet I noticed a sliding door marked PRIVATE and through the gap I could see an industrial-looking space which would surely lead to the cellar.

Our table had two spare seats, and as the pub filled up a couple of Japanese tourists slunk over and asked in broken English if they could sit with us. Two twenty-something females togged up in Gore-Tex and tight jeans and holding half-pints. Danny spread-eagled his arms to welcome them and slid back our wreckage of empty glasses to give them room. Within a heartbeat he was leaning into their personal space and asking them about judo.

"God, here he goes," said Neve. She rooted in her handbag for a cigarette, lit one, tilted her head away for the first exhalation, then smiled at me. "So, man of mystery. What's your story?"

I'd been waiting for this moment ever since I met her. "I'm a complex homo sapiens, Neve."

She laughed. "That's an oxymoron, if ever I heard one."

"You really want to hear my life story?"

"You think I'd rather listen to Danny's chat-up patter?"

To my left, Danny was leaning towards the prettier of the two Japanese girls and had folded his arms in a way that accentuated his climber's muscles.

"It's a long and heartbreaking tale."

"I prefer tragedy to comedy," she said.

So I told her. It was something I had rehearsed subconsciously, and it became a performance, an incantation with a rhythm that was almost like a ballad. She stared at me throughout, assessing me.

The story tumbled out.

I started with my dad leaving when I was a baby.

I told her I never missed having a father when I was growing up, thanks to the love of my mother and her extended family. Growing up in a council house overlooking the North Sea in the village of Pitbirnie in North-East Fife; my grandparents a short jog away and my aunt, uncle, and two cousins a slightly longer jog.

My mother Hazel the art teacher at the local high school, joking that she kept her married name because Kubik sounded like a surrealist offshoot of Cubism, and was more bohemian than McGarrity, her Dundee-Irish maiden name. This, I realised later, also explained the promotion of my Christian name Miro. Another arty name.

Ms Kubik was a much-loved teacher, probably in part because she was young and attractive. She'd had me aged nineteen, so by the time I reached high school she was in her early thirties and had the indomitable spark of an artist who did and said what she wanted to, cared little for what others thought, and carried it all off with a cheekiness that people tended to forgive. Unfortunately

I inherited none of her spark – instead I seem to have been lumbered with my father's genes, his tendency for flight; and perhaps the genetic memory of a grandfather who leapt out of speeding planes into the dark, plummeting into nothingness and leaving nothing behind.

My childhood was a lucky one. My mum, always there with me, reading with me, asking me questions, laughing at my answers, encouraging me in everything I did. My Uncle Donnie; playing touch rugby with him on the beach, the North Sea wind buffeting into me, losing my balance and falling slap-forward laughing into the rough sand. Auntie Sarah, quiet and kind and slipping me secret gifts of football stickers or chocolate bars. My two cousins – Kirsty, Fergus – like siblings to me, sharing sweets and bike rides and fights. My grandparents bringing order to it all with Sunday dinners and birthday cards and stories about an older, greyer, smokier Scotland.

In my second year at university my mum got sick. She lost weight and was tired all the time. Kidney cancer. The treatment appeared to have been successful, then the cancer came back. In my third year it was still there, resisting all treatment, and by my final year the cancer had spread. I had dealt with it all in a fog of denial, believing that she would bounce back. Even when she was bleary and weak from the treatment she still had the spark in her eyes. It was only when Uncle Donnie pulled me aside one day when I was home for the weekend, his grip on my arm stronger than it should have been, and he asked me to look him in the eye and told me in a shaky voice that my mother was dying and I had to get ready for it.

She died on the day I should have been graduating. There were two empty chairs in the Aberdeen hall that day. Instead I was at my mum's bedside with the family, holding her hand until the nurse gently told me I should say goodbye for the last time.

In the weeks after I stayed with Donnie and Sarah, occasionally popping back to the empty house as if visiting a shrine. On those return visits I would lock the door and let the grief out, collapsed face down on the living-room floor until I was wrung out. Then I would walk on the beach for three miles until the sand petered out into rocky shoreline, then walk back, often soaked through to the skin from the summer rain.

One blustery July day Aunt Sarah brought me the envelope with its Robert Gordon's University crest. It was from my former tutor Jane Salzmann, a kind Londoner close to retirement who had followed the news about my mother closely and often asked me to stay back after class. The letter explained that she knew of an opportunity for an archivist at Edinburgh City Council, and would be happy to recommend me for the post. I called her and told her of my loss, and one week later I had an interview. I caught the train down to Edinburgh and went through it all in a daze. Two interviewers in a drab office just off Princes Street, going through set questions, ticking boxes, an air of bored inevitability. The role was at an unspecified location, would suit a graduate, needed flexibility and patience. One week later the letter came to offer me the role.

Uncle Donnie and Auntie Sarah engineered the next steps. I don't remember much about it, but I accepted everything they proposed, because I knew I couldn't spend the rest of my life curled up on the floor of my childhood home. Week by week, we took steps forward. Week one: pack up the old house, throw stuff out, box up the stuff I wanted to keep. Week two: put the house up for sale, look for a flat to buy in Edinburgh. Week three: make an offer on a one-bedroom flat on Lothian Road; offer accepted. Week four: a trip to Dundee to shop for work clothes and stuff for the flat. Week five: accept an offer for the house. And on the weeks passed, a gradual erasure of the old world and an incoming of the new, until by September we were packing boxes into a hired van and hitting the road to Edinburgh.

Neve ground out her cigarette in the ashtray, the last remnant of smoke rippling out her lips. "I'm sorry for your loss."

I tilted my more-than-half-empty pint glass at her and she clinked with her own.

"It's just the truth," I said. "People have it much worse."

More drinks, and the night blurred. It was after eleven on a Thursday, Overspill looming ahead of me tomorrow, and I decided to call it a night.

"Come on Miro, stay out." Neve, again locking eye contact with me, wanting something from me but I couldn't work out what. Something in her eyes told me it was unlikely to be my body.

"Come on Miro, don't be a wussy." Danny with his grin. The two Japanese girls were coming along on the next leg of the evening's adventure.

"I'll call you," said Neve. "What's your number?"

Danny produced a biro from his rucksack, and I scribbled my number and address on a beermat, and slid it over to her.

As I got up to leave Danny blew me a kiss. I thought about giving him the finger but instead raised a hand and walked out from the commotion into the rain.

CHAPTER 9

I heard nothing from Neve for a week. A new routine slowly established itself – work, and Kim's nocturnal visits. A soft knock at my door was always the sign – three slow taps and I would unsnib the lock and let her in. Often, we didn't even talk, just started undressing and got to work on each other. After the first few times I had lost all inhibitions and now we just took what we wanted from each other. She would always leave in the dark spaces before dawn, and by the time I woke the room would be a wreckage of torn condom wrappers, twisted sheets, tossed off clothes, and next to my alarm clock the squeezed-out lube tube. After all those months of being trapped in an inner prison of grief, the rampant animal excess of it all was liberating.

One day at Overspill, just as I was about to close up, the buzzer sounded from above. I opened the door to an unexpected sight. A young guy, maybe five years older than me, dressed like a lawyer or banker. He looked me directly in the eye. "Hello, I am led to believe that you hold a record that belongs to my associates. May I come in?"

I opened the door fully and he strode over the threshold. Navy-blue mohair overcoat, a silver coat-pin, navy-blue suit with a rich depth of colour, blue tie with red diagonal stripes, nape-length hair. Everything about him – accent, manner, dress – telegraphed that he had been schooled with the Edinburgh elite.

I decided I would fuck with him a little, and ramped up my Fife accent. "Whit exactly is it you're looking for mate?"

He pursed his lips, then recovered. "That is somewhat confidential."

"Well, mate. If I dinnae ken what it is you're looking for, how am I gonnae find it. Ken?"

Maybe I'd gone too far. He brushed a little something off his sleeve and feigned interest in the reproduction of Monarch of the Glen hanging in the corridor. "Can we go somewhere to talk?"

I gestured through to the kitchenette.

He took off the mohair overcoat and folded it over the back of a chair. He had the build of a rower – broad shoulders, and an underlying leanness that tightened the suit around his body. "Let me explain. My associates believe a file that belongs to them has been misplaced here."

"Misplaced?"

"It found its way here by accident."

"Well, we're here to help." I already had a creeping certainty that this was about boxfile 467. "The way it works is, you tell me what you're looking for, then I go look it up on our computer."

"It's a record containing lots of miscellaneous information. About an Edinburgh legend."

"Does this legend have a name?"

He adjusted a cufflink. "The Devil's Chamber."

"Never heard of it. But let me go take a look. Fancy a cup of tea?" I held up our oldest, most chipped mug like it was a rowing trophy.

"No thank you."

I gave him a thumbs-up and went downstairs. I sat at my desk and clock-watched for five minutes. This was an interesting development. When I returned back to the kitchenette he was staring at the window. Not *out* the window – but *at* it, like it was an unfathomable object he had encountered for the first time.

"Sorry," I said, shrugging. "Nothing. But the whole point of City Archive 17 is that we're storing the overspill from other archives and slowly getting round to categorising and rehousing it. Something might show up. Could you leave me a contact number and I'll give you a call if I find anything?"

He extracted a silver pen from his inside pocket. "Do you have a piece of paper?"

I tore off a strip from an old Daily Record next to the kettle – a remnant of Bob's last day at Overspill before his fall. The silver pen moved fluidly over the paper in neat script. A name – James – and an Edinburgh number.

He put his coat back on and buttoned it up. "Call me immediately should you find something."

"Will do, James."

He turned sharply and left the kitchenette. The front door swung open and slammed shut with more force than necessary.

I went back downstairs. Mary was clumping around above me so I positioned myself at my desk, logged in to the computer and stared at the flashing cursor. Why would this James guy want the file? Not for the bulk of its contents, which were contradictory and mostly nonsense. He wanted it because he'd heard the map was in the boxfile – that could be the only reason.

The cursor continued to flash, beckoning me. I typed *Devil's Chamber* and hit return.

NO RECORDS AVAILABLE.

I took a moment to compose myself, then dug into the pile of archives waiting to be categorised under my feet. The afternoon dragged by and come five-thirty I hadn't even keyed half of the pile. I packed up for the day and headed out into the chill Edinburgh evening, the granite buildings smeared with frost, traffic fumes hazing in the streetlights. On the way back I stopped to pick up a chicken jalfrezi and peshwari naan. In the corridor I saw Kim and Darren ahead of me, entering her place. She looked in my direction then pulled the door shut. Back at the flat I poured a beer to try to cheer myself up, and was halfway through the curry when the phone rang.

"Miro?" It was Neve. "Saturday," she said.

"Huh?"

"I found the access point. Saturday we go into the Devil's Chamber. Be at the Guildford at ten p.m. Wear old clothes."

I fell into bed and lay staring at the ceiling. Just as I was starting to fall asleep I was startled by a steady pounding from next door, an uproar of grunts and cries, furniture moving. Silence fell and I stared again at the ceiling. Half an hour later the noises came again, and I wrapped a pillow round my head, the world closing in on me.

CHAPTER 10

I stepped through the revolving doors into the Guildford. The pub was busy, and I spotted Neve cutting lemons behind the bar. It took me a while to find Danny, sitting through the back on a stool, battered khaki rucksack at his feet.

"No pints," he said. "You can't be needing a pish when you're on a mission."

I went to the bar and Neve served me. She showed no signs of recognition when taking my order and returning with a double Dalwhinnie. I added a splash of water, and when I looked up she was already talking with another customer. I returned to the table, where Danny was sitting with his eyes half-closed.

"Are you nervous?" he said.

I hadn't told them about my fear of enclosed spaces. A sickening nausea had started to wriggle inside me the day before and had intensified over the following twenty-four hours. I hadn't had any outlet over the last week – there had been no visits from Kim since I'd seen her in the corridor. The thought of the claustrophobia waiting for me under my feet was like a hand slowly squeezing my throat.

"Nope," I told Danny. "Curious, mainly."

"Have you ever used a headlamp before?"

I shook my head.

"Ropes?"

"Did a bit in the scouts."

Danny laughed. "The scouts. Of course."

I sipped my Dalwhinnie. A silence settled over both of us, and Danny closed his eyes completely. He seemed to actually be asleep. I looked around the pub, at the laughing punters telling their drunken stories, snatching at their last bit of fun before work tomorrow. The whisky was helping my nerves. For the first time that week I started to feel vaguely normal.

The bell clanged for last orders and Danny sat up. He rolled a cigarette and nodded towards the back corner of the pub. "When I give the signal, we head to the snug."

Danny was down to the last scrap of his cigarette when he muttered in my direction. "Go."

I followed him as he moved quickly across the pub, punters already drifting towards the door. We scurried into the snug, Danny slung the rucksack under the bench and then crawled in after it. "Quick."

I dropped to my knees and followed. He had cooried in against the back of the space, leaving little room for me.

"Get in, closer."

I crawled in, until we were lying side by side.

"Closer, they'll see you. Don't worry, I'm not going to fuck you."

I edged closer, until our bodies were almost touching.

We lay like that for perhaps ten minutes, my eyes screwed up, imagining myself to be lying in bed at home, anywhere but here. There was a noise nearby – chairs being lifted and clunked onto the table. Inches from my nose, Neve's Doc Marten's. Silence in the pub now, just

Neve's voice, call and response with one of the other bar staff. By now my claustrophobia had eased, and I was edgy with anticipation, the thought of that unknown space below waiting for us.

Neve's voice calling goodbye, the jangle of keys. And then complete silence, just some drunken shouts from the parallel universe outside. Neve's Doc Marten's reappeared.

"Time to come out. Unless you two are enjoying yourselves too much under there?"

I rolled out, glad to get my mouth and nose away from the sticky carpet. Neve was sitting on a chair, amused look on her face as we emerged on all fours. Danny was already unzipping the rucksack, emptying his kit onto the floor, unclipping things. The pub was eerily quiet, and Neve had already turned some of the lights off, giving the place the look of an abandoned stately home.

"Here." Danny fitted a headlamp for me, adjusting the strap until it felt comfortable. "Twist it to turn it on and off. Let's go."

We followed Neve through the sliding door to where a trapdoor hatch jutted open. Neve went first, then Danny. I took a deep breath and followed them down the ladder. Neve guided us towards a door, unlocked it, and ushered us in.

A wall of darkness, the shapes of stacked chairs emerging as our eyes adjusted. Neve shuffled into the room and found a light switch. It flared on, revealing that every available space was taken – chairs, boxes, crates. Neve clambered over the top, using the flat platforms of box tops or chair seats to hop between the islands of junk until she reached the back wall. First she pulled a tea chest away from the centre of the wall to create some space, then yanked boxes back to reveal nothing but scuffed wallpaper, working her way along to the corner. Next she pulled away a stack of chairs, revealing a metal grille screwed onto the wall.

"Listen to this."

She found a broom handle in the pile of junk and slid it in through one of the grille holes. It clanged onto metal, and an echo reverberated far beyond the wall.

"Deep, huh? As if this ventilation shaft goes into a big underground space. The Chamber." She smiled at us.

Danny took an electric screwdriver from the rucksack and removed the screws. The grille was rusted, and when Danny lifted it off, his hands were blackened with thick and oily grime. He crouched and stuck his head into the hole. He re-emerged, determination on his face.

"It's deep. Goes back at least five metres."

Without barely a pause, Danny ducked back into the hole and seconds later his legs disappeared in. Neve hopped down onto the floor and stuck her head in. The noise of Danny's legs and arms shuffling on the metal, then Neve ducked in as well. I got down onto the floor. The beam of my headlamp showed Neve's legs and the soles of her Docs, receding with every movement.

Another deep breath, and I climbed into the shaft.

The progress of Danny and Neve had disturbed years of dust, and I sneezed, the noise echoing in the metal tube. Neve hissed back at me to shut up. I continued to wriggle forward, trying to forget the fact that there was no space to turn around, only one direction to go – forward – and no clue what was waiting for us at the end.

Danny's voice. "The shaft turns right."

Ahead of me, some muttered conversation, and then I saw Neve roll on her side and then shuffle to the right, her legs kicking for purchase on the metal wall. The air quality had diminished and every breath was musty and stale. I reached the turn and slid into the dogleg, aware now of the blind corner behind me, the exit back to the world above now complicated. I kept crawling.

Danny's voice again. "I'm at the end. Another grille."

I kept crawling until ahead I saw Neve's boots and legs. I stopped, the beam of my headlamp on her calf where her jeans leg had ridden up. Claustrophobia forgotten, I stared at her skin until I remembered myself and snapped out of it.

Up ahead, Danny was muttering back to us. "I'll try to unscrew it." He rummaged around in the rucksack, and there was a quiet scratching noise, metal on metal, a spraying sound – WD40 I was guessing – and more laborious scrambling.

Waiting in that airless space I had a sudden awareness of everything above me, the sheer weight of buildings and paving stones and water pipes and parked cars. I could see it all in my head – layers of stone and metal pressing down on me. I bit the strap of my watch until lights prickled on my eyelids.

A clatter as the grille came away and fell to the other side. "Bingo," said Danny.

I heard him climb through, and Neve started moving. My next mental storm came over me, an eerie one, like a genetic memory of my paratrooper grandfather next in the queue to jump out into the black night onto Arnhem fields. I wriggled after Neve until the rectangular hole was in front of me and I was up and through, sliding out onto a stone ledge, the headlamp revealing cracked stonework and fossilised mice droppings.

As I picked myself up, able to stand at last, Neve and Danny were hissing in disbelief. I joined them at the end of the ledge and peered over a short wall.

Below, a staircase winding downwards, tiled on both sides in black and white, a thin wrought iron bannister curling along the wall. We were quiet, breathless. There was no sound from below, just utter silence. Danny swung a leg over the side, tilting his head down to help him plan the best route. He pointed at a crack in the wall, then, using it as a fingerhold, dangled down until his feet touched the railing – from there it was a short hop to the steps. Neve went next, and I followed.

Neve started going down the stairs but Danny grabbed her. He took a red shoelace out of this rucksack pocket and tied it onto the bannister. He pointed at the shoelace and mimed a pair of spectacles and pointed upwards. It took me a few seconds but finally I got it – the shoelace couldn't easily be seen unless you held your head close to the wall, and this was our marker for our exit. I glanced up the stairs, the headlamp beam carving a chunk out of the darkness, but all I could see was the steps curving into a blind corner. I tilted my head downwards and it was the same – stairs, and the black and white tiles.

Neve began to descend and this time Danny didn't stop her. The steps were smooth underfoot, not unlike the steps on the narrow Edinburgh closes leading down from the Royal Mile, polished by centuries of footfall. We continued downwards, utterly silent, and there was the feeling of being not in an enclosed space, but something huge – a cavern. The stairs straightened and a pale light beckoned ahead.

We slowed, wary. The steps stopped and led onto a black marble floor. A space opened up in front of us, reminding me of a church or cathedral, steep walls leading up to an ornate ceiling embellished with corniced brickwork. Two rows of chairs were lined up in front of a larger chair, throne-like. Somehow, a gentle light illuminated everything, an underground moonlight. Our torch beams danced on every surface, intensifying the detail, and a dizzy delight overcame me. Everything about the chamber had seemed like a student prank up until now, a laboured myth, a drunken bet. But here it was – spectacularly weird, and real.

"Look," Danny said. His light pointed to first one archway then another, and he swung the beam across the chamber to show the same on the other side. Four archways, each opening into corridors leading deeper into the darkness.

"Let's try this one." We followed Danny to the first on the right. The archway was bordered by blocks of sandstone, and as we got closer a noise crept out towards us. We stopped, listening. Running water, but not a trickle, more like thunder. We entered through the mouth and the narrow entrance opened up to a broader corridor. A couple of metres further, and a doorway opened out on our left to reveal what looked like a janitor's office: a table, chair, gas heater, empty beer cans and other garbage strewn in one corner. The noise of rushing water was closer, and we followed the corridor for another couple of minutes until the noise drowned out everything else. In front of us, an underground river gushed past, its power concentrated by the narrow tunnel walls on either side, making it resemble a lethal water flume. I leaned out over the rapids and tilted my torch beam upstream – the light showed low ceilings for ten metres or so then faded out into endless dark. In the other direction, more of the same. Neve took my arm and gently pulled me back onto the riverbank – I hadn't realised how far I'd been leaning out.

Danny led us back out into the Chamber. We moved over to the first archway on the left. It narrowed at the neck, red brickwork closing us in, then broadened and opened out into a compact library. Row upon row of leather-bound books stocked the shelves, all in the same caramel-brown colour. Two tables in the middle, chairs tucked in. I walked over to one of the shelves and touched a book, running my fingertip down the spine. Thick with dust.

Danny and Neve had already walked back out into the chamber and I followed them as they moved up to the next archway. Our footsteps were soft on the stone – Danny had insisted on rubber soles and it made me feel more secure to know that we were silent as we explored. My eyes moved away from the shadows and to Neve's messy ponytail and a smudge of grime on her ear. Her childlike fascination was alluring. I continued to stare until she turned abruptly and left me standing on my own.

I scampered after her into the third corridor, and found her and Danny gazing up at a gigantic wooden structure, the sort of huge cabinet you might see in a Renaissance cathedral – built from interlocking blocks of dark wood, maybe ten metres high, the structure fitting perfectly into the space in the wall. The surface of the cabinet was decorated with intricate carvings – birds and snakes and dragons – and behind its dusty windows, its interior was filled with row after row of dark bottles. Danny leaned in close to inspect one. "Wine, maybe."

Neve stepped back and gazed upwards, then back at the alcove archway. "They must have built it here. Piece by piece. It must've taken months."

I walked to the end of the corridor but it stopped short at an ancient brick wall. I pressed my fingers into the seams between the bricks and felt the grainy mortar, a texture that reminded me of church walls and fallen masonry. I returned to the cabinet just as Danny strode off, a man in a hurry. I was conscious of Neve following him, but I remained in front of the carved behemoth, trying to make sense of all these bottles. Wine? But they were unlabelled, and had more of a medicinal look, or perhaps industrial. What could be the purpose of this dark liquid, locked up in the guts of the city? Maybe it was absinthe, or some sort of vaguely illegal spirit, drunk during the meetings of a hellfire club?

I re-emerged back into the chamber. Danny and Neve were inspecting the chairs up close. I counted them – thirteen, not including the throne.

"Look," Neve pointed at the arms of the throne. They were silent as I approached. I saw what had transfixed them. Metal rings on each armrest, with straps attached, and the wooden surface scarred with scratches. After Danny and Neve walked off, I stood staring, unable to tear my eyes away from the gouges in the wood.

"Shit," said Danny.

I turned to see him looking at the floor. A pair of crumpled spectacles lay in the dust, one lens shattered. I moved closer.

A noise burst out that froze me in my steps. A cough. Danny and Neve stood in front of me, not moving. Again – a hacking cough, followed by snorting.

Danny and Neve ran for it.

Frozen to the spot, I watched them sprint back to the stairs, turning off their headlamps as they ran. They disappeared into the mouth of the stairway just as the cough sounded again, on the opposite side of the chamber, meaning that the cougher was likely emerging from the fourth and unexplored archway at any moment. I switched off my headlamp and dived back into the corridor with the bottles.

Heart hammering in my chest, I huddled tight against the archway, obscured from view. The cough again, and this time a few muttered words, uncannily loud in the open chamber. Then a scraping noise, repeated once, twice, three times. The sound was familiar but I couldn't place it. Unable to stop myself, I leaned out and peered into the chamber.

A bulky man, extremely tall, bear-like with a slight hunch, was picking up chairs – two at a time – and moving back to the corridor with the storage room. I caught a glimpse of his face – stubbled chin and fluffed up hair on his ball-like head, a scowl tightening his small eyes. He turned and headed back towards the alcove, and I made the split-second judgement that he must be depositing the chairs in the storage nook, giving me at least thirty seconds to make a dash for the stairs.

He disappeared from sight, and when I heard the cough I emerged out onto the marble floor. Should he glance back the way I would have to cross his sightline to get to the stairs. I ran for my life. As I reached the chairs I heard the cough again, closer. In that micro-second, crossing the chamber, I saw the remaining chairs in all their fine detail – red velvet cushions, gold braid, dark and weathered wood – and in the next moment I was across the floor, the stairs in front of me. I leapt into the darkness, feet moving nimbly up the steps, and the cough sounded again, behind me, and, I hoped, oblivious.

After turning three or four corners up the spiral staircase I edged my headlamp on at low beam. Black and white tiles, the wrought iron bannister, and nothing else. Panic rose in my throat, the claustrophobia slipping its claws into my skin. Somewhere down below, a voice sounded – a cry of surprise, or outrage. My mind whirled. Had he seen footsteps in the dust?

I collected myself and tilted my head close to the bannister. Step by step I climbed, until I saw the red shoelace tied on the railing. I looked above at the wall of tiles. How the hell was I going to climb back up? I ran my fingers across the surface, feeling only smooth ceramic and grout lines. I repeated the process, this time finding a single finger-hold in a broken tile. I swung a leg up onto the railing and braced myself. In a lurching movement I got my second foot on the rail, and swung wildly with my trailing hand for purchase, flapping at first against blank stone, then snagging into a hand-sized hole. I wobbled for a second, about to fall, then regained my composure. I could see the end of the wall above me, and presumably at its end, the ledge, which would give me the handhold I needed. It would mean a mad scramble. I pulled myself up and grabbed at the darkness.

My hand caught the ledge. Pain stretched across my bicep, tearing at the muscle. I swung my other hand up and then I was hanging, dangling, feet pedalling against flat tilework. From somewhere a surge of strength propelled me upwards and for a second I was hinged on the edge of the ledge, the waistband of my jeans pressing into my pelvic bone, until I tilted forward and fell headfirst onto the cold stone. Dizzy and stunned, I crawled forward to the gaping hole that led to the tunnel. In I slid, fumbling my way down onto the metal floor of the shaft, and wriggling along in a commando crawl. At one point I had to stop, a gag reflex jack-knifing my body, but the vomit never came, just a dry heave. I continued crawling on my elbows, head down and past the dogleg, until I ploughed headfirst into the wall at the other side.

A pair of hands reached in for me, under my armpits, and helped me leverage up and through the hole. I slipped out like a landed trout onto a pile of cardboard boxes and crumpled into a heap at Danny's feet.

"You made it," said Neve.

I lay on the floor, lungs heaving, heart convulsing.

"What happened?" She leaned over me, hair dangling close to my face.

I pointed upwards. They took my arms and pulled me to my feet, and together we scrambled over the clutter in the storeroom and out the door. I was dizzy climbing the ladder and took it one rung at a time until I emerged from the hatch and felt the satisfying texture of the pub floor under my fingertips.

Neve took three glasses and poured us pints of Tennent's. I sat on a barstool and chugged the pint in three gulps.

"What happened? Come on, tell us."

I told them, words spilling out so fast they had to ask me to slow down.

Danny had his hands on his face, looking for a moment like Munch's Scream. "That place was unbelievable. Unbelievable."

"I need some air. Can we go outside?"

Within five minutes we were standing at the door as Neve locked the pub. The street was quiet, but some twenty metres away we could see a few people walking and taxis passing. In silence we walked onto the brightly lit Princes Street, where the few late-night wanderers paid us little attention, oblivious to our discovery. We crossed in front of the Balmoral Hotel and headed up North Bridge, wind buffeting us. A sheet of rain descended, and we increased our speed until we found ourselves outside the Royal Oak.

It was last orders, so we got a double round, pints and whiskies. A guitarist bashed away in the corner, out of tune and hollering about distilling moonshine. We took a table in the other corner and just as I was getting comfortable, Danny unzipped his rucksack and removed one of the leather-bound books from the chamber.

"Fucking hell." The words spilled out of me, surprising everyone including myself.

"Chill," said Danny. I huddled closer, Neve on the other side, until we were hunched over the pages. Careful not to let the book touch the beer-stained table, Danny pried it open to reveal what looked like ledgers written in microscopic black handwriting. In each column, words and numbers, difficult to make out in the gloomy light of the pub.

"What is it? Accounts?"

Neve shook her head. "Names… Gordon… MacAllister…Hamilton… but the numbers, I don't know. Not money. This is pre-decimal, imperial currency maybe."

Danny flicked through the book, the pages purring over his thumb, all of it the same in neat regimented lines.

"Hang on, give it here." I motioned to Danny and he passed me the book. I checked on several pages, and then slapped it shut. "Every entry is for the thirteenth of the month. What date is it today?"

It took them a moment, then Neve spoke. "The thirteenth."

"Whatever happens down there, it just happened," said Danny. He reached for his whisky and downed it.

We were silent. I took a sip of my pint. My fear had subsided, but now I was trembling with a new sensation, something between elation and clarity. I had been underground into this weird place and survived. I was the one who had run the most risk.

Danny was grinning. "Want to see something else?"

He opened his rucksack and removed a dark bottle, placing it in the centre of the table. In the amber, smoky light of the pub the bottle revealed little of its contents; its surface was dusty and the dark liquid was filled almost up to the cork stopper.

"Two souvenirs," said Danny. "Two puzzles to solve."

CHAPTER 11

On Monday morning I got to work fifteen minutes late, bleary and sleep-deprived. I unlocked the door and paused in the hallway to listen for Mary. Nothing. I took the stairs slowly, careful not to step on one of the creaky ones. I got to the basement without any signs of life from above, and relaxed, cocooned in its safe space. I slung my jacket onto the coat stand and sauntered over to my workstation. Then I saw the pair of legs sticking out from underneath my desk.

"What the fuck!"

The legs spasmed and there was a thunking noise as some unseen head hit the underside of the desk, nearly toppling the monitor.

"What the fuck!" echoed a muffled voice.

The legs wriggled out, followed by a torso and head.

"You nearly gave me a coronary." A balding man in a Red Dwarf t-shirt and baggy jeans emerged.

"Likewise. Who are you?"

"Cammy from IT. Who are you?"

"Miro. Overspill."

"Well, Miro. It's your lucky day. Today you get access to the new consolidated city archive database. And the internet. Two for the price of one." Cammy disappeared back under the desk.

I went upstairs to the kitchenette and made a cup of tea. My project to categorise all of Overspill's records in advance of the new database going live had failed. Scary Mary would surely be expressing her disappointment at some point this week, but I had a feeling that the city archive central controllers already knew that Overspill was a lost cause. Anyway, I had bigger worries. The Devil's Chamber had loomed large in my dreams the previous night: the scratches on the armrest of the throne, the crumpled spectacles.

Some twenty minutes later Cammy popped his head in. "That's you all set up. I left instructions on your desk. Don't look up anything naughty on the internet – I'm watching you." He winked, then wandered off, whistling.

I made another cup of tea and returned to the basement. This was undoubtedly the third most exciting thing that had happened in my three months at Overspill, bar boxfile 467 or Bob's accident. I opened Microsoft Explorer and the home page loaded. No more internet cafes for me. I clicked around the BBC Football page for a few minutes and made it my first bookmark. A new world was opening up – being able to sit at my desk and not work, but should Mary arrive unannounced, be under the appearance of working.

My eyes settled on the A4 print-out next to the keyboard with full instructions for the use of the new city archive database, accompanied by apocalyptic warnings about the potential impact of the Y2K bug. I clicked back to my desktop and launched the program. Within seconds it loaded, my new work landscape unfolding in front of me, an obvious upgrade on the previous version, with a pleasant light grey and blue colour scheme compared to the original black and harsh flashing green text. There was a new function – SEARCH ALL. In the old world I could only probe around the virtual world of Overspill. I keyed in those two words – *Devil's Chamber* – and hit return.

One hit.

A book called *Edinburgh's Infamous Legends*, stored in City Archive 15 – the rare book vault at George IV Bridge. I clicked on the record and the page loaded. There was only one copy of the book, it was written by a J.Q. MacQuarrie, published in 1898 by Blackwood, 326 pages, and it had been borrowed twelve times. I clicked on the borrowing history.

The most recent was Harry Robertson, more than two years ago in September 1997.

I knew that name from somewhere. I clicked on the underlined name and Harry's record loaded. He lived in Edinburgh, was born in 1941. One word, in capital letters, gave the game away. STAFF. *Your predecessor.* That was what Bob had said to me in the hospital. I scrolled down through the other names – none were familiar.

"How is the interweb?"

Mary, standing by the stairs, looking at me, arms folded.

"I'm just familiarising myself with the new database. It's really good."

"Just as long as this new technology isn't misused. I've heard things." She peered at me with X-ray eyes, and then clumped back up the stairs.

I clock-watched for twenty minutes until noon then grabbed my jacket and ran upstairs. As luck would have it, a bus rolled up just as I got to the stop at Shandwick Place, and I flashed my pass at the driver and found a seat. As we chugged along Princes Street and swung up onto the Mound I had the distinct feeling of heading towards answers.

At the library I took the stairs to the basement and showed my staff card at the entrance to the rare book vault. The vault was empty save for one anorak looking at nineteenth-century railway timetables. I keyed the book name into the computer and up it popped – *Edinburgh's Infamous Legends*: Rack D, Shelf 6.

I located Rack D and walked into its insulated silence. For a second I got that heady rush, a sensation I hadn't felt for a couple of years – the smell of old books, a deep quietness, a sense of the past that was almost tangible. I had that urge to trace my hand over these tomes, feel each spine brush against my fingertips, feel that concentrated oldness, like thousands of lost lives had been boiled down into a concentrated essence, and here it was, manifested in books.

I found *Edinburgh's Infamous Legends* on its designated shelf – it stuck out a little, a centimetre more than the other books as if it had been recently handled and reshelved carelessly. I slid it out and enjoyed its heft in my hand. I found a corner table and let the book slap open from its own weight.

That smell. Old glue, faded paper, worn leather, ancient ink. The pages were wafer thin, luxuriously glossy. I flipped back to the contents page and scanned through the well-known and lesser-known tales – the White Stag, the Leith Lynchings, Deacon Brodie, the

Piper's Ghost, Major Weir, the MacKenzie Poltergeist, Mary King's Close, the Black Dinner, Burke and Hare. And there it was on page 276 – *The Devil's Chamber*.

CHAPTER 12

THE DEVIL'S CHAMBER

The Wanderings of a Colonial Merchant – a Mysterious Potion – Unforeseeable Truths Revealed – the Hidden Chamber – Missing Urchins – a Cabal of Merciless Merchants – Vanishings Continue

In 1805, Edinburgh merchant James Cardonald Sutherland embarked upon a voyage to the Orient. He hailed from an esteemed Edinburgh family that had profited immeasurably from the sugar trade in the West Indies; the Sutherlands were famed in the New Town for their opulent townhouse, their coterie of Negro and half-caste servants, their dinner parties and collection of trinkets and souvenirs from their colonial exploits.

James was twenty-six years old and a known adventurer; already in his young life he had served one campaign with the Scots Guards in India, overseen an expansion of the plantation in Jamaica, and spent time at the family offices in Baltimore. His parents were keen for him to marry, to take his pick of the daughters of the Edinburgh elite and settle into a life of nurturing their wealth and the next generation of heirs. Yet for James, a life of domestic banalities was not enough for his wayward spirit, and without his father's knowledge he accepted an offer from Ebeneezer Gow, a fellow member of his gentleman's club, to explore opportunities in the burgeoning opium trade in the Far East.

James Sutherland vanished for three years with no word of his whereabouts. Rumours abounded in the city's tea rooms and servants' quarters – James had perished at the hand of Chinese pirates; he had lost himself in the opium dens of Shanghai; he had fallen in love with a governor's daughter in Sydney and was living under a new name; he was wandering, boggle-eyed and mad, in the deserts of North Africa; he was still in Edinburgh, living in the basement of the family home under the watchful eye of his father, forbidden to leave home.

The truth was revealed in 1808, when he landed at Leith docks. Three ships, laden with booty from his travels. Those that knew him well whispered that he had a blank glint in his eye, that he was the same James Cardonald Sutherland to look at, but something in the way he moved and spoke suggested his soul had been stolen and replaced with a surrogate spirit. For weeks, he was the talk of the town – the Edinburgh scion who had returned with priceless porcelain vases, bags of gold and sacks of valuable spices, dragon sculptures and bamboo furniture, and a squadron of coolies to transport it all to the family premises.

After a few days a new rumour emerged. One of the ships had contained a cargo of claret wine, hundreds of dark squat unlabelled bottles. Word came from the servants that the other antiquaries were stored in the basement of the family home, but nobody knew where the wine had gone. James withdrew behind the granite façade of the townhouse and within two months had married one of the merchant daughters recommended by his parents. In his gentleman's club his absence was bemoaned, and gin-befuddled aristocrats speculated that James had succumbed to the delights of the Siamese wine he had stashed in some hidden cellar.

A year passed. The city's gossip peddlers moved on to new pastures, to the illegitimate children fathered by wealthy philanderers, to fortunes squandered by dissolute gamblers, to the misbehaviours that awoke in the city after darkness fell. James was spotted on occasion at church, or at the theatre, always accompanied by his young wife Agnes, who as the year wore on could no longer disguise the bump of their first child. Word had it that the Sutherlands were doing well – they had expanded their business into the cotton trade and further investments in the colonies. Work began on a new townhouse overlooking the Water of Leith, and as the seasons came and went, James and Agnes moved into their new mansion and three healthy children were born. James returned to his gentleman's club after an absence of three years, but he was not the same ebullient spirit they had once known – instead he was aloof, reserved, and insisted on speaking to his fellow members only in the private rooms on the upper floors and never in the smoking-room.

Soon, new rumours emerged – James Sutherland had formed an exclusive club of his own. One by one, he had approached Edinburgh's wealthiest merchants, and persuaded them to accompany him in this new venture. It was said that only those with both money and a ruthless streak were brought into the fold. The loose talk originated from those who had been rejected from the initiative – they complained that this new cabal had some special knowledge of the market, for every investment they made was fruitful beyond belief. This secret society was quietly accumulating more wealth than any merchant bank.

Yet another new story reached the hungry ears of Edinburgh's high society. The glittering rewards the cabal reaped from their colonial investments was not from some special inside knowledge; it was Sutherland's oriental wine that provided them with the power to see into the future. Two drops of the claret in a glass of water gave them a sharp and unwavering vision into the movement of the markets, and by drinking this potion they were able to choose where to put their money – into commodities that would, in short time, return their wealth fivefold.

The curious citizens knew from the Sutherlands' servants that there was no wine in the family townhouse – and for all the rumours in flight across the city, no-one yet knew where the wine was stored or where the cabal drank it. One thing was for sure, it was in a location out of sight and hard to find. Finally, on one dark February night, a bedraggled and half-mad vagrant collapsed in through the door of the White Horse tavern, pleading for help. The landlord took pity on him and as he positioned the unfortunate at the fireplace with a mug of ale, a small crowd gathered to hear the tale.

The vagrant explained that his name was John Hotchkis and he was a former miner who had fallen on hard times, yet was a proud man who spent his days looking for work, often knocking on the doors of New Town establishments and doing odd jobs for a few coins. He had been on one such trip with his friend Sandy just two days ago, and upon knocking on the door of a grand townhouse, it was opened by a stern gentleman who examined them carefully while he listened to their story. The gentleman asked them if they were of fixed abode and they confessed that they were obliged to move around frequently due to their difficult circumstances. On receiving this information, the gentleman's face brightened and he invited them in, explaining that he needed work done in his garden.

They followed him down a staircase towards a room at the end of a corridor where they could hear voices. As they stepped into the room, Hotchkis was surprised to see a collection of gentlemen seated around a table, flanked by two large red-faced men with the look of farm hands. The gentleman spoke to his colleagues thus – "It is our lucky day, my Chamberite friends."

Within seconds the two farm hands had pinned Hotchkis and Sandy to the ground, and the next thing Hotchkis knew was the awful sensation of a rag soaked in foul vapours forced over his face. He woke many hours later in a small cell with Sandy slumped next to him. After some time the door to the cell opened and the same two farm hands pulled them out. They were in a grand office with a trapdoor in the floor, and the farm hands forced them down into darkness, where they stumbled over dark steps leading deep into an underground chamber. A row of hooded figures stood in silence in front of them, and Hotchkis watched in horror as they took Sandy and lashed him to a heavy chair. Sandy screamed as the Chamberites forced his mouth open and poured a black liquid into his throat. As Sandy yelled and babbled, Hotchkis noticed that the farm hands were busy watching the spectacle, and took his chance. He ran for an alcove behind him and plunged into its black maw. They followed him in hot pursuit, but his experience as a miner held him in good stead, and he wriggled through tunnels until their voices grew distant. For a day – perhaps two days, for he had lost all track of time in the underworld – Hotchkis had crawled through narrow spaces until he found a broader tunnel and saw a glimmer of light ahead. He had emerged through a drain into the city, starving and parched, but miraculously alive.

Hotchkis's audience pressed him for more details – which address had the stern gentleman lived at? Would he recognise the farm hands again? Could he show them the drain he'd crawled out of? But overwhelmed by their questions and trembling from his ordeal, Hotchkis could not go on any further. The landlord sent a boy to get the local constable, who led Hotchkis away to a nearby lodging house.

And so the White Horse tavern became the hothouse of new rumours, for it was not long before the drinkers connected Hotchkis's tale of the black liquid and unfortunate Sandy with Sutherland's rumoured oriental wine. The whispers grew louder that many of Edinburgh's rootless poor were disappearing, led underground by the cabal to drink the potion and reveal hidden truths. Nothing was heard of Hotchkis again, and some said he had been tracked down by Sutherland's henchmen and taken back underground permanently.

As the years passed, the stories shrank into the shadows. The British armies triumphed at Waterloo and Napoleon was vanquished; slavery was abolished; Queen Victoria came to the throne; Edinburgh's quiet prosperity grew and multiplied with new buildings of austere granite, while the poor suffered in their forgotten Old Town tenements. James Sutherland aged gracefully, and his sons learned the family business and began to find their own paths. The Sutherland heirs expanded into the burgeoning business of the railways, and manufacturing, and by the time James Sutherland passed away at the grand old age of ninety-five, Edinburgh was a jewel of the north, a beacon in the age of Enlightenment.

Yet still, in our modern age where two-thirds of the globe are under Her Majesty Queen Victoria's watchful guidance, there remain hidden corners and dark places in our best-known cities. In forgotten taverns down Edinburgh backstreets, drinkers whisper advice to each other about avoiding certain routes home, lest an unwary walker fall prey to the cabal.

I sat there with the book in my hands open at that final page for many minutes. The anorak in the railway section was carrying a stack of books over to the librarian and asking for photocopies. I waited until she'd finished, then asked for copies of the Devil's Chamber chapter. She handed back the still-warm sheets of A4 paper and I headed back upstairs into the darkening city.

CHAPTER 13

The rain had done little to quell the appetite of Friday night's carousers – the streets were busy with students and tanked-up office workers, en route to clubs or pubs or curry houses. I dodged the crowds hogging the pavements, keeping an eye on the address numbers as I went, counting up the way, and stopped outside a battered tenement door on George IV Bridge. I pressed the button marked GUNN and heard a crackle of static, then a low buzz. The door unlocked and I stepped into a dank and unlit hallway. I pushed the light switch but nothing happened.

Danny's disembodied voice floated down from high above. "It's broken. I'm on the top floor."

I gripped the bannister and made my way upstairs. On the first floor a door swung open. The burst of light surprised me and I froze. A man stood scowling at me, faded tattoos on his arms and neck, thinning hair spiked up haphazardly. A gouged scar the shape of a comma disfigured one cheek.

"The fuck you looking at?"

I bundled on up the stairs, hauling myself up by the bannister until I reached the top floor. Danny stood in his doorway, beer-can in hand, and next to him in the landing's dead-end was a stack of hiking boots and ropes and a mountain bike chained to the railings.

"Home sweet home," said Danny. "I see you had the pleasure of meeting Mad MacAskill." Danny peered over the railing down below. Mad MacAskill's door slammed on cue. "He's a crazy fucker. Junkie and a thief. Bane of my life. I feel like fucking Billy Goat's Gruff every day having to pass the troll on the bridge."

Inside the flat, the smell of tents that hung around Danny was even more intense. I stepped into a narrow hallway with a crumpled poster of Glencoe tacked to the wall and followed Danny into the living-room. Neve stood by the window, looking out. She turned and smiled.

The living-room resembled the garret of an eccentric lighthouse keeper – the walls were crowded with shelves and stacks of books, a sofa peered out from the wreckage with a tiny TV opposite, and on the other side the kitchenette was cluttered with pots and pans and spice jars. The window looked out onto a city afloat in the rain-lashed darkness.

"Grab a seat," said Danny.

We did as told, perching on the sofa as Danny produced the bottle of claret, a jug of water, a pipette, and two glasses. On the lower shelf of the coffee table I could see the photocopy of the Devil's Chamber chapter I'd given to each of them a couple of nights ago. Danny's copy was crumpled and dog-eared, transformed from the crisp sheaf of A4 sheets I'd given him in a polythene folder.

The compact size of the sofa meant that Neve and I were sitting close together, legs touching. She sat back and her upper arm touched mine – we were almost snuggling.

Danny sat on an overturned beer crate with a pillow on top. "You ready for this?"

I nodded. We had agreed to be the guinea pigs, and Neve would be on hand to deal with anything bad happening.

Danny gripped the cork and twisted it gently. It eased slowly out of the neck of the bottle, and with each twist he coaxed it out a little more, veins in his arms flexing, until the cork slipped out with a tired pop. We watched Danny as he raised the bottle to his nose and sniffed; his face wrinkled, and he gently placed the bottle back on the table. Neve leaned over and sniffed at the bottle – I followed. The black liquid smelled of dust and ash, with sharp undertones of something chemical.

Danny poured two glasses of water, then took the long pipette and lowered it into the neck of the bottle, emerging with a thin sliver of liquid in the vial. He held it up to the light and it looked like blood one moment then blackcurrant wine the next. Danny dripped two drops into each glass and we watched it unfurl like ink, merging with the water until there was nothing but a pinkish trace.

We were silent. From somewhere outside, a lone drunken shout called out.

Neve started speaking. "Are you sure…"

But by then I'd already reached out, picked up the glass, and downed it in one.

It tasted of nothing, of water, but after I swallowed my throat tingled and my vision danced with black spots.

Danny was watching me. I leaned back, Neve's arm pressing into mine. She got up and crossed the room, arms folded in front of her, head tilted downwards. I stared at Danny until he also grabbed the glass and tipped it back.

After a few seconds a vertigo swooped over me and the box-like living-room tilted, like it was on stilts in a high wind. Involuntarily I sucked in a deep breath. My fingers dug into the sofa cushion and my line of vision locked onto the bookshelf, my head fixed into position and unable to move in any direction, staring at the spine of a book called MOUNTAINS OF SCOTLAND, the words becoming sharper the more I stared despite being a full three metres away, the book getting nearer and nearer despite me not moving from the chair until I could see the smudge of sun-bleaching on the edge of the lettering. And then the world tipped, and I fell off the edge.

Muffled darkness. Red shadows. Shapes began to form, then faded. Wave after wave of form and fade. Until one shape assembled, and hardened and sharpened, and then light leaked into the space behind it, and I saw my desk at Overspill and the racks of shelves behind, but the shelves did not finish at the mildewed wall behind the Jungle but continued deep into a vast room like a never-ending warehouse, row upon row of shelving illuminated in a weak grey light. As the picture settled I lurched forward, and I was stumbling on the floor of this Other-Overspill, like someone had pushed me from behind and I had fallen down a couple of steps into this new world.

I walked forward past the familiar shelves until I reached the point where the wall would normally be. After this, the new shelves stretched out. The books and boxes on the shelves were far tidier than in Overspill, and I reached over to inspect the first rack. I lifted a book out but could make no sense of it – the pages were printed with Arabic-like squiggles interspersed with numbers. I checked another book, and another – all the same. My feet carried me forwards and deeper into the space, and when I glanced sideways along the racks I realised that the shelves were not straight but curved, so that I couldn't see the end of each shelf but instead just the point where it curved out of sight. The archive seemed to be shaped like an onion, and I was at the centre. The silence was underpinned by a distant hum, a white noise that was barely audible.

A movement up ahead startled me – someone walked across the aisle, and a head, shoulder and leg disappeared behind one of the shelves. I continued towards the mystery person, unable to stop walking. As I progressed the aisle broadened, and I looked above for the first time to see that the ceiling was so high that it was almost out of sight, a vague solidity beyond a complex lattice of metal girders. The archive walls were also hard to make out – from what I could see they were lined with bookshelves and criss-crossed with a network of pulleys and ladders. I reached the shelf where I'd glimpsed the person disappear, and for once my feet obeyed me and I stopped. In the vast silence I could hear a noise close by – somebody sliding books in and out of the rack.

I stepped forwards, and at the same moment the person moved into my view.

She hadn't changed much.

"Hannah," I said. My first girlfriend, five years since I'd seen her last. She was dressed tomboyishly in rolled-up jeans and a flannel shirt; her hair was pinned up Japanese-style. She was smiling at me, a spark of mischief and something else in her expression.

"I was so sorry to hear about your mum," she said.

She reached over and hugged me. I responded and held her close, an apricot-perfume at her hair and neck that nearly overwhelmed me with its memories. We broke from the hug and she held on to my hand, interlocking her fingers with mine.

"Don't go any further." She nodded in the direction of the vast archives. "Just go back."

I stepped away from her. My feet were moving of their own accord, stepping back and away, then turning sharply and advancing up the aisle. I forced myself to turn and glanced back and saw her watching me.

The aisle sloped downwards and the archive deepened, shelves getting higher. My feet knew where they were taking me. By now my heart was thudding and my breathing was ragged. As the light dimmed I came to a halt next to a smaller bookcase with a yellowing 1983 calendar pinned to the side. The calendar was open at March, the rows of days underneath a picture of a Highland cow, its face obscured with sandy hair. The bookcase contained VHS tapes with titles scrawled on their white labels. My eyes were drawn to a tape in the middle with the words JOHN KUBIK written in spidery block capitals. Without pausing I slid it out of its position and walked with certainty further along the rack, following its slow curve until it levelled out at a TV and video player mounted on a portable trolley. I slotted the tape into the machine, which swallowed it hungrily.

A snowy landscape fizzled on the screen, then settled into a clear and lucid picture of a man sitting in a room not unlike a police cell. He was balding, wearing glasses, and a cheap leather jacket and t-shirt. Despite having no memories of him, I recognised him from photos. My father, John Kubik. He lifted a Styrofoam cup of coffee to his lips, winced, then started to speak. "The truth always hides behind many layers. If you peel those layers back, eventually you get to the heart of it all. And then there's no hiding."

The picture fizzled into snow again. I stepped closer, the blizzard of static louder and louder. I saw that the screen was not made of glass and in fact had no hard surface; it was soft like condensed light and I pushed my fingers into its misty greyness, then my hand and wrist at which point I felt a loss of balance and I tilted into its angry fuzz, my head and shoulders following, and I sank into an underwater gloom in which I floated and bumped around into unseen objects, my voice singing out into the fog until I began to scream.

I opened my eyes. Neve was staring at me, her face just inches from mine. Her mouth hung open and I realised I was lying on the floor and she was leaning over me, her hands gripping my arms.

"Are you OK?" she said.

I sat up and took a moment to check. "I think so." My mouth was parched and I reached for the water. Danny was standing by the kitchen, rubbing his eyes.

"Fucking unbelievable," he said.

I called across to him. "What did you see?"

He smiled and shook his head. "I need some time to digest it. But it was amazing."

I noticed the kitchen clock showed half-past-nine. "I was out for an hour?"

"About that," said Neve. "You were just sitting there, moving around a bit like you were having a bad dream, then at the end you fell out the chair and were… convulsing. I thought you were dying."

I drank more water.

"What happened?" Neve looking at me again, a hint of concern in her eyes.

I stood up. I had a need to walk around, and paced to the corridor and back, then did it again. Danny joined me on the second lap, laughing.

"It's like there's this energy I need to get out of me."

"But what happened?" Neve stood in my way, blocking my route.

"It was hyper-real. I was in a different dimension. This world but not."

Danny laughed. "Same."

"I was at Overspill, but an alternative Overspill. It had miles of racks and records, like the secrets of the universe were stocked there and I had free reign to explore. But it was in a language I couldn't read. It was so real. I could touch and feel everything. Hear stuff." I stopped before I said too much.

Danny opened the fridge and pulled out three cans of lager. "A toast. To Sutherland's claret."

I opened a can and clinked. Neve did the same, but I could sense her tension, her need to taste the claret.

Danny sensed it too. "Next time you're up, Neve. We just need to make sure first there are no side-effects."

We drank a couple of beers and Danny told us more about his trip.

"I was suddenly on a mountain-side. It was a summer's day, but breezy. I could feel it all, smell the dry ground and sense the wind in my face. I began to go higher up this rocky path, working my way over the scree. I reached a cave. At the entrance there were a few ten-pound notes on the ground, crumpled and dirty. I could see more inside the cave so I went in. It was big enough to stand up in. I walked down the track for a few minutes and the walls were glittering with some weird mineral. Eventually the track stopped at a dark pool. On the other side I could see a leather-bound book, a bit like the one we nicked from the Chamber. Behind it I could see stacks of cash, thousands like. There was no way to walk around the pool – the walls rose up all around, and they were smooth and un-climbable. The only way to get to the book would be through the pool. So I stepped in. I could feel the water soak into my shoes and jeans – ice-cold but not unpleasant. I waded in, but when I reached the halfway point the floor dropped away from under me and I stumbled underwater. So I started to swim, the water weighing down my clothes. I was shitting myself to be honest, it seemed close to the other side but no matter how hard I swam I didn't seem to be moving. But then something shifted and my feet touched a rock shelf and I was able to haul myself up onto the other side.

"The book was on some sort of plinth. The cover was hard and cracked, and had some sort of scales on it, like it was made from some weird animal hide. I opened it and inside there were these amazing pictures. It was like a Book of Kells sort of thing – all these diagrams and bright colours, and text swirling around. But when I tried to read it, I couldn't – it was like my eyes slid off the letters. I kept trying, again and again, until I lost my balance and fell backwards. I hit the water and the next thing I knew I was on the floor in the kitchen."

They asked me to go through my trip, every detail of it. I told them everything, up to the point of seeing Hannah, her warning, and the video of my father. I ended the story with me stepping through a gap in the bookshelves and falling headfirst back to the real world.

Danny got us more beers from the fridge and we sat mostly in silence.

"Do you think these visions mean anything?" said Neve.

"It must be some sort of psychedelic," I said.

Danny looked at me. "I think it's like a personalised acid trip, you go into your subconscious and find things out. Stuff that's important to you."

Neve butted in. "Caves, old books, money?"

Danny laughed. "Didn't we just spend six months at work in that dead-end office, fantasising about finding a big pile of cash and never having to work? Having enough money to travel the world for years, staying in five-star hotels as we go?"

Neve turned to me. "And you, Miro? What did it mean?"

I shrugged. "I need some time to think about it." But I already had a feeling that I had started something that could not be stopped.

CHAPTER 14

The side-effects of the claret kicked in that night.

I woke with a lurch, like an adrenaline shot had been injected into my heart, bolt upright in bed and wild-eyed, gasping for breath and clawing at the sheets. Memories slalomed into my head at alarming speed, images and sensations strung together, movie reels and flashbulb photos, my past hurtling towards me.

I saw my mother in our old kitchen, so vivid I could reach out and touch her, feel the cashmere touch of her sweater and living flesh below. She was smiling, glad for this chance. "It's just a few seconds, but it's nice," she said, and squeezed my wrist. My heart stopped.

The harbour in Pitbirnie. The heavy slap of the tide against the seawall. Holding the stub of a joint close to my lips, sucking scalding smoke into my lungs and holding back a splutter, passing the hot roach over to Hannah, who pinched it between finger and thumb and inhaled. Rippling smoke and grey-blue skies, gulls wheeling overhead. An hour since we lost our virginities together. I reached for her hand and her fingers closed on mine.

A shudder, and I was in a new place. Aberdeen. Granite walls and cobbles slicked with sea-mist, a doorway ahead and I climbed stairs up to a flat that was unknown yet known, a place I had never been to in real life but had visited in dreams many times. She stood by the window looking out onto King Street and the buses and fish lorries jostled past. I moved closer. I realised it was an alternative pathway to a future narrowly missed – a girlfriend I almost had. She was unaware of my presence. I saw who she was – Caitlin Gartside, a Sociology student I had an almost-date with in my second year in the city, falling together on a night out with mutual friends and talking for two long hours about life and outer space and dogs, comparing scars, my fingertip tracing the white lesion on her pale arm where she fell off her bike onto a barbed-wire fence aged seven. We were about to kiss when her friend came and dragged her to the toilets for a conference and my friends insisted on moving to the next pub, and despite seeing her on campus from time to time the moment was lost and we never spoke another word to each other except for hello.

She looked out the window, brown hair hiding her face. I moved forward to get close to her and tipped headfirst into an accelerated montage of our lost life together – naked and fucking on white sheets sunlit by a blinding Aberdeen morning; rain pounding the windows as we huddled together under a duvet watching a boxy TV; arguing on the streets of a perhaps American city, skyscrapers looming above and inducing vertigo as she yelled in my face, tears streaming down her cheeks; and at my mother's funeral, the reassurance of her touch and knowing that I must stay with her, this good person, someone who will pilot me through my grief.

The visions faded and I lay in bed looking at the thin line of streetlight bisecting the curtains. I drifted off to sleep for a few minutes but woke again, unable to shake the feeling of those half-dreams, and gradually dawn leaked into the room, stealing away the night. In the shower with water pummelling my scalp and my eyes closed I could still see that room with Caitlin Gartside looking out the window, feel the rumble of traffic outside, sense her loss and mine.

I got to Overspill early, before Mary. I'd picked up a bacon roll on the way in and ate it at my desk. When I finished I looked up and saw the back wall and my vision tilted and for a moment I saw the vast warehouse of Alternative Overspill open up in front of me, the racks and shadowed aisles, and then I blinked and it was gone.

Mary arrived and did her usual tour of the racks, tutting when she spotted smudges of dust or badly filed records. I tapped away on the keyboard, searching for random entries, knowing the computer intimidated her and she would be too embarrassed to ask what I was doing. She muttered to herself and disappeared upstairs.

I made myself a strong cup of tea, letting the teabag steep for several minutes. The post-claret sensation was not unlike a hangover – not the physical aches and seedy nausea, but the feeling of dislocation, of gnawing anxiety. Back at my desk I rang Danny's work number.

"Settlements, this is Danny?"

"It's Miro. How are you feeling?"

A soft chuckle. "Fine. Nothing I can't handle."

"Did you get any… flashbacks?"

"I did."

"A bit freaky, right?"

Another laugh. "Luckily I'm a veteran of multiple narcotics. I expect it won't last long."

I stared into my computer screen. Typical Danny. There was clearly no chance of any solidarity here.

"It's all coming together Miro. We're finding out crazy stuff here. Absolutely crazy stuff. And it's only the beginning."

"What do you mean?"

"We need to explore these other worlds more. I'm going to take the claret again tonight. You up for it?"

The thought of going back into Other-Overspill made me physically unwell – I took a moment to drink some tea, breathe, and steady my guts. "Not tonight. Too soon."

Danny muttered something inaudible. "You know what? We don't need you anymore. You helped us find the Chamber. Me and Neve will do the rest ourselves." He hung up.

I slammed the phone down and stood up. That dickhead.

I aimed a kick at an old box of telephone directories that already bore two previous imprints of my shoe (once in existential rage from the sheer boredom of Overspill, the second time when I got a paper cut from an Edinburgh City Archives memo about the regrettable change of pension policy for new employees) only this time my foot followed through, ripping the box at one side and spilling the contents sliding onto the floor, a mini-avalanche of meaningless out of date data.

I bit my lip, then allowed myself a semi-controlled "fuuuuck."

I got down on my knees to clean up the mess, and immediately saw it staring up at me. A highland cow.

Attached to a 1983 calendar, the month: March. I knelt in front of it motionless. A part of Other-Overspill, appearing here in Actual-Overspill. I picked it up and flicked through it. It was a toffee company promotional calendar, no scribbled notes, no evidence of a previous owner, just a twelve-month calendar featuring sugary Scottish kitsch. I tossed it to one side. Underneath was a slapped open phonebook, splayed out at 'K'. My eye ran down the names and settled on *Kubik, John*. I checked the cover. Edinburgh 1995. Four years ago. I flopped back to the K page. An address in Leith and a phone number.

My dad. Lived in Edinburgh. Maybe still did.

I had of course checked the up to date phonebook. I always checked for Kubiks wherever I went. It was a tic I had – any directory or index, I would scan the Ks. And there were never any. And here one was, at an address in Leith. My knees started to hurt so I rearranged myself on the floor and sat amid the wreckage of the burst-open box until I heard Mary's footsteps above and realised I had been sitting on the 1983 calendar for half an hour.

That night, the dreams returned. They were less fully formed, like the claret's effects were working their way out my system, just shrapnel compared to the previous night's memory bombs. As I slept I caught glimpses of my past and future – my last year at school and a dark night on Pitbirnie harbour after the pub had emptied, ceilidh dancing with Hannah and others, laughing and stumbling over drying fishing nets; a stunning Aberdeen evening, the sun slanting in through the windows of the pub where a local grunge band were setting up, the light catching the unfurling brown molecules on my still-settling pint of Guinness, waiting for friends who had since moved on from my life, but I felt that sharp need mid-dream to speak to them again, a need so sharp that I sat up in bed and called out, awake for a few seconds before I fell back into my dream coma; and next it was the unrecognised future, a drawn-out wander through an office with oversized screens and flashing colours, an empty floor of a skyscraper that could be Chicago or Hong Kong or Frankfurt. The dreams eddied and circulated all night, flashes and glimpses, until I woke sweat-drenched ten minutes before my alarm feeling oddly regenerated.

Never again, I thought. Fuck that claret. Then I thought: maybe just one more time.

I decided not to contact Neve or Danny. I wouldn't blink first. A week passed, and I was relieved to have a mundane existence again. November crept towards December. In the evenings I sat watching TV, waiting for the phone to ring, waiting for Kim's knock. Neither came.

Finally, just when I was about to cave, Neve called me.

"Hello stranger," she said. "We need to make plans."

"What for?"

She laughed. "The next trip to the Chamber. See you at the Ensign Ewart on Friday at eight."

Neve and Danny were already there when I arrived, parked in the furthest corner. Yet another different pub as a meeting place. This was in keeping with Danny's policy to never meet in the same bar twice, although I suspected he just liked trawling around the city's endless boozers. The Ensign was an odd hybrid of tourist pub and dive bar – a short walk to the castle but also an oasis for Edinburgh's thirsty worthies in the tartan-and-shortbread wasteland of the Royal Mile. A permed guitarist strummed folk classics in the corner, while a cluster of American tourists watched hesitantly, their request for a bar menu already rejected by the hatchet-faced barmaid.

"You need a PIN code to get into the fucking toilet here. Welcome to Scotland," said Danny, leaning down to suck the froth off his Export.

I placed my Guinness on the rickety table and manoeuvred out a barstool. Neve made brief eye contact with me, and there was something different about her. Something different about both of them.

"So, you took it Neve?"

She nodded.

"Eight times we took it," said Danny. "A lot's happened since you disappeared."

I looked down at my Guinness. The pint was badly poured and had an inch of white froth instead of half an inch. Three squiggled drips spoiled the otherwise immaculate surface. I felt a sense of rejection, and something else – jealousy, I realised. Two gulps of Guinness rinsed away some of the bad feeling.

"And? What's your alternative universe Neve?"

She shifted in the chair. The guitarist was attempting some banter with the Americans and it was going completely over their heads. There was a moment of silence and Neve waited for him to start twanging his guitar again before speaking.

"New York," she said. "I go to New York. An empty New York though."

Danny was doing his fidgets – one knee bouncing, rolling a cigarette, grinning and looking around the pub. I wanted to punch him. Slam my fist into his nose and bounce him back off his gnome stool.

"Each time it's been the same," said Neve. "I drink the claret and I go through this dark grey tunnel and then emerge from underground onto a wide avenue. Skyscrapers, wide street, traffic lights. Shops. No people. It's autumn, there's a fresh breeze. Golden fading sunlight. I walk and feel everything. Like, really feel it – the tarmac under my feet, the braille on the pedestrian crossing buttons, the yellow aluminium of parked taxis, spits of rain on my face. Every time, no matter which direction I walk in, I end up in this little park with a square and an arch. Like it's at the centre of the labyrinth, the heart of the riddle. There are fallen leaves on the ground. Something takes over my feet and I can no longer walk in any direction I want, instead I go in a loop around the park, always close to the benches. Sometimes I see something on one of the benches in the distance – a person, a paper bag – but it's always vacant by the time I get there. The third time I got close to seeing the person's face. It's a man. Black hair. But that's all I can see so far. Then each time I've got dizzy from walking, sit on one of the benches and kind of melt through it. Then I'm back."

She takes a sup of her wine.

Danny sparks his roll-up. "As for me, I'm getting close. The cave? The book? The money? I can now read some of the text in the book and actually feel the money, pick up the bundles and feel the heft of those notes. Fucking thousands, man."

"What about the text?"

He shrugs. "Just words, not joined up. *Stairs. Falling. Garden. Light.* Isolated words. But it feels like the answer is within touching distance. We need to persevere."

My Guinness was nearly gone. "Maybe the claret is just a freaky trip. Like LSD but it links to your subconscious and weaves a story. Maybe there is no meaning."

Danny shakes his head. "Nah. I feel it here." He stabs a finger at his heart. "It's big. It links into time and alternative realities and dimensions. We are clueless in life, we make decisions based on poor instincts or advice. I think the claret opens up the channels. Takes you down into possible futures. You just have to be smart enough to interpret it."

"I keep reading that chapter you photocopied, Miro." Neve reached over and touched my arm. For the first time I noticed how haggard she looked – grey shadow under her eyes, a slight sag in her cheeks, an absence of light in her eyes. "My theory? Sutherland must have stolen it from some religious sect. Deep in the Chinese interior, or Tibet or Thailand somewhere. A monastery that had built a religion around the properties of this wine, or whatever we call it. And that religion kept this community prosperous and blessed and chosen. They understood the world somehow. And Sutherland came along with his band of pirates and pillaged the lot from them."

"And this sect has transplanted itself in Edinburgh in an underground chamber?"

Neve tilted her head. "They've discovered its full potential too. Whatever it is they do down in the chamber."

"Oh, we'll find out soon enough," said Danny.

The guitarist was hollering out Bonnie Dundee, and the Americans were tentatively tapping the table. The barmaid brought them toasties – a compromise had clearly been found.

"Must be your round, Danny?" I jerked my thumb at the bar.

"For once you might be right." He slapped his thighs. "Same again?"

I watched him go to the bar, his gait a little unsteady.

"Were you guys drinking before here?"

Neve nodded. "Had a couple. We've both found it helps with the comedown."

"I got these… intense memory dreams. A bit freaky."

"I get dreams too. But it's more a replay of the trip. Like swooping through it again at an accelerated speed. Rollercoastering through New York streets. I've been waking up feeling very unusual."

Part of me wanted to say it. *I met my mum again, and it was real, she touched my arm.* But I held back.

Danny returned from the bar. More punters had arrived and a steady hubbub had built up. "So," he said. "To business."

He cleared a space on the shiny zinc panel on the table. We could see our warped reflections as we leaned in, faces twisted and discoloured by the bar lights. Danny built a model of the Devil's Chamber using objects at hand. A beermat represented the body of the chamber; a neatly folded Rizla doubled as the stairs down; four matchsticks represented the corridors leading out of the beermat-chamber; and at the end of those four matchstick-corridors, a one pence coin was the library, another penny doubled as the claret cabinet alcove, a bus ticket and trail of matchsticks mapped out the corridor leading to the underground river, and the loose ends of Danny's pockets – a paper-clip, a sweet wrapper, a peanut and a raisin – provided an ambitious visualisation of the unexplored final corridor.

"Here's the plan." He cracked his knuckles. "We get down there early. We go in to the Guildford with Neve in the morning – she's opening up the pub on the thirteenth, first one in – and you and me Miro hide out in the store-room until the bar manager Raymond gets in. Then Neve sneaks off, and we head down to the chamber. We have no idea when they start their ceremony or whatever it is they do down there, so we need a hiding place, somewhere we can see what they're doing while we're unseen. So we find our spot and get ready. It might be a long wait. But it'll be worth it."

Danny dragged his hand through his makeshift map, deconstructing it back into random junk.

The music got louder, the guitarist yelling out *American Pie*, the American tourists singing back at him, and even the dour barmaid joined in, standing on a chair and flapping her arms overhead. Just as the song was finishing another posse of Americans entered the pub, similarly decked out in pastel-coloured Gore-Tex, and converged on their compatriots in a storm of high-pitched greetings and laughter.

It was my round, and I moved quickly before the Americans could get to the bar.

While waiting for the Guinness to settle I opened my wallet and checked my cash situation. I noticed the crumpled edge of something protruding from one of the leather slits and teased it out with thumb and finger. It was a picture of Hannah I must have secreted there on some long-lost drunken night, a trimmed snapshot of her laughing at the camera some four or five years ago when we were seventeen or eighteen, her cheeks flushed with drink but shining with youth and fun and energy. It was a picture I'd always loved and I'd forgotten about it. I remembered meeting her in Other-Overspill and that feeling of her body close to mine.

I took the drinks back and Neve got up to go to the toilet. Danny was grinning, like he couldn't wait to tell me something.

"Cheers," he said. "To new beginnings."

I clinked pints with him.

"Something happened this week," he said. "Me and Neve? We're an item."

My guts curdled.

"We talked for ages after taking the claret for the first time and things just happened. We got close, I suppose. Shared experience and all that. She stayed over." He winked at me. "We made the beast with two backs."

"Congratulations," I offered.

He beamed. "You're not pissed off?"

"Nah. I'm seeing someone now. Good luck to youse."

Neve returned and the pub became even noisier, and we drank three more rounds before spilling out into the night and I watched them walk away, moving down the Royal Mile together. When I got back to Lothian House I tapped gently on Kim's door and she opened it with fury in her eyes, told me I'd broken the rules and what if Darren had been there when I knocked, what would happen then? She lunged at me in the corridor and we kissed, teeth clacking. We waltzed backwards through my door and into my bedroom.

In the dark I fucked the anger out.

She came twice.

We lay in the soupy half-light, watching the headlight patterns on the ceiling.

"Do you want more than this?" she said. "I'll leave Darren."

I turned away from her and closed my eyes.

CHAPTER 15

Neve and Danny were already waiting outside the Guildford when I got there on the morning of the thirteenth. When they saw me Neve took a small step sideways away from Danny. By the time I reached the pub she had unlocked the door – I followed them inside, and in one fluid motion Neve slammed the door shut again and double-locked it.

The pub was unnaturally still, the lingering whiff of cigarettes and spilt beer heavy in the air. Neve moved quickly behind the bar and opened the hatch. "You guys go to the toilet now, it might be your last chance for a while."

Danny slung his rucksack onto the bar and walked off in the direction of the gents.

"What's tripping your face?" Neve asked, looking at me.

"Nothing."

"Are you ready for this?"

"Yeah. And you?" I returned her stare. "The new romance affecting your focus?"

She flinched. "Danny? What did he say?"

"Says you're an item."

"Jesus. It's not…" She stopped and pressed a hand to her forehead. "Forget about it. We need to all keep our wits about us today."

Danny reappeared, complaining that there was no soap. Neve gave me a bottle of liquid handwash, and I went to the toilet but couldn't pee. I stood at the urinal trench staring at the cracked white tiles trying not to think about what was waiting for me under the floor.

Back at the bar, Danny was already climbing down into the cellar. Neve ushered me to follow.

"What's the plan?"

"You guys hide out in the storage room until I come down. I'll wait till Raymond shows up then I'll sneak down to join you."

"How do you explain your absence to Raymond?"

She showed me a handwritten note: SORRY RAYMOND, WOMEN'S TROUBLES, BACK LATER, FIONA. "Go," she said.

I climbed down the ladder. Danny had left the storage room door ajar. When I entered I could see him lying on some chairs close to the ventilation shaft. "Make yourself comfortable," he said. "Neve will probably be an hour or so."

I took up position opposite Danny on a pile of boxes. I used my jacket as a pillow and closed my eyes. I was sleepy after an unsettled night and dozed on the makeshift bed. Danny's voice startled me awake.

"You're lucky, you know."

I let his statement hang for a few moments in the darkness. "What you on about?"

"Neve told me you don't have any parents."

I couldn't put a sentence together. "Lucky?"

"You are free in this world. Untethered."

My fingers dug into the cardboard underneath me.

"Ah, maybe I'm not explaining it well. Look, we're on the brink of something here. Of finding out something massive. It's going to change our lives. You can just up and go anywhere you want, vanish. This is what my main claret dream is about – the money. If we can crack it, unravel that riddle, there's a fortune waiting for us."

"I have family. Grandparents, aunt and uncle, cousins."

I could almost hear Danny's derision in his pause. "It's easy to escape those bonds. My mum and dad? Established Edinburgh middle class, always snooping around, they know everything about me even if I hardly ever see them. I've been the big disappointment in the extended family ever since I started high school. Daniel and his poor exam results. Daniel and his lack of focus. Daniel and his marijuana. Daniel and the crashed Mini Metro. Daniel and his not real university, the polytechnic pretending to be a university, and Daniel not even capable of finishing his course in that pretend university. Daniel and his dangerous climbing. And on and on and on."

Silence. A vacuum.

"So that's my point," said Danny. "I'm not saying it's a good thing that your mum or dad are dead, I'm just saying this will be a totally new beginning for you. Your bad luck will become your good luck."

My eyes had adjusted to the darkness and I could see his shape about two metres away from me, lying in a half-slouch, his feet perched on a nearby barstool.

"You know nothing about me, Danny."

"Oh, I've guessed plenty. The way you always looked at Neve, for example. That told me lots."

I said nothing, glad he couldn't see the flush in my cheeks.

"You're caught up in all of this by accident, Miro. A pretty girl that you liked, and you did stuff that you thought would get you close to her. And now all of this craziness. And now you realise that you're not an adventurer like us. Neve is not the sort to become a girlfriend, which is what you day-dreamed about in your boring-as-fuck days in Overspill, imagining going on dates with her and running across the Meadows hand-in-hand, and maybe even you imagined sex with her. But your daydream is all an impossible fiction, and now you're starting to slowly understand."

"Fuck off." My voice came out weak, a half-whisper. I tried to process everything he'd said, formulate a killer reply, but instead one thing he'd said snagged in my head. *Main claret dream*. "You said *main* claret dream. You've had other dreams? Not just the cave?"

He raised one arm above his head, like he was trying to see his own hand in the half-dark. "Yeah, I've had other dreams. Early days but I think the claret has three gears. Past, present, future. You can visit either one. It all depends on how you train your mind going in."

We lay in the dusty silence, the room lit only by the crack of light under the door from the main cellar.

"Look, don't get upset about the Neve thing," said Danny. "I know it's uncomfortable for you, but just deal with it. It's part of growing up."

"Oh, and at twenty-six, four whole years older than me, you're a fucking veteran of life?"

"No. I'm not. But right now I feel like you're ten years younger than me. Are you a virgin? I suspect you might be."

I closed my eyes and got a flashback of Kim clawing at my back, biting my ear. I stayed quiet until he sighed and shuffled around on his chair-bed into a new position.

Voices upstairs. Five minutes later the door eased open and Neve snuck in. "Come on," she said. "Let's get going."

Danny pointed at the ventilator shaft. "Miro. Your turn to go first."

I clicked my headlamp on and tucked in my shirt. As I ducked my head into the hole, the smear of our limb movements in the dust from the previous trip looked like the trail of a dying animal. I pushed away my fears and crawled as fast as I could, elbow over elbow, knee over knee. I reached the dogleg and turned right. The others were behind but I was determined to outpace them. When I was close to the end of the tunnel I dimmed my headlamp and stopped, straining my ears for any sounds of revelry. Nothing. I edged forward until I reached the gaping mouth and slipped through its gap out of the ventilation shaft and onto the concrete ledge. Still no noise. Getting bolder, I stood up, turned my headlamp onto full beam and leaned over the edge.

Below, my torch cut a swathe through the darkness, illuminating the stairs and the tiled wall. Neve and Danny appeared behind me. I clambered over the ledge and swung myself down. The red shoelace was still in position on the bannister. I dropped down to the stairwell, the stone satisfying under my feet after the metallic claustrophobia of the tunnel. Danny dangled above me then he dropped down too. He reached up to help Neve but she refused and swung herself down onto the stone step.

We stood in silence for a moment, and then Neve spoke.

"What's up?"

I didn't understand what she meant at first, but then saw her gesturing up the stairs. Danny nodded for us to follow. We climbed the steps for perhaps three minutes until they ended, merging into the ceiling. Our torch beams showed a wooden trapdoor with heavy hinges. Danny moved close to it and pressed with both hands. It didn't yield. "Locked from above," he whispered.

We stood and listened, expecting some signs of life, but the silence only deepened, and Neve was the first to move off again. Back down the steps, our torch beams wobbling and splashing light onto the dusty tiles. Danny pointed out the red shoelace and adjusted it slightly to make it less visible from up the stairs and more visible from below. "Just in case we need to run for it," he said.

The memory of last time and my mad lunge for the shelf returned to me. For a second I thought about climbing back up, wriggling through the tunnel and out into the pub, but something made me stay.

"Remember," said Danny. "Be careful with the headlamp. At the first sign of others, aim for a hiding place, then switch it off."

As we approached the bottom of the steps the strange luminescence crept out to meet us. I went first and popped my head out.

The chamber was empty of life but waiting for its masters.

Two rows of chairs were lined up in front of an oak table and the heavier throne-like chair. I scanned the rest of the chamber, each of the corridor mouths and walls, but could see no movement. I beckoned for the others to follow.

I counted the chairs – thirteen in all, same as before. Meanwhile, Neve was wandering the chamber, looking up. She motioned for us to follow, and pointed up some five metres above, where a small balcony jutted out from the stonework. We hadn't noticed it on our last visit.

"We need to get up there."

"It must be through the fourth archway." Danny pointed over to the one unexplored corridor.

Five metres into the tunnel, a doorway opened on the left, breaking into other spin-off tunnels, some with steps leading down, some up. Neve pointed at the second and I ducked in after her and Danny. Quickly the stairwell narrowed into a tight throat, so narrow that to climb these steps you had to use your hands as much as your feet. The wall crumbled under our fingers as we climbed, showering fragments of stone and cobweb down into the space below. I was aware of Neve and Danny both exiting the stairwell and soon I was joining them, stepping out onto a ledge of stone with a narrow balustrade. Down below was the chamber and the formation of chairs. Neve smiled and gave a thumbs-up – this was our spot.

We took a couple of minutes to get organised. Danny placed the rucksack at one side of the doorway, then we lay down on our bellies, each of us facing the side of the balustrade. Through a gap in the latticework we could see the chairs. The stone floor underneath was uncomfortable but after a couple of minutes we settled. Neve was in the middle, and I was at the outermost edge of the balcony – the furthest from the exit. This was already bothering me, but Danny would have the additional burden of the rucksack, so perhaps we were all equally disadvantaged for a sharp exit. My agitation was further stoked by Neve's close presence – her arm was touching mine, and when she moved, strands of her hair spilled onto my elbow.

"Where does the light come from?" Neve whispered. "So weird."

I tilted onto my side and let my head rest on the stone, looking high above to the ceiling of the chamber. There was no sign of any openings in the ceiling from which the light could emanate; instead, it was like the walls themselves had a sickly glow of moonlight. With the headlamps switched off my eyes had adjusted to the pale light and I could see everything in disconcerting detail. The ceiling was rounded, like in the naves of the cathedrals I'd visited in Italy with my mother as a sixteen-year-old. The walls were structured from granite blocks and bricks, seamless at a distance but on closer inspection assembled with geometrical precision. It was hard to imagine how they had brought craftsmen into this underground space and transported materials down here. More worrying at the moment – why had it been built?

I rolled back onto my front and rested my head on my forearm. The only sound was the sea-like noise of the others breathing, a soft rise and hush. Despite the weirdness of all of this, I felt strangely at peace, protected from the real world under layer upon layer of stone. I closed my eyes and drifted off to sleep.

CHAPTER 16

I woke with Neve's hand clamped over my mouth. Her finger was pressed over her lips and her eyes were frantic. I understood – I was in the Devil's Chamber, and I should be quiet.

There was noise from below – footsteps, and hushed voices. Neve's grip on my face slackened and she turned to look through the balustrade. I was dislocated from the unexpected sleep, trapped between two worlds, and not sure which was the more unsettling. Heart pounding, I tilted my head to look below.

A cluster of men moved towards the seats. A chill prickled on my skin when I saw what they were wearing – long black robes, and hats with sheep-skulls mounted on the scalp. I recognised the man-giant I had seen arranging the chairs; he was a head taller than the others, and moved slowly, his barrel-like torso encased in a black shirt. With him was someone who definitely didn't belong in the chamber – a small, child-like man with spiky fair hair and ripped jeans. He was sobbing and being held firmly by the giant.

The men in the sheep-skull hats sat, organising their robes around their legs until they got comfortable. The giant forced the fair-haired guy into the throne and tied him to the chair arms and legs. The sound of the captive cursing in a high voice resonated through the chamber, until a brief scuffle with the giant silenced him. There was a moment of quiet then the giant stepped to one side, and one of the sheep-skulls stood up and moved over to the throne.

In the hand of the lead sheep-skull was a bottle of claret. He moved around in front of the throne, obscuring my view, but I soon understood what was happening – the giant had levered the prisoner's jaw open and Sheep-skull was forcing a cup of the liquid into his mouth.

A sound of spluttering and choking, and voices urging him to do as told. I sensed Neve and Danny tensing beside me. Sheep-skull stepped back, revealing the fair-haired man again. His mouth and chin was stained dark and he was moaning in pain.

"Let the claret speak," said Sheep-skull.

The prisoner slumped in the throne, as if asleep, and the others sat facing him, waiting for something. I looked over at Danny, who was staring at the scene in deep concentration. When I looked at Neve she sensed my attention and glanced over at me, her eyes wide with fear.

Sheep-skull moved over to the throne and whispered something in the fair-haired man's ear. He flinched. Then, slowly, as if possessed by a spirit, he began to buck and writhe in the throne, nonsense words spilling out of his mouth. His alien voice sounded out across the chamber.

"Sogar moot lignin pollet, rig poh thar…"

Neve put her hands over her ears.

"Rag lando jick metno par kinto gool…"

Sheep-skull slapped him, and he rocked in the throne, but continued babbling. Sheep-skull slapped him again, and again, and again; now his face was darkened with blood along with the wine.

"Reveal the truth. Reveal the truth!"

The hostage took a gulping breath, and another, then two words rang out loud and clear.

"Savage Hill."

He began to convulse, in some kind of fit. The words again: "Savage Hill! Savage Hill! Savage Hill!"

Then dark liquid erupted from his mouth, spilling down his front and splashing onto the ground. The men in the chairs sat and watched, impassive. A full two minutes the fit lasted, until finally the prisoner bucked one last time and was still.

One of the other men stood up and moved to the oak table. He removed a book from the folds of his robes, opened it, and wrote something inside. There was a moment's pause, as if he was waiting for the ink to dry, then he closed the book with a heavy thunk. Chairs screeched on the stone floor as the congregation stood up; the lead sheep-skull left first, heading towards the stairs, and the others filed after him, carefully slipping into formation as if there was a defined order of seniority. The giant stayed behind with the hostage. The chamber echoed with the sound of footsteps as they climbed the stairs, fading into the distance until silence returned.

We were absolutely still. Below us, the giant was untying the prisoner. With what looked like a dishtowel he cleaned the blood and wine off the victim's face, then hauled him up over his shoulder in a fireman's lift. He turned in our direction and walked towards our narrow balcony. With every step it became more apparent that he was coming towards the same tunnel entrance that we had accessed. As he got closer I could see the poor state of the dead man's clothes – mud-stained jeans and ancient Adidas trainers, his hair matted from lack of washing. The giant disappeared and next thing we heard his footsteps below us, scuffling about in the corridor. I remembered there were three or maybe four different turnings – surely he wouldn't come up to the balcony with the body?

My eyes locked with Neve's, and we stared at each other. The footsteps receded.

"Let's go," whispered Danny.

I reached out and put a hand on his shoulder. "No. Sit tight. He'll be dumping the body somewhere, then he'll come back."

We lay there in the silvery silence, the stonework of the balcony caging us in. Neve had closed her eyes and was concentrating on her breathing. Danny, by contrast, was fidgeting, ready to run, a livewire.

Maybe five minutes passed, but then we heard the scuff of feet on stone, and below us the giant emerged back into the chamber. He picked up two chairs at a time and ferried them back through the archway, until at last all that was left was the table and the throne. He stood looking at the throne, hands in pockets, and laughed. "Stupid wee junkie." The voice was surprisingly child-like.

He hoisted the table above him and balanced it on the top of his head and walked it out the chamber. He returned for the throne, and even for him its weight was a struggle, as he grappled with it for purchase and lugged it step by step balanced against his thigh. It took longer for him to reappear, and he was visibly out of breath, wiping sweat from his forehead. He stood in the middle of the chamber and contemplated its emptiness. "Fucking chamberites," he said. He ducked his face against his upper arm to blot more sweat, then sloped off towards the stairs. His steps were heavy all the way up, until the dull thud of the trapdoor closing resonated across the underground space. We lay still for a couple of minutes, listening for more, but nothing came.

"Let's get the fuck out of here." Neve was on her feet, stepping over us, already skipping down the stairs. Danny slung the rucksack onto his shoulder and I followed them both down the narrow spiral staircase. Neve paused at the bottom, chopping her hand to indicate that we should also stop – we listened, heard nothing, then moved on. We repeated this at the entrance to the chamber, then scampered quickly across its smooth floor. I tried not to stare at the black splashes but it was no use. The dark liquid glinted in the moonlight glow, still drying. It occurred to me that the giant had perhaps gone to get a mop and this made me move even faster, falling into step next to Neve as we took a few steps then paused; a few steps then paused. We switched on our headlamps and the hyperactive swoop and spin of our torch beams as we climbed the stairs made me dizzy.

"Here," said Neve. "Here." She pointed at the bannister to where the red shoelace was tied. I gave her a foot up and she launched herself at the ledge. Using the palm of my hand as a platform I pushed her foot higher until she was over the lip. There was no sign of

Danny but I wasn't going to wait around. I used the same tactic as last time, launching myself up at the cracked tile and gaining a fingerhold, then balancing two feet on the railing. A pause for breath, then I made a scrambling jump for the ledge; first, my right hand gripped the ridge, then my left; the tearing pain as I strained for purchase, and then the triumphant feeling of pulling my head up to the edge, swinging a leg over, and gravity doing the rest as I tumbled onto the concrete.

Neve was already clambering into the ventilator shaft and I followed, the claustrophobia and the hollow bump of elbows and knees on metal familiar by now as we burrowed our way back. I misjudged my exit and fell headfirst out into the storeroom, but my descent was cushioned by an empty cardboard box. I wriggled up onto an old carpet and collapsed, panting like a dog.

"Where's Danny?"

Neve was somewhere nearby in the darkness. "When did you see him last? I don't remember."

"Fuck."

CHAPTER 17

We lay there, not speaking, alone with our thoughts. Minutes passed. The noise up above leaked down to us – the pub was busy, voices and the clink of glasses and a raucous laugh. Another noise began to encroach, a bumping and scurrying, and in the half-light I could see Neve smiling. Danny's head popped out the ventilator shaft, and slowly he slid the rest of his body out, tumbling onto the storeroom debris.

"Where were you?" said Neve.

Danny grinned where he lay, chest still heaving as he got his breath back. "Exploring." He slung an arm over his eyes, as if to block out the sun.

"Fuck's sake Danny," I said. "You broke the rules you gave us. We're supposed to stick together."

He tilted his hand and gave me the finger.

"That was murder," said Neve. "We were witnesses to a murder."

That word – *murder* – felt unbelievable and almost over-dramatic, until I remembered again the final convulsions of the dying prisoner.

"How do we get out of here, Neve?" said Danny.

"I'll go upstairs, surprise them. Then I'll bang on the ladder three times when there's a good moment. When you hear the sign, move quickly. First I need to get changed."

She removed a plastic bag out from behind the door and slid out carefully folded clothes. We must have both been staring, because she scowled at us. "Can you maybe give me some privacy?"

We both turned away, heard her undressing and dressing again.

"Okay, I'm decent." She was stuffing her dust-stained clothes into the bag, dressed again in a fresh version of her Edinburgh barmaid outfit of white blouse and black jeans. "Stay by the door. Be ready."

We waited, me and Danny, inches away from each other. I stared at the door handle, not wanting to make eye contact. We must have waited for a full ten minutes until we heard the metallic clang three times.

Out the door and quickly climbing the ladder. I was up first, and at the top of the hatch stood Neve, pointing to the left.

I sauntered through the gap in the sliding door out to the bar area. There were maybe twenty drinkers at tables near the bar but not one was looking in my direction. I sensed Danny behind me as I strolled to the toilet.

At the urinal trough I exhaled as I peed, finally able to go after five hours in the chamber. Danny stood at the far end from me. At the sinks we washed our hands, cleaned smudges of dirt off our faces, all the time avoiding eye contact.

"I'll go out first," said Danny. "Want a pint?"

"Deuchars. Whisky as well."

I waited a minute, then headed out into the Guildford. It was a pub again, and I was just an innocent punter. I wandered up to the bar and stood next to Danny. In front of us, Neve/Fiona pulled two pints of creamy IPA, and glugged out two measures of Oban.

"What flavour of crisps?" she said to Danny.

"Salt and vinegar and a cheese and onion."

Neither gave any sign they knew each other. We took our pints and drams and chose a table in the far corner. Danny held the rucksack close and tucked it under his feet when we sat down.

The first mouthful of ale was amazing after those underground hours, and I tipped back a larger gulp. The memory of their victim came back to me, choking up black poison, writhing in the throne. "What now?"

Danny looked at me, and for once I saw fear in his eyes. Then his smirk returned – that annoying, punchable smirk. "Don't be so nervous, Miro. We've got to stay cool."

For a brief microsecond I was about to upend the table and swing knuckles into his face – but the moment passed. "Okay smartarse, tell me the plan."

He picked up two beermats and began manoeuvring them round the table top. "Right, let's focus on the good stuff first. Those fuckers didn't see us, they don't know we were down there, even if they find out that someone came down from the pub cellar they can't trace us, hundreds of folk pass through here every week. So we're under the radar."

"But what we saw down there? We have an obligation to report that."

"How long do you think we'd last before they got to us? We'd be dead before the ink was dry. Those fuckers obviously don't fear the police."

"So what is it, then? We just walk away and forget it?"

Danny looked at me as if I was mad. He leaned in close. "Come on, this is the biggest adventure you'll ever have in your life. I've climbed the Forth Bridge at night, I've driven a motorbike at two hundred miles an hour on the M8, I've been to a Russian mafia orgy in London. This is going to be the biggest rush of them all."

The anxiety burrowed deeper inside me. There was not going to be an easy way out of this.

Danny's voice became gentler. "What we saw… clearly these are evil bastards. I have no idea what went on down there but we need to find out more, then expose them at the right time. We'll find a way to do it anonymously and watch the impact from a distance. Imagine this story hitting the papers? It's all about timing though."

I took a mouthful of the Oban, and let it burn slowly down my throat. "That guy died. And he wasn't the first – if this happens every month, then we're talking mass murder."

"Maybe."

I looked at the table next to us to check for eavesdroppers, but it was two young male students, already half-drunk and talking too loudly about sitcoms. Emboldened, I continued. "Listen, think about what we know. They meet on the thirteenth of every month down there. It must have been around one o'clock, which would make sense – thirteen hundred hours. Thirteen, thirteen, and there were thirteen of them."

Danny nodded. "Fuck, you're right."

"Obviously they're into symbolism. The sheep-skull, the black robes, something a bit satanic about it all. They need someone to…" I couldn't get the word out at first but took a breath and spat it out. "Sacrifice. The wine plays a part. They get something from the exchange, whatever it is gets logged in the books. They go away and do whatever they do with the information. If you give me the book, I'll do more research, see if I can make any sense of it."

Danny raised his pint glass and we clinked. His smugness had gone again, and our camaraderie quelled my dread a little.

"Shall we get another?" said Danny. "Neve finishes her shift in an hour. We might as well wait for her."

She took longer than expected, and by the time she walked around the side of the bar and nodded at us we'd had three pints. She went out first, and after a couple of minutes we followed. She waited for us at the top of the Waverley steps as planned and moved into our slipstream as we passed. We had agreed her colleagues shouldn't see her with us. After what had happened, it felt right to be paranoid. Now that the skies were darkening I felt unsettled, like maybe someone was watching us. The city had eyes, I knew that; it was small enough to run into people you knew all the time.

We walked over North Bridge and turned towards George IV Bridge. Danny told us to wait outside his tenement building as he dropped off the backpack.

"Curry?" said Neve. "I'm starving."

We hailed a taxi and headed down to Haymarket, to a little restaurant Neve knew well. It was around five o'clock and early enough to take our pick of tables. Huddled in the back corner, a full three metres from the nearest people, we had enough space to talk freely.

Neve shook her head. "I'm struggling to take it all in."

Danny loaded a scrap of poppadum up with lime pickle and crunched into it. "So fucked up."

"We need a plan," said Neve. "They do this once a month, right? So January thirteenth is the next one. We have to find out as much as we can and as soon as we can."

"So we go back down?" My voice wobbled, and the others heard it.

"Yes," said Neve. "We go back down. We need to do a few things. Take photographs. Explore the corridors. Find where the big guy took the body. Draw a map. Find where the stairs come out. We need to divide it up among us and try to do it before Christmas."

The mention of that word brought a rush of sadness so acute that I had to take a few seconds to compose myself. I had done no Christmas shopping, and had avoided watching television and listening to the radio. I had been glad to work in Overspill and avoid the office party Christmas hysteria which was now infecting the city. But now, after the emotions of the day, the mention of Christmas brought it all home to me: I had seen a man being killed today, and next week I would go back home for a family Christmas without my mother.

I took a swig of Kingfisher and pretended to focus on the poppadums.

The curries arrived, three sizzling Balti dishes with a stack of naans and a steaming bowl of rice. It was good just to eat and forget – all of us were famished and within ten minutes the dishes were empty and we had pushed our chairs back. The physiological pleasure of eating hot food had helped me recover my composure, but now a new need had arisen – sleep. After yesterday's late night and the events of the day I needed to sleep badly.

We decided to walk back, and Danny proposed I come to pick up the book and take it for safekeeping. We arrived at Danny's tenement and he opened the door and waved us in. Loud music drifted down the stairwell. The Clash, with 'Lost in the Supermarket.' As we reached the first landing, Danny nodded to the door of Mad MacAskill, which was slightly ajar. The music was far too loud even for a party – it was loud just to provoke. Danny shook his head and we continued up the stairs.

I almost walked into Danny's back when we reached the third-floor landing. He was staring at his door, which was burst open at the lock.

"Fuck."

We froze, all three of us, and Danny edged forward, and nudged the door open further. There was no sign of life in his place and we crept into the hall and then into his tiny living-room.

He pointed at the table. "The bottle. It's gone."

I tried to stay calm. "Did someone follow us?"

Danny was looking at his shelf. "Nope. My CDs have gone too. And the tenner I had in that jar. Mad MacAskill."

We stood there, listening to the Clash belting out in the corridor.

"Is that your CD?" Neve asked.

Danny looked worried. "Yep."

We descended the stairs in the gloom, the music getting louder step by step. Outside MacAskill's door we paused, waiting for guidance, but none came. Amid the music a voice was audible, the cadence of a drunk, too fast and the tone lurching up and down. Danny pushed the door open into a drab corridor with an ancient brown carpet. The voice was coming from the door at the end of the hall. Danny went first and we followed.

MacAskill was sitting in front of an electric fire, talking to nobody but himself. He was wearing shell-suit bottoms and a Hearts top at least five seasons out of date. On the table in front of him was the bottle of claret, uncorked, and next to it a scrunched-up ball of tinfoil. MacAskill was alternately laughing and gulping for breath. He saw us and lurched to his feet.

"It's the fucking climber!"

He staggered over, and up close I could see that the whites of his eyes were a salmon-pink colour. The comma-shaped scar on his cheek oozed pus. MacAskill pointed at Danny. "Thanks for the wine you wee prick."

MacAskill started laughing, and a slurry of words tumbled out his mouth, inaudible gabbling that slowed to a whisper. Then he seemed to buckle, as if someone had cut all of his sinews and tendons, and he slumped back on to the sofa. A noise somewhere between cough and hiccup came out his mouth, followed by a spillage of dark red liquid. He wheezed and then was still.

We stood there without moving, the dark liquid oozing from the corner of MacAskill's mouth and dripping onto the Hearts top, darkening its maroon fabric, as the music continued to belt out the speakers. Danny moved over to the stereo and switched it off, then began stowing CDs into a plastic bag.

For the second time that day we had seen a man die.

"Let's get out of here," I said.

Danny cradled the plastic bag of CDs against his belly. "Wipe any surface you touched. You can't leave any fingerprints."

"What about the claret?" said Neve.

"You grab it, Miro."

The landing was quiet, and Danny slowly closed MacAskill's door. We slipped back up the stairs and into Danny's flat, where he produced a bottle of Highland Park from a cubby hole in his pile of books. We took a glass each, but its smooth burn offered little comfort.

Danny spoke first. "We should avoid seeing each other for a while. Think things through."

Neve pointed at the floor. "What about MacAskill? We can't just leave him."

"We can," said Danny. "It's best that way. Someone will complain about the smell in a few days and the police'll find him. Just another junkie death."

Neve was crying. She rubbed her sleeve over her face as if to pretend she just had something in her eye.

Danny produced the book he'd stolen from the Chamber, wrapped it in a plastic bag, and handed it over to me. "See what you can find out."

"What next?" said Neve.

"I'll phone you with a plan," said Danny. "Then you phone Miro. Until then, no contact."

CHAPTER 18

At Overspill, the day was as boring and non-eventful as ever. For the first time since I had started working there, I felt a kind of contentedness, an appreciation of how ordinary and safe this dusty and dank corner of Edinburgh was. I was glad for my desk and rack of pens, my framed photograph of the family reunion three years ago showing all of us on the beach in Pitbirnie, smiling at the unseasonal sunshine, my mother standing next to me defiantly grinning away the cancer. I was glad for my desk drawers, and the notebooks and clutter of paperclips and staples, the books and magazines that I now took less effort to hide.

I doodled on a scrap of paper and mentally mapped out the coming days and weeks. I had one week left at work, and then I would break for Christmas and New Year. Next Tuesday I would catch the train with Fergus and head back up to Fife, the first time I had been back since moving to Edinburgh. I would stay there for ten days or so and return to Edinburgh for Hogmanay, and two days later start back at Overspill. And after that? There was only one date that meant anything. January the thirteenth. The next meeting of the black-robed men in the Devil's Chamber.

I decided to go and get some lunch, and as I put my jacket on I caught sight of the stack of phonebooks from the box I'd kicked open last week. I picked up the 1995 phonebook and dropped it on my desk.

KUBIK, JOHN. I wrote down the phone number and address – a quick check of the A-Z revealed it was in Leith – and folded it into a tight square. I put it in the zip pocket in my wallet. It would stay there, I decided, until I knew what to do.

In the mid-afternoon doldrums, Mary appeared with a stack of mail. She brought it all the way to my desk, handed me the petty cash envelope, and peered at me through narrowed eyes. "For the afternoon pick-up," she said.

It was the usual pile of correspondence going to various other archives and libraries and city council addresses. I had once suggested email to Mary and she looked at me as if I'd suggested she take up hip-hop dancing on the weekends. But there was one letter of interest: Harry Robertson, Private & Confidential.

Auld Harry Robertson. My predecessor. The last person to borrow the *Infamous Legends of Edinburgh* book.

The Edinburgh A-Z was still on my desk, fresh from my reconnaissance on John Kubik, and I flipped to the index. Robertson lived on the Dumbiedykes estate, not far from the Holyrood Tavern where I'd met Neve on our non-date. I bundled all the mail into my rucksack, decision already made.

I stopped at the nearest post office and paid for all the other mail to be sent, transferring the receipt and the small change back into the petty cash envelope. Instead of turning back towards Overspill I kept walking along

Princes Street, hopeful that Mary wouldn't venture downstairs again this afternoon. The city was a kaleidoscope of Christmas lights and the glow of shop windows; it was close to four o'clock and already dusk had seeped into the air, bringing with it a chill that pervaded the heat spilling from the open shop doors. I cut down via the train station and passed the homeless posted out front like sentries, spaced out every twenty paces and each in the uniform of the street-sleeper: stained khaki jacket, beanie hat, sleeping bag, and cardboard sign.

When I turned onto the Royal Mile a savage wind buffeted into me, knocking me backwards for a brief moment. For the first time I felt an apprehension about knocking on Harry's door. But my feet carried me forward, around the corner and past the inviting lights of the Holyrood Tavern. The monolithic concrete blocks of the Dumbiedykes estate were visible on the other side of the road, their bulk cutting shapes out of the grey skies. I knew their reputation – not quite as bad as the schemes on the outskirts of the city, Wester Hailes and Niddrie and Saughton and the Banana building, which the average Edinburgh citizen designated as no-go zones – but Dumbiedykes still had the taint of the scheme, with facades the colour of wet cardboard and a dishevelled air that translated through middle-class eyes into drug dealing and alcoholism and teenage motherhood. I had grown up in a council house and knew the assumptions only too well. That didn't mean I wasn't wary when I stepped into the stairwell of Harry's building and smelled the fossilised nicotine and tinned soup odours.

I worked my way up the landings until I reached Harry's floor. Unlike the other floors, this one was well-lit, smelled of lime antiseptic and was brightened by flowers in window boxes. I could see movement through the glass door of number 22. I removed the brown envelope from my rucksack and pressed the bell.

A well-dressed woman in her fifties answered. "How may I help?"

"Hi, my name's Miro. I'm from the city archive. I've just got something to drop off for Harry."

Her face brightened. "He's out right now but should be back in a wee while. Why don't you come in and wait?"

I followed her through a narrow hall into the living-room. She introduced herself as Theresa, told me to make myself comfortable, and disappeared to the kitchen to make tea.

The living-room had been lovingly tended to, an undercoat of hard times disguised by tasteful paintings and accessories. The sofa and armchairs were covered with bright blue throws, and on the mantelpiece above the glowing electric fire an array of photographs revealed an extended family of two graduate sons in gowns and mortar-boards, a family reunion with some twenty people crowded round a table in a Mediterranean holiday spot, a wedding picture of one of the sons and his redheaded wife against a backdrop of a Scottish castle, and a much younger Theresa on stage in front of a microphone next to a guy perched on a stool with a banjo. The window looked on to a stunning view of the Salisbury Crags, their black volcanic silhouette jutting into the dusk. In front of the fire a tabby cat was curled into a tight ball. It felt like home.

Theresa returned with a tray of tea and biscuits. I was glad for the sugar and a hot drink. As I munched my way through the chocolate hobnobs Theresa quizzed me about Overspill, and I soon realised that her husband had told her little about his workplace or the manner of his departure.

"It was so sudden," she said. "One day he just came back and told me that he would be taking early retirement at the age of fifty-nine and it would be best for everyone involved."

I played dumb. I told her what was pretty much the truth, that I'd started two months ago and it was a job, a start for me, but I was mainly just doing data entry and making trips to the post office and it wasn't exactly what I'd hoped for. This seemed to reassure her, like Harry's job had been dumbed down after his departure. She asked about Mary and Bob, so she at least knew something of the environment, and when I told her that we'd got a new computer system in and a new database something in her face altered, as if she realised this might be the true reason for Harry's departure.

In the hallway the door opened and somebody bundled in.

"Here comes his Lordship," said Theresa.

Harry didn't seem that old. I suspected Bob called him Auld Harry to deflect from his own thinning hair and sagging belly. Harry stood in the centre of the room, thick grey hair spiked up and face red from the cold, and looked down at me. "You a Jehovah?"

"No, I work at Overspill."

"Oh Christ. What now?"

"Come on, Harry." Theresa's voice was gentle. "Miro just brought over a letter for you. He's doing you a favour."

Harry slid a chair out from under the dinner table and rotated it towards me. He held his hand out and I passed him the envelope. "Ever heard of the post office?"

He ripped it open and unfolded the sheets of paper. "Pension stuff." He placed it on the table with a deflated sigh.

Theresa stood up. "Right, time for me to go to my class. Your dinner's in the fridge. I'll be back around nine. Why don't you take Miro for a drink, thank him for dropping by?"

Harry looked at her as if she'd lost her mind.

"It was nice meeting you, Miro. Pop by again sometime." The front door clicked softly as she left.

"Theresa's doing a night class in Economics. Smart woman. How long you been at Overspill then?" Harry, arms folded, legs crossed at the ankles.

"I started in September."

"What you doing?"

"Data entry. Cataloguing everything into the new database. Making tea. Running to the post office."

"Home deliveries too, eh."

For the first time I felt the stifling heat of the electric fire, was aware of the distance to the ground from the sixth floor.

Harry's voice softened. "Why are you here, Miro."

"Boxfile 467."

He unfolded his arms. "What's that?"

"The Devil's Chamber."

His face remained emotionless. "I'm not following you."

"I've been there twice. The Devil's Chamber."

This time, a barely perceptible flicker in his eyes, a wobble of an eyebrow.

"Twice," I said. "I found instructions on how to get there in Boxfile 467."

He leaned forward and rubbed a hand over his face. His voice, quiet. "You were there? Twice, you say?"

"Aye."

Harry stood up and walked over to the window. By now the view onto the Crags had dissolved into blackness, and our reflections stared back at us.

"Do you know the kind of danger you're in?"

The cat crossed the room and leapt onto my lap. I let it settle, head tucked in at my knee.

"This makes things very complicated," said Harry.

"In what way?"

He remained standing at the window.

"Someone came to Overspill looking for materials on the Chamber," I said. "Posh guy. James somebody."

Harry returned to his chair. I noticed his hand tremble.

"What did you tell this James guy?"

"That we have nothing related to that topic."

He bit into a biscuit and chewed. "Two things you have to do, son. The first? Continue saying nothing if folk come looking. The second? Never go back to the Chamber."

"How did James know where to look?"

"I don't know, son. You need to go."

I gestured at the cat, now spread-eagled in my lap. "Can't move."

He laughed. "Smart arse, eh?"

"Have you been to the Chamber?"

He looked away. "No."

"Why not?"

"Too much to lose."

"It's amazing." I rubbed the cat under its chin. "Spooky as fuck."

Harry sat hunched over, looking down at his clasped hands. "Tell me what you know about what happens there."

I told him everything I'd seen. The rows and rows of claret, the library, the corridors, the murder. I didn't mention Neve or Danny, or Mad MacAskill. He sat in silence throughout, nodding from time to time.

"And you?" I said. "Boxfile 467. What's the story?"

"OK. I'm telling you this for one reason only – for your safety. And mine."

Back in the sixties, Harry had been a big deal on the folk scene in Edinburgh. He could play the banjo and guitar and sing, and was a bit of a local hero. He gigged with Billy Connolly and other legends and was out most nights in the famous folk pubs, The Waverley and Sandy Bell's and the like. One of those drunken nights he met Theresa, who was a folk singer also of some repute. They soon became inseparable.

They struck up a friendship with another couple on the scene, Doug Pebbles and his fiddler wife Jeannie.

Doug styled himself as a folk singer but didn't have the voice or the musical skills – his talent was for storytelling, and soon enough he stepped away from singing and was writing songs for others, or reciting folktales during lulls in the wild pub sessions. In his day job he was a PhD student in History at Edinburgh University, and his two lives increasingly blended together after he chose to specialise in the folk culture of the Edinburgh slums in the nineteenth century.

The two couples remained friends as the years went by, kids came along, and soon the only time they were performing was on the occasional night out. Real life had taken over by this point and their musical skills had all taken a back seat, but Doug was still relentlessly pursuing his obsession about slum songs and stories.

One night in the late eighties, perched on bar stools at Greyfriars Bobby, Doug told Harry about his fixation with the legend of the Devil's Chamber. It had all happened by accident; it had started with one ballad, and as the months and years had gone by, when researching archives and interviewing elderly Edinburgh citizens he'd stumbled across more and more material. His office at the university was little more than a broom cupboard but now he had covered one wall with stacked boxfiles containing photocopies of every scrap of information he'd found. At first, the wildly varying accounts of the Devil's Chamber had drawn him in, creating a puzzle for him to solve. It was often the way with folk legends – a story had been born, maybe from the kernel of some true event, and then that story was reinvented time and time again by storytellers huddled around a tavern fire, or folksingers inserting new elements of the story to create a rhyme with other original lines, all of the story's architects and renovators striving to create that perfect arc, seeking to scare or shock or amuse their audience, until after many years all the remixes of the story bore little resemblance to one another.

But underneath all the layers of melodrama and superstition and metaphor, all the stories that referenced the Devil's Chamber hinted at one essential truth – that people disappeared from the overcrowded tenements, and had been taken to some underground chamber in the heart of the city, never to be seen again.

Over a pint of Tartan Special and a bag of salted peanuts, Doug told Harry that the Devil's Chamber was no legend, and not only this, he'd located the Chamber and had found out that people were still disappearing into its black hole. He drank more pints and got increasingly incoherent – the Chamber was run by a cabal of investors, they used a psychedelic liquid to trigger visions, and they forced their captives to drink an excessive amount in a kind of ceremony. Harry listened with as much patience as he could. Doug had always had a soft spot for fantastical stories, and also had a tendency to vanish down a rabbit hole when researching a story he liked. But more importantly, Theresa had told Harry that morning that Doug and Jeannie were having troubles in their marriage, and Harry saw this reflected in Doug's glimmering eyes and jittery movements. He decided to humour his old friend, and when he'd finally talked himself out, Doug slumped on the bar and stared at his empty glass. "If anything happens to me," he'd said, "will you look after Jeannie?"

As they left the pub he walked Doug to a taxi rank, and bundled his old friend into the back of a black cab. It was the last time he ever saw him.

A couple of months later Jeannie got in touch to say that Doug was missing. The police were involved. He had gone to work one Thursday and never returned, taking nothing but the clothes on his back. His briefcase and wallet were also missing, but there were no records of any bank withdrawals. Colleagues told the police of Doug's increasingly erratic behaviour, talking to himself and scribbling weird sketches into notebooks.

One day Jeannie showed up at Overspill. She had aged visibly in the months since Doug's disappearance, hair greying and dark circles around her eyes. She told Harry that she knew something about Doug's vanishing; that it was linked to a folk legend he was investigating; and that she needed Harry to take all the boxes of papers out of Doug's office and keep them somewhere safe. Harry drove up to the University with Jeannie and carried down eight numbered boxfiles crammed with photocopies. They drove back to Overspill in silence and after he had unloaded the car she gave him a wordless hug and drove off into the afternoon traffic. Harry hid the boxfiles deep in the unexplored shelves of Overspill's lost interior, walling them in with piles of other junk and forgotten papers.

Two months later, Jeannie's body was washed up on the shores of the Firth of Forth. The newspapers mourned the tragedy of the Pebbles family, a few hack articles with pictures of Doug and Jeannie performing in pub backrooms in the sixties including a shot with Billy Connolly in the background, the journalists speculating that Doug's disappearance pointed to a suicide that Jeannie followed with her own. The Pebbles' two grown-up kids were at university and showed no interest in commenting to the newspapers, and within a couple of years had moved away from Edinburgh and faded out of view.

"That was around ten years ago," said Harry. "Nineteen eighty-nine."

The cat jumped down off my lap, and I shifted on the sofa, taking it all in. "So why now? Why are they sniffing around Overspill?"

Harry shrugged. "Have you been talking to other people?"

I shook my head. "Nobody." He was looking at me closely. I wasn't carrying this off, because I had always been a bad liar. But Harry's body language told its own story. He wasn't telling me the truth either.

Harry was quiet, computing something. "What do you want?"

The question hung there in the silence, and I was confused by it. What did I want? I had never asked myself this once in the turmoil of the last year. All those sleepless nights, building myself up from the rubble of grief, scraping my way from day to day and ensuring the basics were covered – eat, take a shower, talk to other human beings. And once a kind of steady existence had been achieved, I had slipped into the world of the Devil's Chamber.

What did I want? I didn't want anything specific. A different life, mainly: a job I liked, friends around me, a girlfriend, things to look forward to. Lost in normality, my biggest problem a vague ennui about what comes next. Instead of this. Sliding into a downward spiral towards a black hole, gathering speed, addicted to the buzz.

"I want to stop them," I said.

"Very noble," said Harry.

"And you? What do you want?"

He shook his head. "To forget all of this. Don't you see? If they find out you were down there, they'll connect it to me. And my family."

"Why didn't you just destroy the boxfiles?"

He fidgeted. "Overspill is probably the best place to hide something in Edinburgh. And I felt I owed it to Doug and Jeannie. That somehow, sometime, the truth would come out, hopefully after I'm long gone, after I die of natural causes and not in the Devil's Chamber. Maybe you should hope for the same."

I stared at the carpet.

"So do you promise me?" said Harry. "You talk about this to nobody. And never go back to the Chamber."

I got to my feet and stretched out my hand. "I promise."

When we shook he looked me in the eye, two liars making a useless pact.

CHAPTER 19

The train crept forward, inching away from Edinburgh. Fergus sat opposite me and we were going back to Pitbirnie for Christmas, a ten-day escape from the city and its shadows.

"Where oh where have you been, Miro? You still haven't answered that crucial question."

Fergus eyed me with suspicion. He had already asked me when we met at the Malt Shovel for a pre-train pint, and also in the queue at the off-licence for the on-train carry-out.

He popped a can of Stella. "You're a fucking enigma, man. A dark horse."

I knew I was blushing, so took advantage of it. "My personal life is none of your business, mate."

Fergus shook his head and took another swig from his can. "I'll get it out of you at some point, ya dick."

It was true that I had been flying under the radar since meeting Neve. In the last six weeks or so, I had seen Fergus twice, and the whole family only on that Sunday when they all decamped down to Edinburgh for lunch. I had the impression they were all secretly a little pleased that I had been out of sight – it meant I had found new friends, was building a new life, was moving on. But it didn't mean they weren't also a little hurt but my absence, and I saw it that day at the Italian restaurant – the fondness in my grandparents' eyes, Uncle Donnie winking at me, Auntie Sarah flustered and tearful. I would make it up to them all over the next few days, I'd resolved. They needed me back in the family fold, and after everything that had happened in the last few weeks, I needed it too.

At Haymarket the train filled up, and the seats next to us were taken by an elderly couple. Fergus talked on regardless, not moderating his language or volume, a habit of his that had always embarrassed me. He stabbed a finger at his open newspaper. "It's been, what, more than two years since she died? I get it. It's a tragedy that Diana died, but this big fucking meltdown as if everyone knew her, well it's getting a bit fucking embarrassing. I mean, get real, she was a fucking princess, you know? Let's not pretend she was the girl next door." He shook his head in outrage. "Fucking royals. First against the wall when the revolution comes, first against the wall…"

I held eye contact with him and gave a micro-nod in the direction of the old couple, but he just looked at me quizzically and diverted his monologue to the 'fucked up drunken shenanigans' at the work Christmas party. Only when I kicked him under the table did he finally click and stop talking. He sighed and took a swig from his can.

He was two months younger than me and we'd grown up like brothers rather than cousins. We'd been to the same playgroup, the same primary school, and the same high school. All through that time we had maintained the love-hate intensity of siblings. Our friendship had gone through some tests over the years, including a two-year spell in our early teens when he had barely spoken to me other than at family gatherings, preferring to ignore me in the corridors of school – because, he told me once, I was a weirdo. The relationship got back on track when we were fifteen and both obsessed with Guns n' Roses. This common bond spiralled off into other shared interests – going to gigs, drinking illicit cans of lager on the beach, Twin Peaks, playing pool.

Fergus drained his can. The train picked up speed, accelerating through the Edinburgh suburbs. The elderly woman was engrossed in her book and her husband had fallen asleep, and Fergus took his turn to kick me under the table.

"Get me another tinny," he said.

I passed him a Stella.

He grinned at me. "Need some intoxication to survive the family for ten days, eh?"

"I'm looking forward to it. Home cooking, see some familiar faces."

"Ah yeah… maybe Hannah will be home, huh?"

"Maybe." I decided to roll out the heavy artillery. "What about you, Fergus? Maybe you'll get a chance to meet up with Sandra Goldie?"

His expression darkened. Aged seventeen he and Sandra had been caught in the act on the beach in front of the main car park. Someone turned their car headlights on and there they were, mashing away at each other, Fergus's jeans and white jockeys twisted round his ankles. Sandra was the daughter of Big John Goldie, a grizzled alcoholic fisherman, and for months afterwards everyone had wound up Fergus about Big John coming for him in the middle of the night with a fishing hook and a net.

Fergus went quiet, and I half-regretted raising the topic. The train clanked onto the Forth Bridge, and for a brief second the carriage was quiet, everybody peering out into the falling darkness at the rust-red girders and the slate-grey water below. Houselights glimmered on shore. It had always been a moment I loved, edging out onto the bridge – because it meant going home, or in the other direction, escaping home.

Fergus shoved his newspaper at me, pretending he wanted some quiet time, but Fergus never wanted quiet time. *In the huff*, I thought. I began flicking through. I was a few pages in when I saw the article.

POPULAR BIG ISSUE SELLER MISSING

Friends and family have appealed to the public to the whereabouts of Malcolm Gallacher, 26, an Edinburgh resident and recovering heroin addict familiar to many commuters as a Big Issue seller outside Waverley Station. Gallacher, known to many as ''Wee Malky', was last seen on Thursday 11 December in the city centre and failed to return to his housing association flat as expected that evening. "Malcolm has had many troubles but he has recently turned the corner," said his mother Jean. "He is a loving son and is always in touch with us every couple of days to let us know how he's getting on. I'm beginning to fear the worst." Anyone with information regarding the whereabouts of Gallacher is requested to call the missing persons hotline on 0800 162 162.

In the photo, the fair-haired man tied to the chair in the Chamber smiled back at me. It was unquestionably him – something in his slight frame, scrawny neck, the tilt of his head. I stared at him until I became aware of the granular specks of newsprint that made up the picture. Monochrome dots creating the image of a dead man. The picture the last memorial to him on the planet, because wherever he was now, he would never be found.

Fergus was plucking at his ringpull. *Ting... ting... ting...*

I reached into the bag for a can.

We got off at Leuchars. Uncle Donnie was waiting for us under the station canopy.

"Boys. I hope you're not the worse for wear."

He was, as ever, dressed in discount hiking gear – a battered Javelin fleece and khaki trousers. His day job as an accountant saw him leave the house in pinstripes and brogues; within ten minutes of arriving home, he reverted to his natural state.

"Just a couple of refreshers," said Fergus.

"Aye well, sober up in the car, because everyone is waiting for you."

Donnie and Fergus talked football on the journey, and I was glad to sit and absorb the familiar landscape unfolding through the darkness. The car swooped up and down gentle hills, the headlights arcing over the woodland and fields that I had grown up with.

Donnie pulled up in front of the house, car wheels crunching over gravel. A few years back Donnie had dubbed the house 'Gull View' because the only thing you could see from its upper floor was 'bloody seagulls' and the name had stuck. Gull View was ablaze with light, every window illuminated and augmented by strings of Christmas lights. Fergus jumped out and the front door opened – from my position in the back seat I could just make out Auntie Sarah, and behind her, others. Someone opened my door and hands reached in and grabbed my lapels.

"Cousin Miro! Long lost Cousin Miro!"

It was Kirsty, Fergus's older sister. I tumbled out and hugged her. She pulled me close and pressed her cheek close to mine with a forcefulness that surprised me. I had not seen her since last Christmas. She had moved to London two years previously to work for the Civil Service and her life was famously a mystery.

Somebody else threw an arm around us too, and a commotion of voices surrounded me. After my solitary life – and the loneliness of Overspill – it was a pleasant shock to be attacked by so much love.

The house was overheated. Cheeks flushed, I was ushered into the dining-room where my grandparents provided the next round of greetings. We took our seats – seven of us – and Sarah brought bowls of lentil soup, thick with boiled ham and potato. Within a couple of minutes it was like all the troubles had been erased – the Devil's Chamber no longer existed, just this room of hot food and well-known voices.

CHAPTER 20

The next morning I woke early in my grandparents' house. The small room was familiar to me from many childhood nights, sparsely furnished and damp-smelling, but always a place of sanctuary. I had never questioned how often I stayed here as a child until my late teens, when it clicked that I had been offloaded here when my mother was dating somebody. Not that I objected – coming here always meant a full Scottish breakfast, unbridled access to the biscuit tin, and a somewhat naïve permit to the TV in the back room.

I checked my watch – 6:20am. I couldn't get back to sleep, and with a slippery dread my thoughts returned to the Devil's Chamber. For some twelve hours I had been liberated, but now the memories were back. I got up and threw some clothes on and left a note to say I had gone for a walk.

Pitbirnie was empty at this time of the morning, more so because of the wildness of the weather. I walked the beach head on into the driving rain, letting it cleanse me of my hangover. The sea tumbled and crashed onto the shore, frothing towards me as I walked the line between wet and dry sand. Far out on the dark horizon, the light of a ship blinked in hope. Next stop Norway. Yesterday I had only travelled by train for just over an hour, but Pitbirnie felt a million miles from Edinburgh's sooty granite and hidden spaces.

The rain stopped just as I looped back up into the town. I took a diversion down my childhood street and came to a halt outside my old house. The new owner had ripped out the hedge and painted the windowsills powder blue. I wanted to feel something but didn't.

By the time I returned to my grandparents' place the hangover had lifted, my clothes were drying out, and I felt again the joy of being home. My Gran was up and insisted that I sit down for a cup of tea and a bacon roll.

The day passed in a fug of comforting normality. I spent the morning chatting with my grandparents, the afternoon watching videos in the back room. Just as the skies were darkening my cousins called – Fergus and Kirsty intent on drunken mischief.

We took the short walk to the village's only pub, The Lost Creel. In the summer it attracted the golf crowd from St Andrews, Americans and Japanese, but at this time of year it was resolutely local. We entered into a festive bubble – Wednesday night but three days before Christmas, enough of an excuse to start drinking. We took a corner table underneath a suspended lobster creel.

Kirsty elbowed me as we sat down and wriggled a little closer to me. I couldn't understand this new closeness. We had always got on well but she had been the most distant of the cousins in the previous two years. She hadn't come back for my mother's funeral, which I was okay with, because it was one less person to receive condolences from.

Fergus brought our drinks over, then headed to the toilet. The two of us, alone. Kirsty leaned in. "So you escaped too."

"What do you mean?"

She pushed fingers into her forehead. "You're getting away. Properly. Not like Fergus, with his bunch of suit mates. There's something different about you."

I flapped a hand at her.

She was looking at me. Her black hair a bit too straggly, yet respectable; dressed in clothes that spoke of sophistication yet worn with slight disregard; blue-grey eyes that lacked confidence.

"You've been through a lot, Miro. You should come to London. You'd like it."

Fergus returned. "Your old flame is in the pub, Miro. The lovely Hannah."

Indeed, there was Hannah at the corner table with some other girls from our year at school. She raised a glass and smiled in my direction. I returned the smile, and then ducked down to meet my pint. Within five minutes my glass was empty.

"Somebody's thirsty," said Fergus.

After a couple of rounds the pub filled up with the returning sons and daughters of the village, those who had left for university or for work and would only ever come back for holidays, living new lives that could not be lived on this scrap of coastline. A couple of other old schoolmates joined us at the table, and Kirsty moved round, squashing up against me. Three vodka cokes had loosened her tongue.

"Can you keep a secret?" Her whisper was loud in my ear.

Before I could answer she kept going.

"I've got someone in London. A lover."

I had a feeling I knew where this was going.

"Her name is Molly. She's Canadian." Kirsty's head was tilted over her drink, face hidden by curtains of hair. She had never shown any interest in boys so it was no big surprise.

I squeezed her arm. "Good for you, Kirsty."

"And you?" She looked at me, a little defiance in her eyes. I was maybe the first person in the family she was officially coming out to.

"Sort of." I told her about the Kim situation, all of it, even about her boyfriend, and also mentioned there was someone else that I liked. I told her that I was still emotionally cut up after the last year, couldn't really deal with relationships of any sort. She slung an arm around me, then moved to the bar with a bounce in her step, an ease in her movements. She had told me her secret and I had accepted it. She could be who she wanted to be. I envied her and her future.

Towards closing time I was at the bar buying our final round and Hannah slid in next to me. We hugged, awkwardly. For ten minutes we ran through summaries of our lives, hers involved travelling in Asia and the end of a long-term relationship. I told her about my mum, and my move to Edinburgh. She slipped her hand into mine without saying anything. She hadn't done that for five years but it felt natural, the way her fingers hooked into a snug grip. The combo of six pints and standing here with my first love left me momentarily speechless.

"You know something?" she said. "I had a dream about you a couple of weeks ago. It was so real. I was in this place, it was like a combination between a library and a warehouse, and I was browsing around, then I heard footsteps and it was you. I got this bad feeling that you shouldn't walk any further into the library so I told you not to go. We hugged. You kept walking. I had the feeling of you going somewhere wrong. Somewhere dangerous."

I gripped her hand. These co-incidences, fitting one inside another, like nested dolls.

"It was a good dream though," she said. "I woke up and felt you close. I remembered all the fun times, that connection we had. First love. I'd forgotten it."

"What do you think the dream meant?"

"I don't know." She looked at me, deep into my eyes. I was aware of nothing else at that moment – so it was a surprise to be interrupted by the barman shouting for last orders. "We're at one of those turning points in life, maybe? Don't always chase new knowledge? Stay away from libraries?"

I laughed.

"I'm going to head off, Dora is having a reunion party for the girls. But listen, my parents are away Christmas shopping tomorrow."

She pecked me on the cheek and let my hand slide out of hers as she walked away.

Her parents would be Christmas shopping. An empty house.

CHAPTER 21

The next morning I woke with the sunrise. I had been troubled throughout the night with a fragmented dream of the Chamber, of walking its smooth floors underneath those arched ceilings, and couldn't shake the feeling of anxiety. I lay in the weak light listening to the gulls and the occasional car swish by on the way to the power station down the coast. Eventually the memory of Hannah's words pulled me out of my funk.

Her parents were going Christmas shopping. The mention of their absence had always been a calling card. And now, after five years, the calling card had been delivered again.

I had a lazy breakfast, morning rolls with bacon and tattie scones, and took the gentle reprimand from my grandparents about too much boozing with good grace. My grandpa winked at me once the lecture was over. I was still in the poor little orphan zone, clearly, with a bit of leeway allowed. It wouldn't last forever. My gran went through to the back room to read and for a moment I thought about asking my grandpa about my dad but decided against it. Uncle Donnie would be a better bet.

I showered and put clean jeans on, added an extra splash of aftershave. Hannah was always a stickler for cleanliness. Under the pretence of a beach walk, I looped around the other side of the village where Hannah stayed. The row of houses along the winding back road all had views onto the sea and were among the poshest residences in the area. Hannah's parents were both lawyers and super-active, always off on cycling holidays or canoeing in the Highlands. They usually left the house early and wouldn't come back till late.

The houses were quiet, wisps of haar in the air providing some cover for my illicit mission. Down below, the sea churned against the beach, gulls gliding over the white breakers, a couple of boats further out bobbing on the grey turmoil. Hannah's driveway was car-free. I walked across the gravel and rang the bell.

Movement through the frosted glass.

She grinned to see me, as if she knew I would be unable to resist. She was wearing white jogging bottoms and a tight red t-shirt. No bra. I mumbled something about it being a while but she just shook her head, took my hand, and led me up the stairs. As I climbed up the carpeted steps, eyes drawn to the blue ink of a new tattoo peeping out from under her t-shirt sleeve, I marvelled at the sudden availability of sex. Until Kim I had gone for a year without, and now this glut.

Her bedroom hadn't changed much from five years ago, and even had the same Pearl Jam posters blu-tacked up above her bed. The grin still hadn't left her face, and she pulled the t-shirt up over her head and stood in front of me defiantly. Her upper body was more toned than in the past, tits pert and nipples erect, tattoo of a dragon on her right bicep. I was kicking my shoes off, wrestling out of my clothes, desperate to get started in case her parents should come back and interrupt this early Christmas present.

I got naked first and returned her smile. She looked down at my erection – so hard it hurt – and gave a minute nod of approval. She slipped her jogging bottoms down – no knickers – and entwined herself around me.

Our techniques had improved over the last five years. She muttered commands to me and I complied – after a couple of minutes of our gymnastics we settled down with her on top, rocking against me, one hand on my chest and fingernails digging into me, a claw embedded in my heart. It was dream-like to be back here. In my trance I held on with a newfound willpower, and she came in convulsions and a loud cry like she'd been stabbed. Seconds later I was done, yelling into her hair.

We were both a bit shocked by the experience and lay there saying nothing for ten minutes. Hannah broke the silence.

"Not bad."

She told me to go downstairs and grab a drink while she took a quick shower. "Maybe we should talk about this," she said.

A new kitchen had been installed since my last visit – white worktops, a breakfast bar island with newspapers folded neatly next to a fruit bowl, and a giant fridge. I eased the fridge door open. A six-pack of Staropramen nestled in one of the trays, and I slipped a can out of the plastic loop. I settled myself down at the breakfast bar with a good view of the driveway, popped the can and opened The Scotsman.

I was halfway into the newspaper and the can when I saw the picture. Mad MacAskill's face staring out at me, the second time in three days that the Devil's Chamber had featured in a newspaper.

MAN LAY DEAD IN FLAT FOR EIGHT DAYS

Community leaders have expressed their concern after a man was found dead in his Edinburgh flat some eight days after he passed away. It is thought that Adam MacAskill, 36, died from a drug overdose. "It is the third time this year a deceased Edinburgh citizen has lain undiscovered for a lengthy period of time," said Reverend James Easton, an active figure in the Lothian community group Love Thy Neighbour. "Mr MacAskill may have belonged to the margins of society, but nobody deserves to go unnoticed by their friends and neighbours." MacAskill was known to police and it is understood he was estranged from his family.

I felt dizzy; nauseous. For a moment I thought I would pass out sitting on the high stool and fall to the tiled floor. Instead I got to my feet, grabbed my jacket, and left the house.

I reached my grandparents' place and slipped quietly in and upstairs to the spare room. After getting my breath back I snuck into the hall and dialled Neve's number.

Her flatmate answered. Neve was at work. Could she take a message?

I declined. Seconds after I hung up, the phone began ringing and I snatched it up.

"Hello?"

"Miro?"

It was Hannah.

"You just walked out, without saying anything. What the fuck? Why did you do that?"

It only occurred to me now what had happened.

"Sorry Hannah, I didn't feel well."

"You didn't even tell me. You didn't even leave a note or anything."

Before I could say anything, the line went dead.

CHAPTER 22

By late afternoon I was already parked at the kitchen table at Gull View with Fergus and Kirsty, wine glasses in front of us filled to the brims. They were in high spirits, but I was all over the place. Emotionally dislocated after the encounter with Hannah, my unforgivable departure, and the sight of MacAskill in the paper.

I was trying not to drink too much because I had two burning things to do.

At my feet, double-wrapped in polythene bags, was the leather-bound book from the Chamber. I was waiting for the right moment to speak to Auntie Sarah – like Donnie an accountant, but more contemplative and interested in the intellectual dimension of the job, and probably the better bet to decipher its ancient shorthand.

Secondly, I wanted to ask Donnie or Sarah about my father. I sensed tonight could be the right night – the neighbours coming over for Christmas drinks, Donnie most likely having one too many and ready to share what he knew.

Dinner started, and my resolution to drink modestly was crumbling. Seven of us crowded around the battered old wooden table, a pot of chicken curry in the middle. Fergus topped up my glass. After a few more slugs of wine I was starting to relax, focusing on positives, remembering the amazing experience with Hannah rather than my embarrassing exit, enjoying the buzz of the wine and the feeling that things would work out okay.

After ice-cream and coffee, I noticed Sarah moving to the kitchen to clean up, and I grabbed the chamber book and slipped through to join her.

"Can I dry?"

She smiled. "Thanks Miro. That would be great."

I took up position at the business end of the sink. Her face was flushed, with drink or pride I wasn't sure. "It's so good to have you all back."

"I'm happy to be here."

She passed me the first dripping plate. "We've never had time to talk. Are you alright in Edinburgh? You've been keeping a low profile."

I feigned a chuckle. "It's all good. Carving out a new life."

She smiled. "That's what you need to do."

More plates came my way, and I swabbed them dry and stacked them. The privacy of the kitchen prompted me to take a risk.

"Sarah, can I ask you something? It's a bit awkward."

"Fire away, Miro."

"My dad. I've been thinking about him more and more in recent weeks. I have no interest in contacting him but I just need to know more. What do you remember of him?"

She nodded, as if she'd been expecting the question for some time. "Let's go through the back."

On the way out I grabbed the bag with the Devil's Chamber book.

In the chill of the tiny conservatory, Sarah perched on the windowsill with her glass of wine. "You're old enough to hear this, so here it is. Your dad was a waster. Probably still is. He was mainly drinking and running around with other women while he was with your mum. Oh, he had the gift of the gab, that's true – could talk for Scotland, always had a great business plan, your grandparents loved him at the start. But gradually the bullshit started to pile up."

"What happened? My mum just said he left when I was a baby."

"That's true. Your mum called us a couple of days after he'd popped out to see a friend. He came back a few times though, maybe she never told you that."

Sarah was a bit tipsy, which was uncharacteristic for her.

"Really?"

"Yeah, they made a go of it again for a couple of months. You were probably around two years old."

This new information was shocking – I had always been the abandoned baby.

"What happened?"

"The usual. He made his promises, charmed folk with his chat, he'd changed forever, that sort of thing, then it all fell apart. He had family in Glasgow on his mother's side, and we heard he'd moved through there. Then when you were about eight he showed up one weekend – you were at a birthday party as I recall, but your mother had to literally chase him off the driveway. He was going on about having something for you, your Polish heritage and all that. He would always pull out the Polish paratrooper thing to try to win people over."

I actually remembered that day – a football party in St Andrews, 5-a-side goals set up in this rich kid's garden, then returning home to find unexplained tyre marks on the front lawn of our little council house.

The tears came, and I gave in and let them drip off my nose. I still hadn't sorted out this unexpected fucking crying thing.

"Oh, Miro. Now I've upset you."

I blotted the leakage away with my sleeve. "Let's change the subject. I found this old book at work." I passed it to Sarah.

She was crying too. "Let's see. Let's see."

I focused on my drink as she browsed and composed herself. I had spent an hour in Edinburgh going through it page by page, trying to make sense of it. All I had worked out so far was that there was an entry for each month, and seeded in to the indecipherable shorthand were names and numbers and dates. On the final page the script was faded with time, ink scribbles that had been added to with soft pencilled hieroglyphics. It didn't help that I was unfamiliar with the handwriting standards of the age, the loops and flourishes that merged letters together into a fluid mush.

"Where did you find it?"

"A back shelf. Everything in the archive is pretty much forgotten about. Do you know what it is?"

"It's beautifully bound. Accounts, as you may suspect. But it looks like it's written in some sort of code. It's not any kind of conventional shorthand. Like a secret language." She traced a finger down a neat column of stencilled letters and numbers. "Every entry is on the thirteenth. It looks like an initial payment or investment, and then they leave a gap underneath for what comes next." She flicked through the pages. "Look, here. It must be investments. Thirteenth of June 1904, an investment of eight thousand pounds into a company called Theobald Munitions. Several entries below... some squiggles that make no sense, but according to the final line, it looks like they sold their stake in 1916. Bang in the middle of the First World War. Forty-six thousand and forty pounds, quite the fortune back then."

"So it looks like an investment on a monthly basis?"

"Seems to be." Sarah turned more pages. "It's hard to read but if you look at the final line under each entry there is a figure, and my guess is that's the return on investment. Looks like they were exceptional at what they did. Are there any more books?"

"No," I lied. "Just found the one."

"It would be interesting to find out the name of the investment house, there seems to be nothing anywhere. All very secretive. Oh, look." She turned to the final page and its rows of tiny stencilled symbols and numbers. "Wait here a minute."

She crossed the room to the Welsh dresser and rummaged in a drawer. She returned with a cylindrical object that looked like a mini-telescope and turned it round to show me. "Donnie's magnifying glass for his rocks." Donnie had gone through a spell of being a geology freak, much to Fergus's amusement.

She held it close to the page and peered into its glass eye. "Someone could write really small."

"What does it say?"

"A lot of it's still in code, but this last page looks like some sort of review of the year. Near the top we've got 'Hogmanay 1904/05' mixed in with the squiggles. We've got some other writing in here too… there's a list of industries or sectors – 'railways, steel, automobiles, munitions'… and other fragments of text – 'a toast to the society'… 'another year blessed by God'… 'out with the old and in with the new.' Maybe they also met on New Year's Eve. Like a board meeting or annual review. Or just getting together for drinks and cigars."

She passed me the magnifier and I leaned in to see the text expand, the scratches of ink like spider's legs pressed onto the page. I noticed one fragment of text Sarah hadn't mentioned – "deliverance to the sinful."

"It's a beautiful object. Why did you bring it all the way up here?"

I shrugged. "Solving puzzles keeps me busy."

She slung her arms around me. I returned the hug. Bringing the book here felt like a mistake.

CHAPTER 23

I didn't sleep for three nights in a row – Christmas Eve, Christmas Day, and Boxing Day – and then finally fell into a thirteen-hour sleep once the festivities were over. On the twenty-seventh The Scotsman ran an extended article on the modern-day tragedy of the lonely death of Mad MacAskill. A low hum of dread took over my life. There would be only one solution.

Kirsty was the first to leave after Christmas, togged up in a huge baggy striped sweater. "Did you tell anyone about what I said?" she whispered. I shook my head. As dusk crept in, one by one the older generation fell asleep in front of the TV, and Fergus caught my eye. He nodded in the direction of the sea, our ancient code for a trip to the Lost Creel. Within two minutes we were slipping out the door.

Hannah's friends were in the pub, but no Hannah. They kept looking over at us and I knew Hannah must have told them. When I went to the bar to refresh our drinks, her best friend Dora appeared at my side.

"You're a right numpty, you know that?" she said.

The two pints were placed down in front of me.

"You know how much Hannah cares about you? She doesn't sleep around. She's had a rough couple of years. So what happened was not some sort of ex sex. It meant something. You just walked off? Do you know how much you hurt her?"

"Dora, it wasn't like that. I got sick. It's embarrassing to talk about."

She stared right at me. Through me. "You'll never meet anyone else better than Hannah. It's your loss." She turned and clopped off on her heels back to the corner. I picked up our pints, my shaking hands spilling beer over the sides, and returned to the corner and a giggling Fergus.

On my last day we made a shopping trip to Dundee, and I started planning. Along with some shirts for work I bought a tight-fitting black micro-fleece, black jeans, and a heavy-duty pocket torch. Sunday dinner was epic, a brisket soup followed by roast beef and Yorkshire puddings, and finished off with sticky toffee pudding. It was best for me to eat a big meal now – I would need my strength for later.

After a round of farewell hugs and handshakes, Donnie drove us to the station. For once, Fergus was quiet.

"What's the plan for Hogmanay then boys?" Donnie's voice had a weary resignation to it, as if he suspected the answer would be 'get hammered.'

Fergus looked at me. We had not discussed it, and I realised I would need to get out of whatever he might propose. I spoke first. "I'm meeting a lady friend."

Fergus shook his head slowly, as if this was the ultimate betrayal.

"Who is she?" said Donnie.

"Just someone I've been hanging out with lately. I don't know if it'll go anywhere."

"And you, Fergus?"

Fergus yawned. "Got a few options."

"You two," said Donnie, shaking his head. "It's the big one – year 2000! You'd think you would bother your arses to do something memorable."

"Maybe the Millennium bug will destroy the world," said Fergus. "Midnight, and your toaster will come and kill you."

"Mother of Christ," said Donnie.

On the train Fergus produced two cans of Beck's. It was late afternoon and the carriage was busy with revellers heading south to Edinburgh for the big party. Loud voices, shrieks of laughter, the clink of plastic bags full of bottles and cans.

"So what's her name?" Fergus was peering at me, a glint of doubt in his eye.

"Neve," I said.

"What's she like?"

"Northern Irish, hair a sort of golden-red colour. Smart. Tough."

"Fancy inviting me along?"

I raised a hand in apology. "Sorry Ferg, but I've been waiting for this moment for months now."

The train filled up at Kirkcaldy, standing room only, some people singing already, the girls all made-up and smeared in glitter. Onto the bridge, the dark water below like a giant slab of marble. I was ready for the next step. Tonight I would go into the Devil's Chamber on my own and find the answers.

CHAPTER 24

The Guildford was rammed. Dressed in my new black clothes, the micro-fleece snug against my body, I must have looked like a burglar. In my jacket pocket was the torch, and a spare battery. I squeezed through a gap in the crowd at the bar at the same moment Neve turned to serve me.

"A pint of IPA."

She flinched, then regained her composure and grabbed a glass from the overhead rack.

"We're not supposed to speak to each other," she said, eyes fixed on the filling glass.

"Nothing to stop me coming for a beer."

She looked brilliant: hair tied up loosely, tight white blouse, silver bangles slack on her wrist as she gripped the pump. "Are you planning something stupid?"

I kept quiet.

"Two pounds thirty." She held her hand out. I looked her in the eye. There was something new in her gaze – fury, perhaps. But maybe it was something else. Attraction? A twinge of lust surprised me.

I slowly counted out the price of the pint with all my small change, and then slung it into her palm. She turned away.

I found a corner through the back and sat with a newspaper. The noise grew as the minutes passed, the clock edging towards the new millennium. At around ten to midnight, the punters started drinking up and heading out towards the street party. I saw my chance, and as a couple left the booth table at the back, I scanned the pub, noticed everyone was looking in the other direction, and then walked over, hit the floor, and slid under the bench seat.

I waited as the noise calmed, a few drinkers staying on and cheering as midnight came, then the voices dropped off until I heard the clunk of the doors closing. A volley of fireworks erupted outside. Two feet appeared in front of my face, and a creak above me as the person sat on the bench.

"What are you doing?"

"Going down below."

"On your own?"

"I know the way."

"Danny will be raging."

"Fuck Danny."

A long silence. A sigh. "I'll come back once the coast is clear."

Maybe twenty minutes passed, and I heard one of the doors open and close again, and Neve was down on her hands and knees, peering under the seat, hair spilling down onto the carpet. "Get your arse out here."

When I got back on my feet she was sitting on a chair opposite, head in hands. "Did you see the Mad MacAskill coverage?"

I nodded. "And the guy… you know. The one they killed. Malcolm Gallacher. Missing."

"Something else…" She looked up at me, and I saw that she hadn't been sleeping either. "Savage Hill."

I remembered how those words burst out of Gallacher's throat as if torn from inside him.

"I found it on the internet. It's an Australian mining company," she said. "In the last week the share price increased around one hundred per cent."

I stared at the carpet, its whorling patterns and ancient beerstains.

"They use it to make money, just like it said in that book," said Neve. "If you drink it you can see into the future. They find people who won't be missed, make them drink the claret, get the information out of them and then make investments. It's not a Satanic club, it's a fucked-up bank."

"And it's been running for a couple of hundred years."

Neve nodded. "They must be worth billions."

We sat in silence. From outside, the scream and whump of a firework broke the spell.

"They meet on New Year's Eve," I said.

"How do you know?"

"I found an entry at the back of their accounts log for Hogmanay. Looked like it might be a review of the year."

"And you want to go down there? While they're meeting?"

"I can't sleep. I think about it all the time."

Neve fiddled with her bangles. "I know what you mean. But where is this leading? We can't tell the police. Maybe we just forget about all of it."

"And they just go on killing people?" I stood up. "I'm going down. You don't need to come."

She stared at the floor.

"If I don't come back, then tell the police."

"I'm coming," she said. "Danny won't be happy."

I shrugged.

We descended the ladder together into the cellar. I went first through the ventilation shaft – by now it was second nature wriggling through that narrow space, the dull clang every time I put one elbow in front of the other. I slid out onto the ledge and that now familiar smell of damp and decay. Seconds later, Neve followed, and I pulled her to her feet. She held a finger to her lips and we listened – utter silence.

As I dangled off the ledge and dropped to the steps below I felt a buzz inside me – a happiness almost. Finally, I was back.

We took the steps slowly, my pocket torch lighting the way. As we reached the bottom the moonlight glow of the Chamber seeped out towards us. I clicked the torch off.

"Where are we going?" said Neve.

"We need to see where the giant took the body."

We crossed the smooth stone floor and past the dried spatters of Gallacher's blood. Above us the ceiling spilled its unearthly light and I felt strangely at peace. We stepped through the top right archway.

"Here goes," said Neve. I clicked the torch back on and we walked into its dark mouth.

The beam of light showed up crumbling brickwork and cobwebs. We walked in silence along the curving channel. After two minutes we saw a dead end ahead of us, and in front of the wall, a gaping hole. A small wall circled the hole, and when we got up close it resembled a well. I shone the torch beam down into the black pit, illuminating its rough and craggy walls. A cold and rotten smell crept up to us, and Neve covered her mouth with her hand.

"They drop the bodies down here."

I tried to see the bottom of the well, but the torchlight faded halfway down. "One body a month for more than two hundred years… that's like two and a half thousand people." Neve stumbled away from the edge, and I followed.

We headed back into the Chamber. A noise up ahead made us freeze. Neve slapped a hand into my chest, and I felt her fingers press against my ribs, and I was reminded of Hannah's nails digging into my heart as she climaxed.

Ahead, through the library archway, a soft muttering.

Neve stepped away from me towards the sound, moving steadily but noiselessly towards the book racks. My feet moved and I was surprised to find myself following her.

At first I thought they were dead – a cluster of men face down on the main table and two lying on the floor, an ensemble that reminded me of pictures I'd seen of mass suicides in Germany at the end of the Second World War. But one of the men at the table moved, his head lolling from side to side, and from somewhere a snore vibrated in the vacant silence.

On the table was a bottle of the claret and a jug of water.

We edged closer.

I recognised the nearest man on the ground. It was James Sutherland, his long-ish hair spread out on the stone floor, eyelids flickering as he plummeted through his claret dream. He wore a navy-blue tartan suit and white shirt open at the neck.

Neve was picking her way slowly around the men, peering at them up close. I watched as she reached into the trouser pocket of one and slid out his wallet. She beckoned me over and made a writing motion. I took my notebook and pen out of my zip pocket, hands trembling. She showed me the open wallet and a driving licence – Arthur MacAllister. I wrote down the name, date of birth, and address.

We worked the room, one by one. Each time we checked they were comatose, then frisked their pockets. There were eight of them, and we found six wallets. Three of them wore the same dark tartan suit as Sutherland. I covered two pages of my notebook with names and addresses.

The muttering got louder – it came from the man in the bulkiest chair, whose hair was streaked with grey, high cheekbones making him look something like a Goth Elvis. His name was Carson Gow. His hands were clenching and unclenching. Neve gripped my arm and pointed back towards the chamber and we crept back out. As we re-entered the Chamber we could still hear Gow's muttering behind us.

Neve leaned in and whispered into my ear. "They probably left the trapdoor open at the top of the stairs."

There was no other choice – we had come this far, we needed to take a look. We climbed the stairs back up. I kept the torch beam trained on the railing until I saw the knotted ribbon.

"Okay," said Neve. "Let's count the steps."

Forty-six more steps and we were standing below the open trapdoor. Electric light spilled down from above. The stairs continued up to the lip of the trapdoor, and we kept climbing, stepping up into a basement room with a huge polished mahogany table and bookshelves lining the walls. It was empty of life. Neve ran her fingertips along the soft surface of the table as she circuited the room, and I moved over to inspect the bookcases. Accountancy, economics, investment, history, engineering… all books bound in leather and early editions.

Neve pointed at headed notepaper on the table. *Sutherland Gow Investments*, but no address. She tore off a leaf and folded it into her pocket. Then she went over to the door at the top of the room and tried the handle – it was locked.

"Shit," said Neve. "Look at this."

Between two of the bookshelves and hidden in shadows was a heavy padlocked door. Neve beckoned me over. At head height was a small sliding panel. Neve edged it open to reveal a panel of glass. She peered in.

"Oh fuck." Hand over her mouth.

"What is it?"

She shook her head. Unable to stop myself, I leaned over and looked through the darkened glass.

A cell, with a narrow bed on one side and a bucket in the corner. Stains and scratched graffiti on the walls.

"It's where they keep them," said Neve. "Before the ceremony."

We climbed back down into the darkness again, forty-six steps until we reached the ribbon. A snore was faintly audible from below.

"Here." I cupped my hands together for Neve's foot. She got in position, using me for leverage, and launched herself up the wall, scrambling over the ledge. I placed a foot on the railing and reached up for the cracked tile. One, two, three and I launched myself upwards. I was halfway through the air when the tile crumbled under my grip; I dropped sideways, slammed into the railing, flipped once and landed with a whack onto the steps below.

I gasped for breath, in agony, lungs crushed.

The cold stone pressed into my forehead and I felt myself merge with it, becoming darkness.

Neve whispered down from above. "Miro. Miro."

I moved a little, then turned slowly onto my back. A minute or so later, I wrenched myself into an upright position. Slowly, with microscopic movements, I reached for the railing, gripped it, braced myself, and pulled myself up. I still couldn't stand up straight, the pain throbbing down one side where my ribcage had bounced off the railing.

From above: voices. And footsteps.

I looked up and my torchlight caught Neve's terrified expression in full beam. No choice. I flipped the torch off and descended into the chamber, my feet moving down the smooth steps, hand gliding over the railing, the pain making me dizzy. The voices got louder – maybe three or four men. I reached the Chamber and without hesitation headed towards the first archway. The river. They wouldn't go to the river.

I made my way past the stacked chairs and reached the janitor's cubby hole. I almost cried out loud when I saw the bulk of the giant's back encased in an outsize black Adidas tracksuit top. He was leaning over the table and opening a can of lager.

I rushed forward. It was only when I reached the end of the corridor that I noticed the absence of noise – the thundering water had calmed. Behind me I heard footsteps and baritone muttering, the giant coming in my direction, probably for a piss. I edged out onto the slimy riverbank. The water was now just a sluggish trickle. I switched my torch on again and swung it upstream, then down. I made a split-second decision – upstream would most likely lead to an exit – and I eased myself down into the river.

My feet soaked instantly with ice-cold water. I began to wade through the stream, teeth chattering with fear and cold, but it wasn't as difficult to walk through as I'd feared. I rounded the first bend to see the tunnel open up in front of me, heading back for fifty metres or so. Underfoot my trainers found purchase on a layer of pebbles, and I made steady progress, one foot over another, swinging my arms to maintain balance.

Slosh, slosh, slosh. I moved mechanically, wading ankle-deep, torch-beam playing on the slimy walls. The pain in my side was still intense but somehow manageable now that I was walking into the unknown. The fear and dread that had dominated my life in recent weeks had vanished; now I felt only acceptance. I would probably die down here, if not today then at some point soon.

The tunnel curved and narrowed, until it shrank into a borehole. I ducked my head down and walked into the narrow space in a crouching position, the water faster and deeper over my feet. I was able to reach out either side and touch the walls, hooking my fingers into the mouldy stone. At one point I slipped and fell to my knees, the water chugging around me, one hand sunk into the stony riverbed, the other hand holding the torch, the dark water just inches from my face. I stumbled back to my feet and continued forwards. The tunnel narrowed again. I stopped and tilted my light into the black mouth. Past the glistening, rushing water I could see the next section, a broader open stretch of tunnel. I plunged headfirst into the narrow space, fighting through the churning water, the stink of underground thick in my throat. I slid back, and fell face first into the current, my body grinding against the riverbed, about to be spat out again into the tunnel below but I performed a manic forward crawl, still holding the torch, fingers clutching at pebbles until I found purchase. I huddled down in my awkward tiger's crouch position for a few seconds, getting ready, then thrust myself forward, scrambling into the icy flow, water sloshing and rippling up onto my face, fighting my way forward until I breached the top of the sloped tunnel and tumbled out.

I dragged myself to the side of this new chamber, away from the steady flow of the river. For a couple of minutes I lay on my back, getting my breath back, until I realised that the light from my torch was fading. The water must have damaged the bulb. I sat up in panic, and at that moment saw stairs on the other side of the cavern. Rough steps cut into the gap in the wall, leading upwards. I staggered to my feet and waded across the shallows, the light blinking out just as I reached the bottom step.

Utter darkness.

For a few seconds I crouched with my hands on the step, claustrophobia rising in my gut. Then I calmed down. There was only one thing to do. I climbed upwards, my hands feeling the way on the cold stone, counting the steps as I went. When I reached forty-two the stairs gave way to an open space. I paused, waiting to see if my eyes would adjust to the darkness. Slowly I became aware of a grey shape ahead of me and I crawled in its direction. Moonlight spilled in from some unknown source, and I saw that I was in a mausoleum.

Two pedestals, one on either side, coffins on each slab of stone. As I crept forward I could see more. The coffin on the left had partially collapsed. On the right, the casket was intact. A dank smell hung close in the air. I couldn't help but stare at the coffin on the left, remembering the crypt at St Magnus. A shred of linen stuck out from the crumbled wood, the remnants of a shroud. More death. It was following me.

A sudden flush of moonlight illuminated the way ahead. I saw a low gate made of iron railings, and through it, the Edinburgh night – and freedom. I rushed towards it, grabbed a railing in each hand, and pushed.

Nothing.

In the half-light I could just make out a padlock on the other side. I reached around and fumbled at it, but it was snapped shut. From where I stood I could see the shapes of gravestones, and beyond the lights of the city. I pushed and pulled at the railings. Nothing. I realised I couldn't go back down with no light – it would mean scrambling blind downstream. The pain in my ribs had returned. I could feel the oppressive staleness of the mausoleum behind me, and a childhood fear rose up inside. I was trapped inside a mausoleum – coffins, skeletons, decay. A surge of manic energy hit me and I shook the gate back and forward, a scream building inside.

The railings moved.

I let the scream out and kept tugging and pushing. A grinding noise gave way to a rattling and seconds later the lock broke and fell to the ground. I leaned in with all my weight and the gate edged open. One more push and it nudged forward again. I put my head through the gap and wriggled out, the railings compressing my battered ribs.

In the weak moonlight I leaned back against the outer wall of the mausoleum. Under my fingers I could feel the etchings in the stone and I turned around to read the inscription.

HERE LIES JAMES CARDONALD SUTHERLAND
1779-1874
AND HIS BELOVED WIFE AGNES JANE
SUTHERLAND
1796-1875
SAFE IN GOD'S ARMS

Sutherland. The co-founder of Sutherland Gow, with access to the Chamber in the afterlife.

I got my breath back and tried to get my bearings. The cemetery was an old one, with tumbledown stones and carved angels. The city was close though, streetlight leaking in and casting shadows. I walked towards the light and reached a flight of stairs. Within seconds I was out onto a city street. Waterloo Place. I glanced back and saw the sign: OLD CALTON BURIAL GROUND.

I turned left and walked back to the city centre. The Guildford was around fifty metres away, behind Burger King. I checked my watch – it was half past one. The New Year party had finished around an hour ago and the debris was thick on the ground – cans, bottles, crumpled plastic. Drunken voices yelled out, and groups of stragglers hollered at one another across the empty road. I walked home into the new century, shoes squelching with every step.

CHAPTER 25

By the time I reached Lothian House I was shivering – drenched to the bone, no jacket, and a nervous wreck. I stepped into the lobby, glad to feel its residual warmth. I took the lift to the fourth floor and stepped out into darkness. A bulb had burned out again. I shuffled my way down the corridor, already fantasising about getting into dry clothes and straight into bed.

Someone was sitting at my door, legs stretched out into the corridor. At first I thought it was Kim, but then I noticed the shape of the Doc boots. Neve. She stood up.

"Shit, you made it. You got out."

She reached out and pulled me close.

"You're soaking," she said.

"I need to get out of these clothes." I unlocked the door and she followed me in.

"What happened? I waited for you for an hour."

"How did you know where I live?"

"You gave me your address that day in the Café Royal."

"Give me a minute. I'm going to shower."

In the bathroom I leaned in under the hot water, washing off the stink of death, the chill finally leaving me. I ducked into the bedroom and threw on a t-shirt and jogging bottoms. In the living-room, Neve had helped herself to a can of McEwan's Export.

"Want one?" She waved the beer at me.

"Aye, go on then."

I sat down on my armchair and sank into the cushions. Neve handed me an ice-cold tinny.

"So what happened?"

I concentrated on my beer. One mouthful, another, then I closed my eyes. "I hid by the river. Slipped and fell in. Waited until the voices faded away."

"How could you hear? That river was noisy." Doubt in Neve's voice.

"Echoes. It was a gamble. I sneaked back out to the archway and peered through, made a run for it."

"But how did you get out of the Guildford?"

I lied again without missing a beat. "There was a set of keys near the till."

"What did you do with the keys?"

"Put them in a bin on Princes Street."

She was looking at me like she didn't believe me. I had already made my mind up – the other entrance to the Chamber would be my secret. But as I submerged this secret, willing it to fall into the black depths of my memory, another secret bobbed up – Harry's story. She continued to stare at me and I felt the need to win her back.

"I found out something big before Christmas. About the boxfile. But you can't tell Danny."

The spark back in her eyes.

I told her. My mission to Dumbiedykes, Harry's grumpy denials, then the story of Doug Pebbles the folk collector. Eight boxfiles hidden at Overspill. Two more deaths.

"So this is why Sutherland came to Overspill," she said. "They have a lead. Where is this going to end?" said Neve.

"Maybe now? We could just write down everything we know and send it to a few newspapers and the police."

Neve nodded. "It's an option."

"It's twelve days until the thirteenth of January. If we do it tomorrow then there's a chance we could save a life this month."

Neve took a mouthful of her tin. "That cell. Jesus. The poor fuckers. How long do you think they're cooped up there for?"

"Gallacher went missing on the eleventh of December, so he must have been locked up for two days."

"Christ."

"I'm wide awake. I could start writing it all down tonight. We can draw maps on how to access it. We've got enough to at least get people curious."

"I'll help you," said Neve. "But I'm hungry. You got anything to eat?"

"Bread in the freezer, maybe."

I dug out an A4 pad and put it on the coffee table with a couple of pens. Neve rooted around in the freezer and put some toast on.

"Do you have anything to put on the toast?"

I got up and opened the wall cupboard and took out jam and honey. She reached over and our arms touched.

I moved first and she returned the kiss. Clumsily we put the beers down on the worktop, still kissing. She muttered something about needing to warm up, and we kissed through our smiles, stumbling towards the bedroom. In the dark we undressed. I was remembering the amazing experience with Hannah, trembling with anticipation. In the half-light I could see Neve examining me, her eyes blank and unknowable. The sheets were cold, damp almost in the slowly warming flat, and we cooried tight against each other.

But when we started to have sex, something went wrong. Our rhythm was out – as I thrust she flinched, and she repositioned to get comfortable. I tried again but suddenly my every movement felt clumsy, like I was some lumbering teenager again. I moved into her and she went limp. I tried to swivel my hips, get some motion going, but I sensed her mood changing, like she was about to start laughing. Her hands were no longer on my back.

"It doesn't feel right," she said.

I withdrew. We lay side by side on the bed without speaking, and then eventually she broke the silence.

"I need a glass of water," she said.

She got up and I continued to lie on the bed. I didn't hear much movement from the living-room, but it didn't sound like she was leaving. I lay looking at the ceiling, a clammy shame overcoming me. Should I go talk to her? I lay there paralysed until at some point I must have fallen asleep.

I woke in an empty bed. It was a surprise when I went through to the living room to find her curled up on the sofa, with her jacket as a blanket. I dressed and popped down to the corner shop for bacon, rolls, and Irn Bru. When I got back she was just waking up. It was at that moment I saw the sheets of paper spread out on the coffee table, filled with black ink. I edged closer, the bag of groceries still in my hand, and peered down at the neat writing and diagrams of how to access the Devil's Chamber.

"I couldn't sleep," she said. "So I wrote it up."

"Fancy a couple of bacon rolls?"

She nodded. "I'm starving."

I got to work in the kitchen. She turned the TV on. For a moment it felt like a comfortable domestic situation, the two of us co-existing in tranquillity. I kept glancing over at her on the sofa. It seemed inconceivable that less than twenty-four hours ago I was at Gull View saying my goodbyes to the family.

As we ate, there was a moment when we both reached for our second roll and our arms bumped. But there was no laughter, or banter, just an awkward repositioning, with me sitting back on the armchair and telling her to go first, and her snatching up a roll and dropping it on the floor. Again, no jokey comment, she just picked up the roll and started eating. No chat, just the awkward noise of munching.

When we finished, we drank our tea in silence, watching the news.

Eventually, she spoke. "I think I'll head off. So you'll copy the pages at Overspill? It'll be easier, my office is really busy."

"Sure. So where do we send it? BBC, Scotsman, Herald, Daily Record, Police?"

She put her empty cup on the table. "Yeah, probably. Just make the copies, I'll call you, OK?"

She pulled on her Docs and laced up. I felt a rising panic, the impending solitude approaching me like a climbing wave.

"Listen, last night. Can we talk about it?"

She looked me in the eye for the first time that day. "Miro, let's just forget about it."

She slung her jacket on and thirty seconds later my door snapped shut, leaving me alone.

CHAPTER 26

The next day I was unable to shake that memory of Neve lying on my mattress, utterly bored, as I put my moves on. Combined with the memories of the trip to the Chamber and the lingering feeling of guilt and loss about my family I could barely hold it together.

I tried watching videos but by the afternoon I called Fergus and met him on the Grassmarket. The rest of the day was a blur. Pint after pint, shots, a pizza somewhere, shouted conversations with American tourists, and through it all, a buzz of dread in my bones that wouldn't leave me. I had no memory of getting home, just a tumble of crisps and chocolate on the worktop from the late-night shop the only evidence of a functioning return journey. My hangover was appalling, and I lay on the sofa cocooned in my duvet. One image kept coming back to me: the tiny cell in the Sutherland Gow office, its narrow bed and metal bucket in the corner. Within ten days the next victim would be locked up there.

It was a relief to go back to work on the morning of the third of January. The hangover had gone, my energy levels had returned, and the dread had partially lifted. I unlocked the door to Overspill and stepped into its dusty silence. The lights were on, so somebody else was in. As I descended the stairs to the basement archive, I heard someone whistling.

Bob – the whistler – was sitting at his desk shuffling bits of paper. "Hey lad! Look who's back in action."

His face shone with health, his hair was fluffy and recently shampooed, and his shirt was white – rather than off-white – and appeared to be have been washed in the last week.

"Aye, have a good stare." He stood up and limped off down the main aisle of the archives, whistling as he went.

I had been away for almost two weeks and everything looked and felt alien. So much had happened. In my bag was Neve's carefully stencilled story about the Devil's Chamber, its whereabouts and its murderous meetings. I would make five copies while Bob was on lunch and prepare the envelopes.

I made some tea and had just got settled when the buzzer rang. Some bus-spotter no doubt, looking for the 1982 timetables. I told Bob I'd get this one and went up the stairs.

On the front step: Danny.

"We need to talk," he said. There was a hardness in his eyes and an edge in his voice. I stood to one side to let him in.

In the kitchenette he leaned against the worktop and stared at the wall. He couldn't look me in the eye. "You went into the Chamber without me." His voice was quiet.

I said nothing.

"The agreement was we would wait. I would contact you." Finally he looked at me. "Are you taking the fucking piss out of me?"

I laughed. "So I need your permission to trespass into an underground chamber which has nothing to do with you?"

"You know what I mean. Everything we saw. MacAskill. We have to be so careful."

Mary's voice came from the end of the corridor. "Miro? Is that you along there?"

"Yes, it's me. All under control."

Her footsteps returned back again.

"Give me the letter," said Danny. "The big confession that Neve wrote."

"Come on, Danny. This is all so fucked up. It's the best thing to do."

"No fucking way. Think about it. Neve did something stupid. In the letter we say that the access point is from the cellar of the Guildford. So it's the staff who have access, or at least allow access. So the police then interview the staff one by one. There are six bar staff I think, including Neve. It won't take long before they narrow it down."

"And then?"

"Let's imagine they believe it, investigate it, discover all of it. We'll be in court as witnesses. Maybe face some charges for not talking about it earlier. Imagine if it goes massive, the biggest story in recent years. Do you think you'll come out of it well? You'll lose your job. You won't get another in archives. The tabloids will be all over your life, your family…"

Danny seemed to know that the mention of family would flick the right switch.

"So we do it differently," said Danny. "We need to know where the other access point is. An address. Then that keeps us free from the whole thing. And we do another thing differently. We don't give the story to the newspapers… we *sell* the story to the newspapers."

Danny's eyes lit up. "Think about it. We're all in shitty jobs. I want to travel, Neve wants to travel, you want to… I don't know what the fuck you want, but it isn't this." He waved a hand at the walls of Overspill. "We sell the story. For a hundred grand. You know how I know this will work?"

I was quiet, trying to hold it together.

"My claret dream," said Danny. "Two nights ago, I took the claret and this time I crossed the cave, waded through the water, and the words in the book were in English. I read it all. Everything spelled out for me."

"You want to sell it." My voice was feeble. I remembered the quote in the newspaper from Gallacher's mum, her desolation.

"Listen to me." Danny was getting bolder, and wandered across to me, inches away from my face. "We go down to the Chamber on the thirteenth of January. We'll take pictures. We'll find the other access point. I'll find the right journalist and send them the letter. It'll be done within two weeks. All you need to do is be ready for the call. Got it?"

I said nothing and remained motionless.

"Now go get me Neve's letter."

I remained motionless.

Danny grabbed me by the throat and pushed me back against the wall. For a second we were trapped, straining against each other, then I swung a knee up into his balls. I connected perfectly, my thigh clunking between his legs. Danny crumpled forward and hit the floor.

"I'll go get Neve's letter. All you needed to do was ask politely."

By the time I returned upstairs, Danny was sitting on the lone armchair and putting a brave face on. I gave him the envelope – he pulled the letter out, read for a few seconds then stuffed it back in again. "And you didn't make any copies?"

"No. I was planning to do it around now."

"Just as well I got here in time." He stood up, wincing a little. "You wait for the call. Got it?"

I watched him leave.

The rest of the day passed in one of those long drawn out Overspill eternities that I had grown so used to. Utter silence in the basement other than Bob's whistling, or occasional banging around between the racks; Mary doing her best impression of a prison guard every hour, circuiting the premises to check we were behaving, peering behind shelves as if expecting to find contraband; and my computer screen blinking at me, dark grey lettering on bottomless blue depths, cursor flashing.

At twenty-five past five I was already staring at the clock. I willed the minute hand round until it juddered onto the half-past mark. Bob already had his jacket on – he seemed to have evolved in his twenty-odd years at Overspill to know the time without actually looking at the clock. We left together.

We walked, chatting, for fifty yards until we reached our parting point – he turned right to catch his bus down to Gorgie. I continued on the ten-minute walk home, a monochrome loneliness descending upon me. When I reached the door to Lothian House, I was conscious of someone stepping in alongside me.

Kim.

It had been around a month since I last saw her, and she looked different. Her hair had been chopped back and her nails were painted dark red. "We need to talk," she said.

When the lift door closed behind us, she started speaking.

"It's Darren," she said. The pause went on too long, until she added: "My boyfriend."

"I remember who Darren is."

"He found out," she said. "Not about you as such. But he knows I've been playing around."

"How does he know?"

She was blushing ferociously. "My diary."

I stared at the carpet in the lift. "You wrote about us in your diary?"

"In code," she said.

"Really? What's my codename?"

"Mr X. But that doesn't matter. He knows it's someone in the building. Someone around my age. I told him it was just some fantasy writing, but unfortunately I was a bit too graphic about stuff. Sorry."

The lift doors opened.

"And? What's he going to do when he finds Mr X?"

She shook her head. “He won’t. But I’m thinking of dumping him, and then I’m worried about what he might do. He has anger issues.”

I marched ahead of her, unlocked my flat, and banged the door shut.

CHAPTER 27

It was ten days until the thirteenth of January, and if Danny was to be believed, the execution of his plan. A hundred grand. It sounded ridiculous to me, but as I lay awake I tried to imagine what I would do with the cash. The truth was the money I'd come into from my mother's passing had not been enjoyed much. I'd bought the flat, which felt much like buying into some sort of parallel dimension. There had been a few thousand left over which had mostly gone on work clothes, furniture, my student loan, and other necessary things. It was hard to imagine my life being materially improved by those extra digits in my bank account. Instead a foggy recurring dream came to me in those half-awake nights that followed, a dream that changed every time but was somehow always the same. A dream that maybe was incubated by some residual trace of the claret's poison trickling through the tunnels of my brain.

I dreamt of a place that was near a beach – not some Mediterranean spot, but instead something northern, Atlantic coastline perhaps, a place of fresh breezes and bleached white sands. I would appear and disappear along this beach or the road next to it, and always there would be somebody nearby on the periphery of my vision, laughing in earshot but just out of sight. Sometimes I would go to places in this seaside town and be at peace. A small café with Italian ice-cream, a green bench next to a putting green, a bus shelter looking out onto the tumbling sea, a picnic table outside a pub with a hanging basket. In each of these places I would sit or stand, the voices and laughter nearby, sounding like people I knew but simultaneously had never met. The dream was comforting and when I woke from it the warm glow would linger until wakefulness fully came. And then in the half-light I would count the calamities: my lost mother, the horrors of the Chamber, the disaster with Hannah, the failed night with Neve. I could feel other certainties slipping away too: my ageing grandparents, my cousins leaving home and the only family unit I'd ever known slowly unravelling.

Those final days at Overspill were the worst yet. Sleep-deprived, permanently in a kind of grey mist. One afternoon, paying for lunch at a local bakery, I noticed the bulge in the pocket of my wallet. I unzipped it and teased the folded piece of paper out. As I ate my steak bake at the window counter I stared at the name – JOHN KUBIK – and the address and phone number.

Back at Overspill I sat down at my desk and waited for the right moment. When Bob went to the toilet, I dialled the number and heard my father's voice for the first time.

"Kubik." Gruff and snappy. I pronounced my surname the Polish way – *Koo-bik* – but he said it 'cubic.'

"Sorry, wrong number."

At five-thirty I put my jacket on and walked towards Leith. The city was ice-cold, and minus the Christmas glitz, a dark and angry place. I strode down Leith Walk, counting the side streets until I found the right one.

Number 36 was a battered old tenement with litter strewn in the front garden. At the scratched door I found his buzzer and name. Some of the other names were printed and encased in plastic, but his was naked to the elements, a peeling rain-stained white sticker with KUBIK scrawled in black biro. In that same dream-like state that had brought me all the way here – like a zombie walk to the edge of a cliff – I pressed the buzzer.

The door unlocked without any enquiry. I climbed one flight of stairs, up into a rising smell of damp and cigarettes, and saw him standing at his door. He looked at me and laughed, a cynical smoker's chuckle. "Miro?"

He looked exactly the same as in the claret dream, but I expected nothing less. An average height, thinning hair, silver-rimmed spectacles that had last been fashionable in the early 80s, a navy polo-neck sweater, stubble specked with grey.

"I wondered when you would end up here."

I stood and stared at him, looking for any likeness between us.

"Come in and we'll have a dram."

I followed him into the small flat. A pile of clothes lay on the floor in the hallway, an impromptu laundry basket. I stepped over the pile and into the living-room. There was one armchair, and a table with two chairs. One of the chairs doubled as a TV stand. My father beckoned me to the armchair and swivelled the free chair round to face it.

He opened a wall cabinet and took out a bottle of Bell's and two crystal tumblers. He poured two fingers in each and handed me one in a vulture grip. I was conscious of his smell of stale booze up close.

"Aye, Miro. It's been a long time. You know the last time I saw you?"

I shook my head.

"You were playing football for the school. In that wee town you grew up in. I remember it well. You were in goals. Buckhaven beat you 8-2."

This was a surprise, several years after the 'last time' that Auntie Sarah had mentioned. I remembered it well, our school team, a bit soft, up against the rough kids from down the coast. They blew us away with their snarls and sharp elbows. I had a sudden, eerily real flashback of pulling off a save and landing in a puddle on the red ash surface. Shouts and rain, the warm splat of spit on my cheek.

"You were shite in goals," he said, laughing. "I hope you didn't have hopes of making it professionally."

I shook my head and took my first sip of the whisky.

"What age were you then?"

"Fourteen, probably."

My father laughed again. "God, what a day. Your Uncle Donnie saw me and chased me all the way back to my car. We had a scuffle in the car park. Quite dramatic. But that was the last of it. I found a different direction." He pointed to the mantelpiece. There was a photo of a boy in school uniform. "That's Kieran."

I got up and moved over to the fireplace. I hadn't seen any likeness in my father's face, but this kid looked just like me when I was his age. Black hair and a goofy expression, frightened eyes.

"History repeating itself," said my father. "I met his mother, had a great laugh for a few months, got her up the duff, stuck around for a bit then got bored."

In the photo, Kieran was struggling to smile.

"I heard about your mum. There's a guy who drinks at that pub next to the harbour that I still hear from now and then. He phoned me up. Said, oh your old missus kicked it. The Big C."

I closed my eyes.

"She was a great girl at the start, seven years younger than me, liked a drink and a laugh. Into music and art and all the things you care about at that age. Went like the clappers, too."

I gripped the mantelpiece, feeling its hard ceramic under my nails.

"Then she got pregnant with you. I know I played a part in it, but I blame her, you know? She should have been more careful. Ruined a good thing. But hey, you were like me, a Kubik. Descended from a Polish paratrooper, a hero of Arnhem. So I tried to do the dad thing. And after I left, I tried to come back a few times. But she always chased me away."

I was waking from the dream-like state.

"And you know what, son? It's in the genes. You'll probably do it too. Dump them and leave them. Maybe wee Kieran as well. My advice? Don't even try to be a good guy, because you won't make it."

At my feet by the fireplace was a toolbox. Messy, a few screwdrivers, an oily cloth, and a claw hammer.

"So I got made redundant from the gas board four months ago. Decided that was it for me. I'm just drinking my way through the redundancy money, and hopefully it'll kill me before I run out. But I was hoping you'd show up, so I could tell you the truth. Truth liberates." He jabbed a finger at me. "Don't waste your life with ideas about love and all that bullshit. You were a mistake. Your mum nearly had you aborted, even went to the clinic, changed her mind in the waiting room. Then after you were born, we nearly put you up for adoption. The whole parenting thing, neither of us could handle it. She wanted to give you up and then go to Australia. So don't get all sentimental about her – she wanted rid of you at the beginning."

The claw hammer.

"Take it from me, son. We're alone in this world. Look after number one and extract what pleasure you can. Enjoy the fucking ride. You don't say much, eh?"

In the photo of Kieran I saw myself reflected.

"I just hope the end wasn't painful for Hazel, I wouldn't wish that on her."

I turned around and was out the flat and moving down the stairs. His voice called out behind me. Unbolting the door and a wall of cold air. Prickling snow. Traffic cutting through a thin layer of slush. Walking and walking.

The next day I was operating in slow motion, unresponsive to any question or comment from Bob or Mary. I saw them talking in the corner of the basement, clearly discussing me. Maybe they thought I was on drugs. I didn't really care, because I already knew I would not stay at Overspill too much longer – something would happen one way or another that would end my time here. The thought of it reassured me and made me calm – I would not be here much longer. Here at Overspill, here in Edinburgh. Here on the planet.

CHAPTER 28

The droplet of black wine struck the water, then the second droplet, and I watched as the dark liquid unravelled, spreading, changing from purple to pink to shimmering oily transparency and then to nothing. Dissolved. Ready to drink.

Danny slid the glass towards me. We were in his flat, and I had insisted on joining as he went back into dreamland to finalise his plan. Neve sat opposite me, her glass empty, eyes drooping shut as the claret took hold. She would be in her Other New York in seconds.

An hour earlier, I had met her in The Last Drop on the Grassmarket. The pub that would have once overlooked Edinburgh's gallows. It was shouty and spattered with spilt booze, some sort of meetup underway between a university hockey team and a university rugby team. Screeching laughter and impromptu wrestling matches bundling around us as I tried to rebuild rapport with Neve, skirting around our failed one-night stand without mentioning it, as she positioned and repositioned her glass of wine around the table like a chess-piece, private school voices hollering over us. She listened to me intensely with an expression of pained concentration as if she was trying to read a foreign language she barely knew. I coped with her silence as best as I could and bought another round.

The claret. Danny nodded at me impatiently and I downed the glass in one.

I'd told him on the phone that I wanted to understand the claret better. Wanted to do what I could to contribute to our masterplan.

"Train your mind in advance," he'd said. "Spend the whole day thinking about what you want the claret to reveal. Before you drink, concentrate. Visualise the thing you want and you'll go there."

Before leaving the house I'd done just that. I'd opened my water-stained notebook at the double pages with the six scrawled names and addresses of the Chamberites. I had circled each name in fluorescent yellow marker, and read down the names one by one and back again:

ARTHUR MacALLISTER
JAMES SUTHERLAND
CARSON GOW
GARRICK BREMNER
WALTER McCRIMMON
STEWART RAEBURN

I felt that bitter tingle at the back of my throat. Danny stared at me, watching me slip off the edge.

Utter darkness invaded my head and a new world took shape with startling speed. I was sitting on hard metal, a rail digging into my back, squeezed tight in my seat by others sitting on either side of me. Voices, almost drowned out by the screaming drone of an engine, and a jolt, and another, as the new world shook. Suddenly I could see.

I was in a large metal cylinder. Men around me wearing dull khaki with strapped on packs. The voices were not speaking English, but a melodious language that flowed then chopped short, rose up in emotional peaks and fell away in muttering and what I supposed was cursing.

I knew where I was. I was looking for the words but they wouldn't come into my head. I looked down at my hands and they were not my hands – rougher, a scar on the left thumb, black grease under bitten fingernails.

The words came.

Aeroplane. Paratroopers. Polish.

I was in the skin of my grandfather, and I was flying above Arnhem in 1944.

A door opened in the plane wall and we got to our feet. A voice barked orders, and now I could understand Polish. *Ready. I will give the order one by one. God go with you.*

A wire hooked me to the overhead rail and we shuffled forward. I was standing with a dimpled metal floor under the soles of my boots but could already feel myself falling away from the world I knew. There would be no climbing back from this – no stumbling back into Edinburgh in 2000. The claret had tricked me into another dreamworld. My breathing was ragged, strangled. The first paratrooper fell out of the black hole where the open door was, and another, and another. Flak struck the plane and it lifted us off our feet for a second – we all jumped and landed again, hard. *Faster! God go with you.*

The paratrooper in front of me shoved his rosary beads into a breast pocket and bundled forwards and out, and then it was me – a brief moment of noise and buffeting air and black endless space lit up by explosions and burning aircraft – a moment of hanging in time, no noise, no anything – and then I was falling, swooping through a hurricane of moist air. My fear had gone – it was like I was now free and unburdened – but then my hand moved instinctively to the ripcord and pulled and I jerked down and sideways and up as the chute unfurled and billowed above me, spinning the world out and round, until it settled and my feet pointed down the way and the landscape below me tilted and flattened and I could see burning vehicles and the snake-like gleam of a river. I drifted down. A shell whistled past, followed by the red-hot firefly of a tracer bullet. For the first time I noticed those around me – the other paratroopers gliding gracefully down, dozens of autumn leaves on their downward trajectory towards mud and shrapnel and fire and the end of something.

I reached up for the chute lines and tugged gently so that my direction changed towards open ground, the churned field rushing towards me now, littered with bodies and debris and the discarded shrouds of collapsed parachutes. I saw one man and another land and tumble onto the Dutch soil, and then it was my turn, and I braced myself and knew in that moment of silent focused descent that this would be my last moment of peace for decades.

My feet hit the ground and I rolled forward, tumbling onto muck and stones and tangling up in the chute lines and then the war was gone and I was lying on a carpet with the stink of cigar smoke all around.

"You see, MacAllister," a voice was saying, "it takes a bit of getting used to but really this is the moment in life where you become something altogether new."

I was still wearing the khaki uniform, and the parachute was above my head and tangled over a chair. I elbowed myself up into a sitting position. Orange lights above, and I screwed up my eyes until my vision adjusted. A small room, red carpets and drapes, old wooden tables topped with brass plaques, and a stained-glass window with a thistle motif. It looked like the back room of an Edwardian pub. Three men sat at the main table, chunky crystal glasses and a decanter in front of them.

"I can't get my head around it." This from the smaller man in the middle, wearing a rumpled suit, his thinning hair fluffed up by his hand that he repeatedly rubbed over his scalp.

The other two men reflected each other on either side of the table: sitting poised, one hand on a crystal tumbler, looking at each other knowingly. I recognised them: the one on the left was James Sutherland. His floppy long hair, his rower's build. The air of arrogance that had swept him in and out of Overspill that day.

I recognised the other man because I had taken his wallet out of his inside pocket in the Chamber. Carson Gow, the Goth Elvis. He nodded at Sutherland then leaned in towards MacAllister.

"You need to get your head around it. And quickly." His accent was hard Edinburgh, clipped with a pretend poshness that he had never mastered.

MacAllister took a swig of his whisky and Sutherland topped him up from the decanter.

"But that wee homeless guy. Gallacher, the papers said his name was. He died and we watched. We just watched."

Sutherland glanced over in my direction and looked right through me. For a second he almost made eye contact but my ghost was not visible to them.

"I joined less than a year ago," said Sutherland. "It's a bit of a rollercoaster, I'll grant you that. What age are you, MacAllister?"

His voice was small. "Forty-four."

"Well, I'm only twenty-eight and I realised quickly I had to man up. Become the next torch-bearer for my family."

That's it," said Gow. "Man the fuck up."

MacAllister looked at the table. "Or?"

"We can't take any risks," said Gow. "You're in or you're out. And if you're out… well, that has a certain permanence about it. To ensure that confidentiality is not breached."

MacAllister sipped from his glass. His eyes were not visible but I could tell he was computing Gow's statement and making a decision. "So we do this meeting every month?"

"Yes," said Gow.

"For how long has it gone on?"

"Since 1809, more or less."

"But is it really necessary? When I drank the two drops I experienced quite powerful visions."

Sutherland tapped his finger on the brass-topped table. "It's a matter of potency. A few drops gives a burst of insight that is often reliable. A full glass brings us certainty in an uncertain world."

"There are no riddles with a full glass," said Gow. "We almost always get the information we need."

MacAllister seemed to crumple in on himself, hunched over the whisky glass with hands clenching his head. Face hidden, his voice was muffled. "What information?"

Sutherland and Gow exchanged a glance, their eyes hardened with impatience, like they were already considering a course of action.

"We are a company," said Gow. "We exist for the benefit of the thirteen shareholders. Together we make decisions on investments. The information we… glean… guides those investments."

"Glean?" said MacAllister. "That was gleaning?"

Sutherland stood up, towering above MacAllister. "When we first met, you expressed surprise at the inheritance you received from your father."

MacAllister nodded.

"It was the same for me. An estate valued in the region of ninety million. Overnight I went from a middling trainee lawyer to a global decision maker. I own a townhouse in Edinburgh, an apartment in Zurich, a beach-house in Barbados, and a penthouse in Manhattan. No more nine-to-five, instead a family duty rooted in a tradition almost two hundred years old. I have three mistresses, and numerous high-class whores on speed-dial. Any restaurant in the city will take a reservation from me at short notice. I have six cars. A yacht. And I get to shape the future. All of this, MacAllister, is on a plate in front of you. And you're scared to pick up the plate?"

Gow swigged from his glass and grinned. "A fine speech from young Mr Sutherland. See, the thing about our company is that we are a close bunch. We have our separate lives but our club is at the heart of everything. If you don't want to be in the club MacAllister…"

Gow opened his hands and left them open, as if showing the size of the problem.

MacAllister stared at the table. "What do I need to do?"

"We meet on the thirteenth of every month. You know where. We have ad hoc meetings too, for which you will receive a phone call. All meetings are compulsory, so you should ensure that any other business interests are secondary. These meetings usually concern our strategic investments. We invest for two purposes – firstly for profit, and secondly to re-invest dividends in causes close to our hearts."

"Such as?"

Sutherland moved to the window, peered out, then apparently satisfied, returned to his seat. "When you have a long-term venture such as ours, it's important to ensure that the business climate retains its long-term potential. So we make donations to support this. For my ancestors, this involved investing in the colonies. Investing in *Britishness*, to convince those suspicious of our Scottishness. These days it's about keeping the market free. This involves investing in some fringe interest groups."

After a moment of silence, Gow spoke. "Tell us the story of your grandfather, MacAllister."

"The pharmacist?"

Gow nodded wearily.

"He was a hard worker. Built a small empire of pharmacy shops across Central Scotland. An elder in the Kirk. Family man. I was scared of him, but he was fair. Someone to look up to."

Gow and Sutherland exchanged a glance. Gow slapped both hands down on the table. "Hector MacAllister was a famous company man. He guided our portfolio wisely. A hot streak like no other in the twenties, taking us into shipping, whisky, and automobiles. During Prohibition our money was behind almost forty percent of the illicit scotch shipments into the US. The profits were obscene, and the money came back to us by the truckload. Hector was the man at the front of the company meetings, pouring claret down the throat of one waster after another and gleaning the information we needed to move our money around. And he was endlessly enthusiastic about channelling the company's dividends back into noble causes. He even set up a thriving printing press dedicated to anti-communist publications. It was a sideline but by the sixties it was a respectable company employing a hundred people. This is what we do, MacAllister. It is difficult at times but we bring order to chaos, and structure to what would otherwise be rubble."

"How do we manage it? There are only a dozen of us."

"Thirteen," said Gow. "It's like any business. We are the leaders. We don't engage in the operations. There are many layers below us. Cash in hand greases the wheels, and knowledge of us is lost down the many layers. If we want someone to disappear? Then I'll ask a man who knows a man who knows a man. If you pay thirty percent above the going rate then that usually guarantees secrecy. A small price to pay. So MacAllister, are you in?"

MacAllister clasped his hands in front of him. "I will do my duty," he said.

"Oh, that's good news," said Sutherland. "Your grandfather would be proud."

Gow uncorked the decanter with a soft pop.

The lights – red and yellow – shimmied, and I heard the dull pop-pop of bullets fired and found myself lying in the mud of a Dutch field. High above the planes and gliders slid by, some on fire. Nearby a shell crashed into the ground, spraying up a littering shower of earth and I held my hands over my ears until maybe ten minutes or five hours later I lurched back to life on Danny's floor.

CHAPTER 29

The call came on the twelfth of January.

I had fallen asleep on my sofa, two hours into a deep dreamless sleep. The phone drilled through my drowning slumber and I slung my hand at it.

"It's all set up." Danny's voice.

It took me a few moments to wake up. "Chamber?"

"No you prick, the Queen's birthday party." In the background I heard a female laugh. "Of course the Chamber."

He was with Neve. I could already tell.

"So you organised it like you said?"

"Even better."

"The journalist?"

"Come on, don't talk on the phone like this. You never know who's listening. Be at the pub at eight a.m. tomorrow. Phone in sick."

The phone clicked dead.

I slept surprisingly soundly that night. I woke refreshed and made bacon, scrambled eggs, and toast with a pot of black tea. I had a feeling of certainty that it would end today. I would be sorry for my grandparents and the rest of the family up the coast because I loved them so much. But the feeling of fate was strong.

They were already waiting by the railings outside the Guildford when I got there at five to eight. Neve peeled away first, taking the keys out her pocket. Danny grinned at me with a new smugness, like he knew much more than me and would never tell. Up close as we entered the pub I noticed how haggard they both looked – sleepless just like I had been. But once inside they moved with a precise energy unlike anything I had seen before – slow-moving but focused, Neve almost dancing across the floor and behind the bar to set things up for the day; Danny taking off his trench-coat and folding it into a perfect square.

"Same as before," said Danny. "Me and you go down to the store-room and hide out until Neve can join us around eleven. Then we head down and get in position. Wait until it starts."

"What about the journalist? The story?"

"Trust me," said Danny. "I know what I'm doing."

We took turns to use the toilet as before, then we climbed down to the cellar and into the storeroom. Danny switched the light on and built his bed of cardboard boxes. He was wearing the canvas Dutch Army shirt with pop buttons that I'd grown to hate so much. Once he settled down he asked me to turn the light out. I built my own cradle near the door out of an old armchair and three boxes lined up in front, then flicked the switch to dark and clambered into place.

We were quiet for a long time. Danny spoke first.

"So you got your big chance with Neve, Miro."

His disembodied voice, as always, a missile hitting me square in the ribcage.

"She said you were clueless."

In the darkness I tried to calculate the distance to Danny – if I launched himself at him in one running leap, would I be able to get a few good punches in?

"But that's not important. The claret, Miro, that's what's important. The claret is sensational. We've drunk about a quarter of the bottle now, me and Neve. Very controlled, a drop or two every night, just chiselling out a bit more truth. Chip, chip, chip. And we've discovered a lot."

I stared out into the darkness.

"Last week I took the claret and I was floating above you as you walked down to Leith. I slipped through a tenement door behind you and you didn't notice a thing. I was your shadow. And there he was at the top of the stairs – your long-lost dad. I watched that scene play out – you standing by the fireplace as he told you the truth."

My head lolled back against the armchair. There was no hiding. No escape. I stared up above. I wasn't sure if I was looking at the ceiling or an imaginary grey sky, eyes tricked by the darkness.

"I felt for you, Miro. That was tough news to take – you were almost aborted or given up for adoption."

I said nothing. Paralysed on the ancient armchair.

"I've been on so many trips," he said. "You can't really do more than one a day, it gets too much for the system. So you have to be careful, ration it out. If the comedown dreams get too intense then you need to take a break for a few days. But I've found out so much. For example, Neve gave me some helpful nuggets of information. She told me about your predecessor Harry. The guy from Dumbiedykes. The whole backstory of the folktales and the professor. I concentrated on those details and took a little extra claret – two and a half drops in my glass of H-two-oh. Man, what a ride that was. Like a movie from start to finish. I saw your friend Harry getting duffed up by some Edinburgh thugs. Turns out he's a big gambler and in a spot of bother. Up to his ears in debt to a loan shark. So he's decided to blackmail the Chamberites for a couple of hundred grand. Been sending them threatening letters and the like. But they're onto him. They know the source is Overspill. He's in their sights."

In the darkness I could see that Dumbiedykes flat – the cosy living-room, the view onto the Crags, Theresa eking a home out of straitened circumstances. I remained silent, determined to give Danny nothing.

I woke when Neve opened the door.

"Let's move," she said.

Danny put his headlamp on and was in the tunnel first, knees and elbows clanging on the aluminium.

I was adjusting my headlamp when Neve spoke.

"Honestly Miro, the claret is unbelievable. My family has been a mess the last few years, parents divorcing and all manner of chaos. I see it clearly now. I just need to stay away for two years. Everything will settle down. And Edinburgh is not home for me. New York beckons."

"I'm happy for you."

"You have to drink it again, when we get back later."

"Will we get back?"

She was caught in the beam of my headlight, red-blonde hair glinting, an invincible smile lighting up her face. "Have some faith Miro."

She ducked into the tunnel, and after counting to twenty, I followed.

By the time I reached the ledge she was already scuffling around on the stairs. I swung over the ledge and could hear some distant footsteps down below already. I followed slowly, and walked out into the Chamber's main room, thirteen chairs already set out for the main ceremony.

I looked back to the stairway, listening. The giant would be down first.

Neve had disappeared, and I hung around in one of the alcoves near the stairway, waiting. I wasn't nervous; there was just an anxiety to get it over and done with.

Danny and Neve reappeared at around the same time, as if planned, emerging from alcoves on different sides of the Chamber.

"Let's get in position," said Danny.

We found the narrow staircase and made our way up to the tiny balcony where we'd witnessed the demise of Malky Gallacher. Danny placed his rucksack carefully by the exit and took the position at the edge of the balcony.

I checked my watch. It was only just after ten. Three hours to go.

Neve touched my arm. "You take the middle. I've got your back. Let's all get some sleep."

The weirdness of it struck me in a way it hadn't before – the three of us, lined up side by side, settling down for sleep in advance of a psychedelic poisoning. Nevertheless, something about the Chamber encouraged going with the flow. I lay back, Danny's battered

Timberland boots on one side and Neve's riot of red hair on the other.

"This wasn't what you promised, Danny," I said. "Where's the fucking journalist?"

"Don't worry." His voice was soft.

I let my head rest on the stone and stared high above at the ceiling. Like last time, I felt a strange peace, entombed but somehow protected, a readiness to submit to what was waiting. A grey half-sleep crept over me.

Neve's hand was on my arm.

Through a gap in the balustrade I saw them take their places in their long black gowns. I noticed McAllister's tubby body as he took a chair in the back row. Sutherland was in the front row, legs crossed, looking a little bored. The man standing at the front was clearly Gow – gaunt, and with the same controlled energy I'd seen in the last claret dream. He put the skull-hat on and shifted it for comfort. They were ready.

A raised voice down below, and two figures came into view. The giant, and Harry Robertson.

"This is what happens if you mess with them," whispered Danny. "Harry's getting what he deserves."

The giant manhandled Harry forward. He looked beaten and bloodied, but he was still fighting.

"Aye, you fuckers! You think it ends with this? Other people know."

The giant forced Harry down into the chair and strapped his wrists to the armrests. Harry yelled manically. The giant strode off through the cabinet archway and came back into view with a tray, on it a bottle of claret and a cup. Gow gestured impatiently and the giant poured. In one fluid motion Gow dug his fingers into Harry's spiky grey hair, tugged his head back and chugged a cup of claret into his mouth.

As Harry coughed and spluttered I rested my head on the cool stone. Death would come to me today as well, I was sure of it.

"Tell us!" Gow's voice roared out. "Do not hold back. Where should we put our money?"

Harry's response was garbled, nonsensical. But I could see some of them taking notes.

Gow started hitting him. "Speak sense!"

I closed my eyes. The noise of Gow's blows rang out across the Chamber, one hard slap after another, the frequency intensifying, then as Harry's mutterings slowed and quietened down altogether, the slaps stopped.

I was conscious of Danny lowering himself next to me, out of the line of sight.

Footsteps crossed the Chamber, and I risked a glance below to see the giant with Harry slung over one shoulder. He entered the alcove below us, and his footsteps faded then came back loud again, and faded away as he moved towards the well. Then came a dreadful noise: the distant sound of something heavy landing deep underground.

The chairs screeched on the stone floor as the congregation stood up. There were quiet conversations in small huddles, and one of the men sat at the table writing into a leather-bound ledger. When the entry was logged he slapped the book shut and got to his feet. Gow led the way. They moved off in single file towards the stairway, and the noise of their scuffing feet rang out, diminishing as they climbed.

I was shaking uncontrollably. Danny was talking to himself, incoherent whispers babbling out. Neve slowly got to her feet.

"Let's go back up."

She offered a hand to Danny and hauled him to his feet. They walked out of the alcove, leaving me sitting alone. I remembered that the giant was still somewhere down below – they seemed to have forgotten, already scrambling down the stairwell, Danny's voice too loud.

I sat there, paralysed, waiting.

When I heard them below in the Chamber I finally made a move, slipping down the narrow stairs. At the bottom I stopped and listened for the giant, peering into the dark corridor leading to the well. But there was no sign of him.

Out in the Chamber, Danny stood staring at the claret spillage. It was hard to tell if it was blood or just the wine. I thought about Harry, husband of Theresa and father of two grown-up kids, now a corpse in a dank hole in the ground next to the bones of so many others.

Danny turned to me. "The plan has changed. They know the source is Overspill. You're the weak link in all of this."

"Fuck off, Danny."

He lurched at me and jabbed a finger into my forehead. "I'm inside your head, motherfucker. I own you. From now on you do everything I say."

I swatted his arm away and moved towards the stairs.

Neve was already a few yards ahead of me when it happened.

An explosive shout from behind.

I turned, and there was the giant, mouth hanging open.

"Intruders!" he yelled. "Intruders!"

He began to run towards us in a lumbering stride, picking up speed.

I sprinted towards the stairs, Neve ahead of me, Danny some way behind. Feet pounding, heart hammering, up the stone steps, curling round one bend, then another, my headlamp beam splashing wildly around on the tiles, until I remembered I needed to look for the red shoelace and trained the light on the railing. I saw it and heard Neve scrambling over the ledge at exactly the same moment – and then I made the decision that would haunt my waking nights for the next nineteen years.

I reached out, grabbed the shoelace, ripped it off the railing and stuffed it in my pocket. Then I took four steps back and launched myself at the wall.

The first time I bounced off with a pathetic slap and tumbled backwards onto the stone. I bounded back up on my feet and threw myself at the wall again. The adrenaline boosted me up, and with a flailing hand I caught the edge. I swung my other hand up and found purchase with my toes. Up and over the ledge. Moments later I heard Danny round the corner and – seeing no shoelace – continue up the stairs.

"Intruders!" roared the giant from below.

Voices came from above too. Danny's rapid footfall continued up the stairs, until he met the Chamberites coming back down, and the giant caught him up from behind, and all at once there was a shouting match, but loudest of all was Danny's anguished yell.

I slid back into the tunnel and pulled up the grille behind me, getting it firmly into place. I took a few breaths to calm myself, then crawled back towards the world above, back towards the light.

Singapore, Edinburgh

January 2019

CHAPTER 30

Dawn bleeds into the sky, and I see the eagle on its tireless swoop, circling the skyscraper opposite and plunging against the wall, scrambling against the surface as if trying to catch some phantom prey. It flaps and fumbles off the smooth glass, plummets out of control for a few metres, then resumes flight. Thirty seconds later it reappears from the far side of the building and starts its kamikaze loop all over again.

I have been watching this bird for a few weeks now from my 25th floor apartment on Clarke Quay. It only happens early in the morning or late in the evening when the city's endless flow of traffic has slowed to a trickle. I have often wondered how it survives when it's wasting so much hunting time chasing shadows.

I take a slug of water and the plastic bottle crinkles in my grip. It's five-thirty in the morning, and I have barely slept. I open Neve's email on my iPhone and read it again:

They Found Us

Hi Miro

This is the email I hoped I'd never have to send, and the email I'm sure you hoped you'd never receive.

Last week I was returning home with my daughter and on the front step was a package addressed to me. I opened it, and inside was an old shirt, and a letter. I realised with shock that it was Danny's shirt, the Dutch army one he'd always wear and was wearing on that last day.

The letter was unsigned but I knew it was from Gow. He wrote that he'd somewhat belatedly tracked me down, and also my accomplice Miro McGarrity (formerly Kubik). We are both cordially invited for a drink at the Guildford Arms on the evening of 12th January. Could I "do the honours and get in touch with Mr McGarrity?"

He said that if we don't come then there will be consequences. He also said the consequences would start sooner rather than later.

Please come back as soon as you can. We can only face this together.

Yours
Neve

Trembling, mouth sour, I decide to make some breakfast. The kitchen in my serviced apartment adjoins the living-room, and from where I stand at the hob, stirring my porridge, I can look out onto the city skyline, daylight slowly replacing electric light. I wash raspberries and blackberries and chop a banana and I'm halfway through eating when my mobile rings.

The name on the display hits me like a punch in the guts. My cousin Fergus. He never calls my mobile. I already know what's coming.

"Miro? Sit down. I've got some really bad news."

I slump down hard on the sofa.

"It's my dad. It's Donnie. He was found dead on the beach this morning. They think he had a heart attack while walking the dog."

I can see the beach, the breeze blowing a sprinkle of gritty sand up onto the road. The North Sea tumbling onto the shore, waves folding in on themselves.

"Oh Fergus."

"You'll come home?"

That word; home. And I remember another word, in Neve's email. Consequences. Sooner rather than later.

Five hours later I'm at the check-in queue at Changi Airport. It is the fourth time I've made such a journey over the last twenty years, returning home at short notice. The first times were for the deaths of my grandparents; the most recent time, last year, when Kirsty's civil partnership broke up.

It is still impossible to believe. Donnie. Invincible Donnie. Gone. And that lingering thought at the back of my head. *Sutherland & Gow*.

I leave my suitcase at the bag drop; it's bulked out by my carefully folded suit-bag, the black tie tucked into a zip pocket, and the winter clothes that I never wear in Singapore, only when travelling. Through departures in a daze and on to the KLM lounge. I have paid a small fortune for this ticket, business class the only option, but that is no bad thing. I may not have long left, so I might as well enjoy some small luxuries.

In the lounge I order a Highland Park. I rarely drink these days but it feels necessary, an anaesthetic and an intoxicant. I sip at the scotch, tilting the glass and letting the lone ice cube slide against my lips. I have spent almost twenty years remembering and trying to forget the Devil's Chamber, until it has become a secret part of me, a virus that I have learned to live with, a benign tumour that I cannot tell anyone about. And now, finally, it has reactivated and grown malignant as I always knew it would.

My mind goes back to those days after my last visit underground. I have always avoided exploring the memories, because I know it will take me down a rabbit-hole that only leads to oblivion, but now there is a certain relief in knowing I have to confront it, remember everything. Because maybe the way out lies in some forgotten detail.

Nineteen years ago, and there I was tumbling out of the tunnel back into the storeroom. Neve was lying on the boxes, panting heavily.

"Danny?" she said.

"They got him."

She said nothing. We stayed there for a few minutes, vague noises drifting down from the pub above. It was two o'clock on a Thursday afternoon and it wouldn't be easy to get back out unnoticed. Neve went first, out and up the ladder. I heard her speak to someone, a tone of surprise. Nothing happened for a long time and I realised Gow and the others could be coming for me soon – how long would it take them to find the tunnel? Just as I made my move towards the door, stepping over the tumble of junk, it opened and Neve's face appeared.

"Quick."

I followed her up the ladder and she urged me to move. I walked through the sliding door into the afternoon hubbub. Nobody noticed. A few drinkers here and there, most of them reading newspapers or absorbed in conversation. Neve wandered over to me as if I was a customer. I saw how empty her eyes were – how hollow her cheeks.

"Go home," she said.

The days afterwards I barely remember. I went to work; I must have eaten breakfast, lunch, and dinner every day; I went to bed at night but did not sleep. The attention from Bob and Mary intensified. I fell asleep at my desk at some point and was shaken awake by Bob. I called Neve; the phone rang out. I tried again and again over the weekend until eventually she picked up on Sunday. She agreed to come over. I hadn't slept properly for nine days and everything was dream-like, my consciousness teetering from underwater fogginess to above-the-clouds hyper-awareness.

When I opened my door I could see that Neve had not slept either. She told me about her week. Immediately after the visit to the Chamber she had gone to Danny's flat and taken the claret. She did not explain why she had a key to his flat. She had signed herself off work and each day had drunk the claret, looking for answers. But it hadn't worked – instead she'd seen more vivid visions of New York. Glimpses of a possible future but no insight into the up-ended present. I watched her leave my flat and walk down the corridor until she disappeared.

At Overspill, one morning Bob and Mary were in deep discussion. Bob looked shocked after she headed back up the stairs.

"Auld Harry's gone AWOL," he said.

"What happened?"

"Nobody knows. Just disappeared. He had a gambling problem, so maybe he had debts, did a runner."

I lasted only a few more days. I went home one night and as I was going into the flat Kim's door opened and out came the boyfriend. He barrelled towards me and I knew what was coming, wanted it to happen actually, turning just at the perfect moment to step into his fist and blow after ringing blow. It was over in a minute, Kim dragging him off as he kicked me with his white trainers. The cuts and bruising on my face were pretty bad but I carried on going in to Overspill regardless, knowing that something would change soon. The picture of Danny in the paper tipped me over the edge – a photo of him at the top of a hill, described as a keen climber, pleas for information with a slight suggestion that perhaps the answer lay at the bottom of a mountainside or down a pothole somewhere.

Bob called an ambulance when he found me lying on the floor next to my desk. I was in hospital for three days, diagnosed with a breakdown, then signed off for two months.

I never went back to Overspill.

I spent three months at Donnie and Sarah's, piecing myself back together, hiding behind a story of a burnout triggered by pent-up grief and a relationship gone wrong. I barely left the house except to walk on the beach, and as the summer drew to a close there was yet another moment of reckoning just like one year ago, and this time I knew the only answer was to go far away, somewhere I could bury all my memories deep underground, covering them up with a layer of concrete. I changed my name by deed poll from Kubik to my mother's maiden name McGarrity. I told the family that I wanted the same name as them; that my father's name meant nothing anymore. They seemed proud. The main reason was that I did not want to be traced.

I signed up for an IT postgraduate course in London, sold the flat in Edinburgh, and in September 2000 I was on the train down to a city big enough to swallow my secrets.

I scratched out a new life in London.

I was glad that Kirsty was nearby; my cousin and her circle of friends gave me the support I needed in the early weeks, and soon my studies started to fill the hole in my life. Something about software development appealed to my traumatised inner self – building something painstakingly line by line, understanding more and more as the weeks went by about how data could be brought in from the chaos of the universe and ordered into something almost invisible. I got evening temp jobs in data entry to keep me going, and to keep me busy; the combination of my new coding skills, my archivist's mindset, and the hard slog of keying words and numbers into cavernous databases set something alight for me. The year passed quickly, and I graduated with distinction. I had found some sort of peace through hard work and application, and the Devil's Chamber was a memory discreetly packaged in my head, only creeping back during the occasional sleepless night.

I spent six years in London. Kirsty and her Canadian girlfriend Emma became my closest friends, and I dated one of Emma's friends for more than two years until it ended with some sharp drunken words from me. Three years in and the call came from Donnie: my father John Kubik had been found dead from alcohol poisoning. The world felt like a fractionally better place. London was a million miles from Scotland, and when I returned for Christmas or other holidays I always made a point of never stopping in Edinburgh. Even still, my heart would beat faster as the train passed through, half-expecting to see the giant or Gow standing on the platform waiting for me.

London ended for me one rainy November day. I had passed through Russell Square tube station many times but had never taken the staircase. As I descended the steps something about the damp air and the cracked tiling sent me hurtling back to the Devil's Chamber; I lost my footing, stumbled forward, and fell headlong down the stairs. My fall disturbed the flow of commuters and a few toppled onto me, and for a few panicky seconds I was squished under the weight of other bodies. But it was over quickly, and people helped me hobble to my feet, helped me get back up into the daylight and fresh air. I cracked two ribs, broke the pinkie on my right hand and scraped the skin of my nose and cheek. Alone that night in my tiny Stockwell apartment, I felt the oppressive weight of all those underground spaces below me, a secret London conspiring to catch me out. Everything I'd suppressed came bubbling up again. I spent two weeks recovering, battling the ghosts in my head. And then I knew that it would be best to run away again; just keep on moving.

I got a job in Amsterdam. The utterly different landscape helped – there was not much going on underground, just water. I worked for a major publisher, leading the reorganisation of their IT infrastructure and data categorisation. Again, I lost myself in work, in the comforting glow of a monitor, and took the edge off the long hours with late nights in the city's nicotine-stained cafes. Without any effort at all I got job offers from around the world every few weeks – it seemed every big company had vast lakes of data to be filtered and processed and brought to order. I did not find the thought overwhelming; in fact, quite the opposite. The thought of those uncharted oceans of information reassured me because there was enough out there to drown the noise in my head for the rest of my life.

After two years in Amsterdam, New York came calling. I had travelled to the city many times with work and had always felt at peace there. It happened surprisingly quickly – a one-hour phone interview, an offer emailed to me the next day doubling my current salary, and four weeks later I was arriving at JFK. I rented an apartment in Brooklyn and took the subway over the water to Manhattan every day – my office was in Midtown and looked onto the Chrysler Building. This time it was a large automotive company that wanted me to clean up their data spill. It took a few weeks to adjust to the intensity of the new company – the barked orders, the tantrums, the American gushes of optimism. But very occasionally in life, it pays off to be Scottish. With a laser-eyed stare, a curl of the lip, and a rip-roaring curse, I scared off my assailants. A bit of Scottish street theatre always goes down well in corporate.

I'd been in New York for only two months when the most unexpected thing happened. I fell in love.

I was in Midtown East with a colleague, a half-Korean half-Irish programmer called Sean Lee. I wasn't sure if the Lee was from his Irish half or Korean half and was planning to ask him once we'd had a couple of beers. We went to an old school place on East 45th street called the Comfort Diner for a late lunch, the sort of joint which to me was straight out of the movies – booths with red leather seats, pourable sugar jars, bottomless cups of coffee, pissy waitresses. The place was rammed, but the two of us managed to get a booth for four. We'd just got our pancakes and eggs when there was a commotion at the counter – the waitress had knocked a glass of orange juice over two girls sitting waiting for their brunch order. Sean was always one to spot an opportunity and intervened in the shouting match to offer them a dry spot at our table. Over they came.

I was always doubtful about the idea of love at first sight but this came pretty close. Dana Metzler, petite and black-haired and black-eyed, togged out in jeans and a biker jacket, skin colour a shade lighter than mocha, looking at me with deep suspicion. Until I opened my mouth. I'd learned already that cranking up the Fife accent worked wonders, and Dana looked startled. I barely noticed her friend, who was already deep in conversation with Sean Lee.

"Where are you *from*?" she asked, as if I was from another planet.

"Scotland. But I try to keep it quiet."

That smile. "So cool. Your accent."

After brunch and coffee we went over the road to a dodgy Irish pub called the Perfect Pint, and stayed until Sean could no longer stand. I found out lots about Dana Metzler. She described herself as the ultimate New Yorker, the perfect mix of German, Irish, Dominican, Italian, and Russian Jewish. Her eyes sparkled as she talked. She was a kindergarten teacher. She liked gin cocktails, nineties hip-hop, Thai food, and kayaking. Every time I spoke she looked at me with those curious eyes, and I returned her gaze. We swapped numbers as Sean swayed by the door, and the next day I texted her, sparking a 2-hour SMS blizzard, and an hour later I was in her bed. Within a month, she'd moved in with me.

Seven years I was in New York, and seven years with Dana Metzler. My accent rounded out, absorbed some American flavour. Dana's family became my default family. The newness and ever-regenerating energy of the city made it the perfect place for me, because whenever my thoughts began to backslide towards Edinburgh, something new happened – at work, in the neighbourhood, in the city – and this endless movement meant I could always propel myself forward.

Just like my fall down the tube steps in London, everything came unstuck in one brief moment. October 2015. We'd been talking about marriage on and off, both a little uncertain about upsetting the equilibrium we'd found. But I was thirty-eight and she was thirty-two; it felt like time to make a big decision. And that day, walking the Highline on a beautiful fall afternoon, the mirror-glass windows of skyscrapers reflecting the vivid blue skies, Dana told me she wanted a baby. She also told me that we needed to talk; that she saw in my eyes I was hiding something from long ago, she knew that there were things from my past I never wanted to talk about, but it was important to get these things out in the open and move on with a new life, become parents, give a little one a childhood that was better than mine.

Something about her choice of words caught me off-guard. I had a flashback to that night in the Leith flat when my father told me to not even try to be a good guy, that it was in the genes for me to run away, that my half-brother Kieran would probably do the same…

Our walk ended in frosty silence, and then I was off to Denver for work, after which I had to stay on for a couple of extra days and missed her parents' anniversary meal. It all unravelled quickly after that. She gave me plenty of chances to turn the situation around, but I stayed late at work, went for long runs, kept quiet as we lay awake beside each other in the middle of the night. At the heart of it all, I knew that if I told her about one thing then I would need to tell her everything – and I was conscious of how ludicrous the Chamber story sounded, how if I told her then the outcome would be the same, and on balance it was just better for her not to know.

I moved out in January, on a day when Brooklyn was smeared with dirty snow. We kissed, and there was a feeling of one last chance, but I got in the car and drove over to my new place eight blocks away. In a zombie daze, I worked 70-hour weeks and spent the weekends browsing for my next location. Two months later I was on a plane to Melbourne.

The trick seemed to be to pick a place significantly different from the previous one. The first year was a blur. This time I was working for a food company, rebuilding their infrastructure after a scandal linked to misleading ingredients saw their entire management team cleaned out. Dana emailed to let me know that she was with somebody new and four months pregnant. It was a blunt knife to the heart, but after a few hours to reflect, I wrote back to say I was happy for her and meant it.

For my fortieth birthday I travelled back to Scotland and a party at Gull View. Since the breakup with Dana I had barely thought about the Chamber, and landing at Edinburgh on a bright July day, it felt like a chapter that was closed. The party had been months in the planning, and the weather was kind, gentle sunshine breaking through the clouds just as the first guests arrived.

My cousins had done more or less OK.

Fergus was on good form. After experiencing a lost decade in his twenties – one middling job after another without direction, family gossip about his binge-drinking dominating most conversations – he'd cleaned up his act in his early thirties, knuckled down and done an MBA, met and married an Anglo-Irish physio called Aisling, and they had two daughters and a son. He did something in public affairs for a large financial services firm and used the tenuous excuse of confidentiality to avoid talking about it and hence getting the piss taken out of him. He stood next to me nursing a bottle of IPA, his attention rarely drifting from his kids at the far end of the garden. I clinked bottles with him and he smiled. He no longer had a runaway mouth – he spoke in a measured way, always thoughtful, as if at some point he'd had a major epiphany about his meandering babbling. I suspected both Aisling and his boss had given him some sort of boot-up-the-arse ultimatum.

Kirsty had been through the wars but was coming through the other side. She'd split with Emma, the Canadian, after sixteen years together, and had been through a redundancy not long after. But she had bounced back with a promotion at a new creative agency and a new relationship, tentatively introduced this same weekend. Her French girlfriend Stephanie was working the crowd, and I could hear her fluttering laugh somewhere over by the greenhouse.

The weather held throughout the evening. The caterers served up nachos, fish and chips, cranachan, coffee and mints, gin and tonics, single malts. As the shadows lengthened, the garden got busier, Donnie and Sarah's extended circle dropping by, and soon I was surrounded by people I hadn't seen for a long time, in some cases twenty years. To my shock Hannah's parents arrived – they greeted me warmly, and I asked about their daughter perhaps a bit too keenly. Edinburgh, they told me. A daughter. Doing well. I was surprised how much I yearned for my old childhood sweetheart at that moment. I took the opportunity to go inside to the upstairs bathroom where I wouldn't be disturbed and spent a few minutes just enjoying the solitude, trying to piece my composure back together again. From where I stood I could hear the voices and the laughter – a good party, created by me no less. Sometimes it was a shock to realise that I knew people; that my life wasn't just a hop from one location and job to the next, everything strung together by loose connections and long hours in front of glowing screens.

I breathed in-and-out a few times, the mini-meditation that I'd learned in the aftermath of my London breakdown all those years ago. By any measure, what was happening all around me was indicative of a happy, successful family. Three generations back they had been dirt poor, Irish and Highland migrants who'd relocated to Dundee's jute mills to escape the empty places of the Celtic fringes. The neighbours no doubt saw the McGarritys as a model family in the town. Middle-class and respectable, educated and well-dressed and healthy, throwing a party organised by the family's international jetsetter. It was just as well they couldn't see inside my head.

CHAPTER 31

The thud of the plane's wheels hitting the tarmac jolts me awake. Amsterdam. On long-distance flights I always get weird dreams – this time I was back at Gull View, reliving the fortieth birthday party, but the sea had been just inches away from the garden, and not the marine-grey foam of the North Sea but a much bluer ocean. Dana Metzler had been there in the garden with a small boy. I had been unable to cross the grass, every step gliding me backwards.

I rub the sleep out my eyes and the images of the dream fade. The plane landed on time, and I have one hour before the connecting flight to Edinburgh. I make my way to the gate and order a black coffee. As I sip at its scalding bitterness, I open my email – there is another message from Neve, a simple one line with her phone number and asking me to call her once I'm in Scotland. I wonder how she tracked me down – changing my surname and abstaining from social media have certainly made me hard to trace, but last year an old university friend guessed I'd taken my mother's maiden name and found a photo of me as a guest speaker at a data analytics conference in Singapore. He then correctly guessed my work email. There are always ways to find someone who doesn't want to be found.

The coffee kicks in. I think back to the call with Fergus. Donnie had been found on the beach, alone.

There were some stories about heart problems in the family, but he was a lean and lively sixty-four-year-old. Sarah was in shock but not surprised, if that made sense. Fergus had wanted to understand more about the cause – perhaps to help prevent it for other family members – and wanted to do a post-mortem. But Sarah refused. He's already gone, she'd said. Let's not cause him anymore trouble.

I walk through the possibility of connections to the Chamber. How could they have done it? Caused a healthy man to die in full view on a beach? True, his death took place early morning, while the village slept – Donnie liked his six a.m. dog walks – but still, the risks of being spotted with him seemed high. Had they poisoned him in advance?

I watch a KLM-liveried jet take off. It rises sharply, charging into the sky, taking a hundred people to their next destination – home, work, away from home, to lovers, away from lovers, leaving something behind or moving towards a fresh start. And me? Going back to something, or reaching the end?

At the gate, a stewardess is typing by a monitor and two men in luminous vests stand by the door. Boarding soon. I am going back into the unknown, that's where I'm going. It occurs to me that almost twenty years have passed since I was last in the Devil's Chamber – and there is no way of knowing how many deaths have taken place, how many investments have been made, how many fortunes won.

An idea comes to me. An idea so simple that I laugh out loud.

Despite spending my working life filtering data to make sense of the world, I have been so keen to run away from all of this that I have never once googled the Devil's Chamber.

I fumble with my iPhone and open up a web session. Type 'Devil's Chamber Edinburgh.' The results pop up. The first one is a WordPress site with the tagline – *The myth of Edinburgh's secret underground caverns, and the terrible things that take place there*. I click on it.

The landing page shows a generic picture of an underground cellar with blank concrete walls. The site is a basic Wordpress blog, with a list of posts down the right-hand side. I read the landing page blog first, which dates back one year ago, and introduces an extract from The Scotsman back in the nineteen-twenties, all about the hidden chamber underneath the feet of Edinburgh's citizens. One by one I click the links. An extract from a potboiler novel with Nazi-esque overtones. A transcript of a long rambling poem. And on and on. Every single link a digitalisation of the scraps I photocopied for Neve back in 1999.

I click on the contact page, and at the top is a photo of a boxfile with the number 467 scribbled on its front. I tap on the textbox and start writing.

Hi, my name is Miro, I have been to the Devil's Chamber. Contact me urgently.

Nothing to lose, I figure.

The boarding announcement is made. I pocket my phone and join the back of the queue.

CHAPTER 32

Fergus is waiting for me at Edinburgh airport.

His eyes are bloodshot and his hair ruffled. I go straight for the hug and pull him close. "Sorry, man."

"Me too."

Fergus's grip squeezes a stray tear out my eye.

"He was the only father I ever had."

Fergus nods. "Come on let's get you home."

We are silent in the car until we reach the bridge over the Forth. Fergus fidgets with his iPhone and Sonic Youth's 100% bursts out the stereo. "Mind if I play my nineties mix? We won't have much chance for anything other than sadness over the next couple of days."

"Go for it."

As we cross the choppy water I'm reminded of that other trip nineteen years ago when I saw the picture of Malky Gallacher on the train and Fergus drank tin after tin of Stella. Despite myself, I smile. "Remember that Christmas train journey over the bridge? You effing and blinding about the royals?"

"First against the wall, eh."

"Good memory. You still want to kill them?"

He laughs. "These days, I'm like… let them be. Don't care for them, but… you know."

"You're mellowing in your middle age."

"Life's too short. What's the Bagehot quote?"

"What?"

"Bagehot."

"You've got much more intellectual since that train journey, Ferg."

He rearranges his hands on the steering wheel. In the past he would never have conceded any sort of knowledge whatsoever, for fear of appearing pretentious; but the Scots have softened in my time away, and these days seem almost quietly proud of talking about their feelings and things they know. For emigrants like me it is still disconcerting.

"Walter Bagehot," he says. "He was a sort of autodidact in the nineteenth century. A journalist and businessman. Anyway, he said, let me get it right… 'the monarchy's mystery is its life. We must not let in daylight upon magic.'"

I repeat back to him. "We must not let in daylight upon magic."

He nods and says nothing more.

After a couple of minutes, he gets the chat rolling again with a rant about his boss, and soon we're shooting the breeze like days of old – work stories, football, music. Fife passes by in a blur of brown fields and black dripping trees; we drive through the familiar chain of old mining villages, some which have gentrified, some which have not. When we are ten minutes away Fergus goes quiet for a moment, then comes out with his big statement.

"Maybe you should think about coming home for a while, Miro. Everyone misses you and I think my mum would be glad to have you around for a bit. Especially now."

I don't know how to answer. I am already wondering how to plan ahead if I disappear and my family are left with two absences rather than one.

There are three cars parked out the front of Gull View. Fergus eases into a corner hard up against a fir tree; when I get out a branch springs back and I am whipped with heavy raindrops. The front door is open wide and voices spill out into the winter air.

My arrival is greeted with gentle mumbles, and Sarah hugs me close. Fergus fixes me a cup of tea. All the family is here, except for my nephew and nieces, who are camped out with friends and safely hidden away from the grief. Darkness falls and Sarah insists on opening some wine. An order is placed for Indian takeaway.

Dinner is a solemn affair. Sarah starts crying halfway through and Kirsty takes her upstairs, and it doesn't feel right to go on eating. Fergus is still shovelling up curry with a wedge of naan bread until he feels everyone looking at him and stops. The gathering breaks up – I help organise the dirty plates then sneak out into the back garden.

I dial Neve's number.

She picks up on the second ring. "Hello?"

"Neve, it's me. Miro."

A pause that reflects the passage of time – nineteen years. "Miro. I can't believe what's happening."

"My uncle died, Neve. I think maybe it was them."

"Oh God. I have a twelve-year-old daughter. I mean, what…" She tails off.

"I'm up in Fife for the funeral. Can I see you on Friday?" The eleventh of January, the day before our appointment with Gow and the Chamberites.

She gives me her address, and detailed instructions on how to get there. A farmhouse in the Pentlands, twenty minutes south of Edinburgh, a driveway that's easy to miss.

"I got another letter from them," she says. "A reminder."

"As if we'd forget."

"I'll see you on Friday. Come around lunchtime."

We hang up. I linger in the garden for a couple of minutes, breathing the cold air, listening to the clink of activity in the kitchen, human shapes moving behind the frosted glass. A nervousness has got into me, a fidgety anxiety, and perhaps what's most troubling is that it's not because of Gow and his friends. It's because I'll see Neve again.

Back indoors, the cousins are huddled at the kitchen table, finalising the order of service for the funeral. Sarah is through the back talking to a neighbour who's come over to offer condolences. And all I can think of is that awkward night all those years ago when I fumbled with Neve in the blank darkness of my bedroom, every kiss and touch seeming to fall short, knees and elbows in the way of every movement.

The next day passes in a blur of rain and sighs. By the time the gloaming settles on the town, darkness eking into the spaces between the granite houses, Sarah tells me to take Fergus for a pint. We throw our jackets on and head out into the windy darkness. The Lost Creel is still there, a constant in the village despite the passing of the years, its lights beckoning us down to the harbour. We enter into warmth and noise – fishermen, office workers, farmers, artists, and schoolkids just the wrong side of eighteen. At the bar we get caught up in condolences – *he was a great guy, will be much missed, gone too soon, village is a poorer place without him* – and before we know it we each have two pints in front of us, offerings to the gods. Fergus motions to the corner spot by the window and we make our way over, our barstools tucked in against a window shelf, obscured by a pillar and afforded some privacy.

At first we talk about the business at hand, the funeral on Sunday and the communal sadness, but then as the beer kicks in we drift to other subjects, dragged back to the past by the undercurrent of grief. At one point Fergus nudges me with his elbow. "What I said the other day, about you moving back for a bit – would you think about it?"

I gaze out through the condensation-misted window to where the black shape of the sea is just about visible. "Let's see. I need to sort a few things out first."

We stay at the window seats till closing time, seven pints worse for wear, just like old days. When we get back to the house everyone is still up, huddled in the kitchen with cups of homemade soup. I take a moment to check my email on my phone and there it is – a reply to my message on the Devil's Chamber WordPress site.

Dear Miro

I've been waiting for you to mail me for years. We need to talk.

Your old colleague,
Bob

I check my watch – it's after midnight but I have the feeling that Bob will be waiting for my call. I excuse myself and go out to the conservatory. I dial the number and it's answered straight away.

"Miro?" he says.

"Been a while, eh?"

"That it has."

"Are you still in Edinburgh?"

"Where else?"

"At Overspill?"

He laughs. "They closed Overspill nine years ago. I got moved to the main offices. One year left till I retire, so they leave me to my own devices mainly."

I'm a little shocked that Bob is only sixty-four. Back in my Overspill days he seemed to be at least mid-fifties, but I suppose that was just the booze and the pies.

"So what do you want to talk about?"

"What do you think?"

It was a stupid question. "Shall we meet tomorrow?"

"Yes, come to my place. I've got something to show you." Bob gives me his address, which sounds like the same tenement flat in Gorgie he lived in back in the 90s.

The next morning Fergus drives me over to Leuchars. We're both hungover, and Fergus buzzes the windows down to let in fresh air.

"So what's the big secret?" he says.

"Remember I said I have a few things to sort out. This is one. I'll be back in the evening." He leaves me at a rainy Leuchars and I jump on the train to Edinburgh.

I get off at Haymarket and when my feet touch the platform dread slithers in my guts. This is my first time proper in the city for nearly twenty years. The airport doesn't count and passing through on the train doesn't count. Now my feet are touching the city's stone, my feet are walking over whatever lies underneath the pavements.

I hang a right up Gorgie. The city still smells of malty beer, the breweries still going strong. Gorgie Road appears a bit more upmarket than in days of old, a couple of fancy-looking cafes mixed in with the same old hardcore boozers. I count the streets on the left until I reach the third and find Bob's door.

He's waiting for me on the second-floor landing – thinner than in the past, grey hair snipped short. "Fucking hell," he says. "Time's not been kind to you."

I shake his hand. "You look well."

He waves me in to his flat. "I finally cleaned up my act, more or less. The occasional lapse from time to time, but mostly I'm away from the pub. Found myself a lovely widow."

He points to a picture on his desk of him and a grinning woman standing next to a mountain-top cairn. His flat is clean and minimalist, except for the heaving bookshelves that cover each wall. He makes tea, and we sit facing each other, waiting for the big talk to start.

"So you're a blogger these days, Bob?"

He gives me a sarcastic pout. "It was bait. Mainly for you. I didn't expect to find so many others though."

"Others?"

He raises his eyebrows. "It's a long story. You go first."

So I tell him everything. Remind him of the day he fell and broke his leg, and how he told me about boxfile 467, and the meeting with Neve, and the trips to the Guildford. The missing Malky Gallacher. My encounter with Auld Harry Robertson, and his story about the boxfiles. Danny. As I talk he writes into a hardbacked notebook. When I finish he sits back and stares at the ceiling, all the light in his eyes gone.

"I never wanted to be right about this. But I am."

"Your turn," I tell him.

He sighs. "We'll need more tea. And biscuits."

And so Bob tells me his story.

A few months passed after my departure. Overspill remained the same, but the council had chosen not to replace me – cutbacks – and now Bob was on his own in the basement. The walk-ins had dwindled to a couple per week, so it was always a shock when the buzzer rang.

So this one day Bob goes up the stairs and opens the door and here is this tall, gaunt man, dressed like an undertaker or a particularly stern lawyer. He introduces himself as Mr Gow and asks if he can come in to discuss a sensitive matter. Bob makes him some tea and they sit in the kitchenette. Gow explains that he is looking for some documents that belong to him and his associates and they are currently trying to track these down in the city archives. Bob asks him what the documents are about. Gow gets all serious and says he'd prefer not to discuss the contents. Bob says if he doesn't know the subject he can't search the computer. Gow stands up and goes into the corridor, Bob close behind. Are you on your own here? Asks Gow. Yep, says Bob. Apart from Scary Mary. Gow appears deep in thought and then leaves without saying a word.

Bob spends the rest of the day digging around in the Jungle at the back of Overspill. He rediscovers boxfile 467 and reads through it page by page. None of it makes much sense. Most days he digs it out and re-reads the contents, looking for clues. He gets obsessed and starts to scour the shelves looking for more material. He finds the other boxfiles that Auld Harry had hidden deep at the back of Overspill, some behind a false wall and others disguised under piles of endless shite. Mary is suspicious but pleased. Hard work cures most ills, she tells him in her soft Highland accent.

After several months of tidying and reorganising Overspill, Bob overcomes his allergy to computers and learns how to use the new database. Much like me, he keys in The Devil's Chamber and gets one hit – *Edinburgh's Infamous Legends*. He makes the same journey as I did up to the George IV Bridge library and reads the chapter, another piece of the jigsaw slotting into place.

At around this time he starts to notice something when he's reading his morning paper – the number of young homeless men who go missing, two big issue sellers in the space of two months. He starts to take note of them – names, the dates they go missing, their background – and a pattern emerges. They are all lost souls, most estranged from their families, with no fixed abode. They go missing on the eleventh or twelfth day of every month.

He writes up his notes and one chilly spring day walks over to the police station at the top of Leith Walk. He explains his theory to a gruff detective who looks into his coffee as Bob talks. The detective is silent and asks Bob his full name. Bob gives a false one. The detective writes it down and says that the pattern is interesting but maybe just coincidental. He asks Bob for an address and phone number and again Bob gives a false one.

He is five minutes out of the station, walking back into the city, when he gets the sense he is being followed. A bus with shaded windows slides up at the traffic lights and Bob looks in the reflection – behind him, the bulk of a huge man, six-foot-six with a barrel-like torso.

"Based on your story I'm guessing this was your friend the giant," says Bob.

So Bob crosses the road and sees in the reflective shop front of John Lewis that the giant is about four or five strides behind him. He ducks into the department store and moves quickly, squeezing past shoppers and onto the stairs, up one level and doubling back, taking his jacket off and folding it under his arm, walking around the perimeter of the store, all the time keeping an eye out for the giant. He slips out into the St James's Centre, finally relaxing, and takes the side exit towards St Andrew's Square. He's a couple of steps out the door into the empty street when an arm hooks around his neck and drags him towards a pile of wheelie bins. He is choking and kicking, gradually slipping deeper into the embrace of the giant when he remembers his Swiss army knife. He flips open the blade and stabs it deep into the nearest flesh.

The giant roars out. Bob has stabbed him in the leg, and the giant presses on the wound with both hands. A couple of shoppers come out and glance over at Bob standing in the shadows – the giant is obscured by the row of bins but muttering noisily. Bob strides off towards Princes Street and the safety of crowds.

"After that I took fright. Every day at Overspill I was waiting for the knock at the door. Every night walking home I expected that arm hooking around my neck again. I cut my hair short, grew a beard, got different glasses, changed my look. I had one of my lapses and started drinking at home a lot. Then after a few months it felt like maybe I'd got away with it."

And so a few years passed. Overspill closed, and they packed everything up to be relocated to a warehouse on the outskirts of the city. "I took the boxfiles home. Stuck them in a cupboard. And it all started calling to me again. I searched for you online and figured that you'd changed your name or were dead. Then I had the idea for the webpage, worked out how to set it all up, and uploaded all the content about the Chamber. I heard nothing for the first couple of months but then every few weeks or so I'd get an email. Some were just nothing, you know, people saying they liked the page, or it was a lot of bullshit, that sort of thing. But then some messages came through that seemed to be more. I was wary. One email was from a guy who said he was a collector of materials on old folktales and was willing to pay for any content I have. I ignored it. Then another email came in from a guy calling himself David McMurdo, and he said he'd been to the Chamber and wanted to meet up and tell me his story. We set a time and date and a pub as meeting place, and I'm a couple of minutes away from arriving, and who do I see lingering nearby but our friend the giant. I turned around sharp and went home. Lay awake all night.

"Then I got a series of emails from The Tunneller. This guy said he was an urban explorer and part of a group who were looking for the Chamber. They'd heard people had been there and made it out again. They wanted to know where the entrance was. I wrote back and asked him where else they'd been. He sent me email after email detailing their adventures. I started to trust the guy. It was hard to imagine Gow and his crowd having the imagination to come up with this. The Tunneller's friends started emailing me too. Then others. A guy who said his brother had disappeared from the streets many years ago, and he'd heard a rumour from the homeless community that he'd been stolen away underground. A copper who'd heard rumours about the Chamber. A journalist, looking for a story. In total there are nine of them, and I asked them individually if they'd be ready to go at short notice if I find the entrance. They tell me they're ready."

A ragtag army of nine, plus the three of us. Twelve versus fourteen. It's not a bad ratio. The skies are darkening outside. I remember that it's Donnie's funeral tomorrow, know that I shouldn't be back too late.

"So you meet Gow on Sunday night?" says Bob.

I nod. "The twelfth."

"There is only one solution – look for their weaknesses. I think I might have an idea."

"Me too. Might need more tea though."

We sit for another hour and sketch out the plan. Back on the train, my forehead resting against the glass as dark fields swish by, for the first time I think I might have a way out of this. I repeat that line from Fergus in my head like a mantra: *We must not let in daylight upon magic.*

CHAPTER 33

The funeral cars arrive at eleven. It's a short drive to the kirk, which is perched at the edge of the town looking out onto the sea. Donnie was anti-religion but he walked the dog past the kirkyard every day and was on polite talking terms with the minister, so it only felt natural to the family that we should say goodbye here.

When I get out the car I see her immediately. Hannah, standing at the heart of the crowd milling into the kirk's entrance, dressed in a slim black dress with a black cashmere coat, light brown hair longer than she used to wear it. She looks stunning – forty-two but could pass for thirty. I can't focus on anything else and almost walk into the funeral director who's adjusting his gloves and looking up at the sky. When I look back she's gone inside already.

I try to compose myself. As I walk down the aisle to the front rows I glance from side to side looking for her. Instinct tells me to crane my neck and look to the far left as I get closer to the front and my eyes lock with hers. She stares back with the same intensity. I find my seat and fold my hands in front of me and gaze at the faded wood of the pew. The last mourners are taking their seats, the clatter dying down, until a heavy silence hangs in the air. Next to me, Fergus is sobbing with his head in his hands, leaning in to his wife.

The service is quick. Donnie's life story, a Hugh MacDiarmid poem, and a rendition of his favourite song, *Sunshine on Leith*. Fergus gets up to the pulpit and talks about his father's impact on the local community, his stern kindness, his bad jokes and his fondness for the dog. When he finishes there is a sense of finality. The family get up and file out – despite the sense of overwhelming loss I can't resist a sideways glance and again Hannah is staring in my direction.

Outside in the kirkyard the coffin is waiting for us on its trestle. I am one of the six cordholders; together we take the ropes and lift the coffin over towards the open grave. The funeral director orchestrates our movements, and slowly we lower Donnie into the ground. The minister throws a handful of earth skittering onto the coffin; says his words as a flurry of crows bursts up from the car park; and leaves two hundred of us listening to the sea breeze whipping in over the kirkyard walls. My face is wet with tears.

As the black-clad crowd turns away, I feel a tingle of anticipation, a certainty about what's going to happen next. As I walk back towards the funeral cars I can feel her walking by my side, moving into step with me. I glance sideways, already knowing I will meet her eyes.

She gives me a sad smile. "I'm sorry, Miro. He was a good man."

"The best. You look well. You've not changed."

She shakes her head. "It's been a rough few months. Divorce. Where are you now? Still in Singapore?"

"Yeah, been there two years."

"You don't have much of a tan." That laugh, a laugh I've not heard since a December afternoon nineteen years ago when we got naked and she dug her nails into my heart. And I saw the Mad MacAskill story in the paper and did a runner from her kitchen.

"Will you come to the house for a drink?"

"Sure." She squeezes my arm and slips away, graceful on her heels, careful steps over the gravel.

Back at the house I accept a beer from the caterer and then stand by the stairs with a good view of the front door, welcoming the mourners to the wake with a handshake and sometimes a hug. When she comes in, cheeks flushed from the cold, I take her arm and lead her through to the conservatory, grabbing a wine for her on the way. We sit on the sofa, the dog at our feet, and talk in relative privacy as the noise level slowly cranks up next door.

She tells me her story. Her twenties largely spent in London, working at a marketing agency. Returning to Scotland and meeting her husband at a Thai boxing club. Marriage, a baby girl, life in the suburbs, a year lost to depression, the slow slide of a marriage breaking apart, her daughter's remarkable musical talent, the divorce and an uneasy peace, and the last twelve months finding a new place in life. Ready to move on. Ready for something new.

I tell her my story in return. I start by apologising for leaving that day nineteen years ago; explain that I was going through something that's still very difficult to talk about. I tell her about London, Amsterdam, New York, Melbourne, Singapore. The things I've seen, the people

I've met. I tell her about Dana. I tell her about finding a place in life that is a sort of uneasy balance – a contentedness missing meaning, a something balanced out by a nothing.

The respectful hush of the first hour has fallen away into a clamour of grieving celebration – Donnie would not have wanted glum faces, that will be the story next door, and now it's loud voices and the occasional laugh, the clink of glasses and the grind of chairs against the wooden floor.

We kiss.

CHAPTER 34

I wake on the same sofa where I kissed Hannah. The conservatory windows are smeared in frost, my breath plumes out in the pale dark. I put my hoodie on and snuggle deeper into the sleeping bag, wishing Hannah was with me still. My slight hangover is offset by the thrill of the kiss and mixed in with guilt that Donnie's funeral deserved my full attention. But I think he would have understood.

Late morning, I leave with Fergus and his wife Aisling. I give Sarah a big hug before I depart, wondering if it will be the last. Fergus drives me down to Edinburgh and out of the city limits to the fringe of the Pentland hills. I give them directions – left at the bus stop, up the farm track, the house with the red roof. As I get out the car I see Neve emerge from the front door. Fergus gives me a sneaky smile.

Hannah yesterday, and now Neve. All of my ghosts.

The car pulls away behind me and I walk towards Neve. She looks beyond me, then to either side, as if expecting someone else. From a distance her hair still looks red, but as I approach, in a brief flush of sunlight, I see it has faded into a honey colour.

"Come in," she says.

I follow her through into a compact bungalow. She still has that grace of movement, a natural confidence that intimidated me two decades ago and intimidates me still. She digs around under a chair and comes up with a bundle that she shakes out on the kitchen table. Green canvas. Danny's Dutch army shirt.

"Here are their letters." She hands me two sheets of paper.

I try to read them but my eyes can't focus. I place the letters on the table and touch the sleeve of the jacket. It feels slightly waxy, and an ancient water stain blots the shoulder.

We sit in silence for a while. I start to notice the details of her new life. The photos of her daughter everywhere, a brown-haired girl climbing, dancing, smiling, doing handstands, playing badminton. The kitchen sparsely furnished but done well – a modest income partially hidden by good taste.

"I haven't slept for a week," she says.

"You need to get your energy up. I have a plan."

She looks at me with that familiar mix of disdain and amusement. "Really?"

I wave my hand at the table. "Who writes letters anymore?"

"Huh?"

"They're traditionalists, Neve. They do everything the same way they've always done it. That's their weakness."

She continues to look at me, and I feel my heart beat faster. But my heart is beating for a different reason than all those years ago – I'm thrilled because the spell is broken. She no longer holds any power over me. It's Hannah. I will get through this and go back to Hannah.

I tell Neve Bob's story and walk her through the plan step by step. The skies turn monochrome and edge towards dusk. Her expression changes and I see my own renewed confidence reflected in her eyes. This could work.

Neve's daughter Kerry returns from school, and I wind up playing Scrabble with her. She has her mum's smile. I suggest to Neve that I should take a taxi into Edinburgh and grab a hotel but she insists I take the spare room. She cooks pasta and we sit around the same table where Danny's jacket was laid out like Exhibit A. It's dark outside and the wind rattles the windows. Neve fiddles with her bangle, pressing each chainlink between finger and thumb. I ask if she has any wine and we open a bottle. Kerry goes to bed, and we swap notes on each other's lives. At moments I forget the circumstances and find myself enjoying her stories of backpacking in Australia, temping in Glasgow, teaching in Dubai. It is no surprise that she has also spent her adult life running away. To our surprise we discover that we were in New York at the same time. Something in her expression changes, and her enthusiastic monologue loses altitude and plummets into silence. I realise why. Her claret dream about New York.

"Did it mean anything? The New York dream?"

She nods. "The dream came back to from me time to time, years after it all happened. I'd been teaching in Dubai and had saved a fair bit of cash and was at a loose end. One night the dream came back stronger than ever – empty New York, the square with the grand old arch, the glimpse of a man with black hair sitting on a bench.

I had to give the school an answer about renewing my contract the next day and I just decided on the spot to jack it all in and go to New York. I rented a studio apartment in Queen's and spent the first few days exploring the city. Eventually I found the square."

She tops up her glass. "So I'm walking through Manhattan on this autumn day, turn a corner and there it is – the arch, and the park. Washington Square Park, it's called. There are red and brown leaves all scattered around, and a fountain in the middle that I didn't remember from the dream. It's busy, lots going on, hot dog vendors and kids running around, when I see a man with black hair sitting on a bench. I walked towards him, like I had no choice in the matter, just went right up and sat down on the bench next to him. He glanced at me and physically recoiled in shock, like he literally jumped an inch off the bench. *You're the redhead*, he said, *the redhead in my dream*. Turned out he'd had the same dream as me for years."

I remembered all those years ago in The Lost Creel, Hannah telling me she'd dreamt of seeing me in a sprawling underground library. Other Overspill. Another shared dream.

"We talked for three hours until it started to get cold. Then we went for Vietnamese food and kept talking till the restaurant closed. His name was Jackson Tilburg. Three years younger than me, a fellow teacher off work on burnout, looking for new direction. He came from old money on his mother's side so luckily for him there was no wolf at the door. For the next two weeks we met every day and he showed me around the city. It had such inevitability about it, like we were caught up in something that was irresistible, a current behind us that was forcing us forwards. We drove up north for a weekend away and when we came back I moved in with him. Got married two months after that. Eight months together, then one day it was just blank between us, like the electricity had gone. My dad was sick so that was an excuse to fly back to Northern Ireland. A couple of weeks later I realised I was pregnant. My dad got better and I decided I would keep the baby. Kerry. But I didn't tell Jackson."

She sees the look of surprise on my face.

"I know what you're thinking – that sounds like Neve, forever selfish, never doing the right thing." Her eyes are hard. Bottomless green. "But it was again like this feeling of a flow, of things just moving in a direction they were meant to go in. And Kerry – you know, she's absolutely the best thing that ever happened to me. She brought my parents back together, healed things in the wider family. I have this absolute feeling of purpose because of her."

"So why did you move back to Edinburgh?"

"What's that saying? Keep your friends close and your enemies closer? I applied for a job here and when I came back it felt right. Like I was more anxious away from the place."

"And Jackson?"

Neve pauses for a moment. "He got back in touch with me again recently. Widower, got a son. Wants to talk." She blows out a sigh.

"Sorry, I didn't mean to probe. Or judge."

She shrugs. "I just wanted to answer your original question and got waylaid. What about your dreams?"

"I only took the claret twice."

"You never told us much about your experiences."

I nod. "The first dream… I told you something about it at the time. A warehouse archive, sort of like Overspill but huge, stretching out into the distance until the shelves faded from view. I saw my ex-girlfriend there, and she told me not to go any further. But I kept going. Saw my dad."

"What did it mean?"

"I think the archive was a store of everything about me. And I wasn't meant to explore it. It was better to just let it be."

"And the other dream?"

"Sometimes I still dream the first part. I'm in my grandfather's skin, in a plane high above Arnhem, about to parachute out into the blackness. I'm in that moment, trapped in it, and there is no escape. And then I'm falling down to this landscape of burning tanks and wrecked bridges. When I hit the ground I was suddenly in the backroom of a pub, with Sutherland, Gow and MacAllister."

Her eyes are locked on mine. I never told her about this.

"MacAllister had just been down in the Chamber for the first time and was having doubts. The other two talked him out of it. Basically threatened him. They talked about how their money can buy anything, how the stain of their deeds never taints them because they pay a man who pays a man who pays a man."

Neve clasps her hands. "So there was no metaphor that time. Just a window into reality."

"I guided it. Spent the day memorising their names and addresses and visualised the list when I drank the claret. It's like what Danny said – there are three gears: past, present and future. But you can never be in charge of where it takes you. Ultimately it owns you."

Neve drains her glass. "Here's what I think – the claret connects you in to different paths you can take. It's not magic. There's a capability we all have deep in our subconscious that can see into multiple realities. We don't know how to tap into it. Some people are better at it than others, some people call it spirituality or religion and get glimpses that way. The claret is just a stimulant that opens the channels and shows you what's possible. It's foggy, and you have to work to reveal the possible truth, but with patience and practice you can unlock those realities.

"For me, the claret guided me towards my destiny. That was the purpose of the New York dream. To create Kerry. It's an amazing thing to have experienced, and it's a power for good. That was the original use of the stuff, those monks in some remote temple sipping it to go on missions into possible futures and shaping the world in the image of benevolent gods. But those fuckers" – she stabs a finger at the letters from Sutherland Gow – "those fuckers twisted it towards something else, locked it away underground and use it to make shitloads of money."

The Chardonnay bottle is empty. Neve shows me to the cubby-hole of a spare room with a single bed tight against the wall. There is a moment when she looks at me with curiosity in her eyes – a pause waiting to be filled with suggestions – and I tell her thank you. Good night. She tells me good night too and smiles. I hear her door close and slide into the damp-smelling sheets. As I lie in the dark I feel the pieces of the plan assembling, clicking into place one by one.

CHAPTER 35

We walk into the familiar noise and warmth of the Guildford Arms.

The pub hasn't changed much, and still retains its beaten charm. I spot the giant's bulk at a table through the back, meet eyes with Neve, and she nods. We walk across the pub towards them.

Gow stands to meet us. "At long last," he says. "We've waited so long for this moment."

There are five of them huddled round the table.

It is an odd feeling to get a close look at Gow after all these years. He has retained something of his Goth Elvis look, although his hair has receded into a narrow grey landing strip on his greasy scalp. He is dressed in what he probably thinks of as smart casual – black suit trousers, a grey blazer with elbow patches, a greying white shirt. His eyes are watery and determined. A man with things to do.

The giant looks ridiculous, sitting on a tiny stool, dressed in discount jeans and a battered old ski jacket; he gazes vacantly at me with a moronic sneer, his dark curls faded to granite grey. Next to him is a small man who looks like MacAllister, the new boy with doubts all those years ago; he crouches over a half pint of ale, face screwed up in disgust. Sutherland is there too, the youngest of the bunch, his rower's build bulked out with middle-age chub. The two others have the air of disappointed accountants, dressed in out of date suits and practising their best hardman stares.

There is an otherworldly moment as we look for chairs, as if we're a bunch of colleagues getting together for an afterwork drink. Gow even lifts a stool over for me. Everyone rearranges themselves around the table.

Gow raises his pint.

"To absent friends."

I grip the edge of the table.

"Do you know how we finally found you?" Gow is staring at me. "It's quite a story. Naturally we were very worried to encounter your friend Danny in the Chamber that day. We tried to get the truth out of him –" at this moment he smiles at us – "but that was a dead end, pardon the pun. In its concentrated form the claret forces out the facts, and Danny did babble a little after a glass and a few fists. *I'm here with the other two*, he said. *Urban explorers*, he said. But he wouldn't tell us who you were or how you got in. Died halfway through mumbling something."

Gow sips his beer, enjoying himself. "It took us a while to identify the breach. We were looking for secret doors in the corridors out back. It was only when we forced MacAllister here to climb along all the edges that we found the ventilation shaft."

MacAllister gives me his tough guy look and I stare him down. His eye contact wavers and he goes back to looking at his beer.

"So we figured out the tunnel went to the Guildford," says Gow. "And worked out that it had to be a member of staff to get such easy access to the cellar. Our detective had a boozy chat with the bar manager Raymond, who was somewhat bereft about the sudden disappearance of his favourite barmaid Fiona. But with the lady giving a false name, and a cash in hand arrangement meaning no paper trail, we hit a wall quickly. It only took us nineteen years to strike gold, but we got there."

I can feel Neve bristling beside me, her old prickliness rising up.

"So put us out our misery, Mr Gow."

"I struck up a friendship with Raymond. This was around 2001. He was easy to get to know, mouth running away with him all the time. It seems he had quite a thing for you, Neve. It was a running joke over the years, usually the first thing I said to him by way of introduction – *Have you seen the disappearing barmaid? The one that ran away with your heart?* It always cracked him up. I must have come in here every couple of weeks this century. The fucking geek was still in love with you after all this time. Then last month I come in and there he was, drunk at the bar. And he'd found you! A picture of you in the Evening Times, the proud mother of Kerry, winner of the Edinburgh District Girls' Badminton Tournament. Raymond's getting all juiced up at the bar, saying you'd never lost your looks, and what did I think, should he contact you? Ask to catch up?"

Sutherland cuts in. "Turned out Raymond didn't have many friends or family. Turned out he wouldn't be missed much. So he paid a trip to the Chamber just before Christmas."

Neve's confidence has gone. She stares at the table.

Sutherland laughs. "Raymond didn't take too well to the claret. Couldn't hold his drink. But he gave us a good lead, I think."

"And me?" I fix my gaze on Sutherland.

"Once Raymond gave us Neve Pinkerton, we got our detective on the case again. Back in 2000, he'd broken into Danny's flat and stole his address book. Messy thing, lots of scribbled first names and no surnames. But written under NEVE was MIRO. Unusual name, Miro. I have a good memory and made the connection. We exchanged pleasantries at Overspill in late 1999. We couldn't locate Miro Kubik, but it's quite easy to find out if someone changed their name. And *voila* – Neve Pinkerton and Miro McGarrity, our two mystery urban explorers."

"I believe you know what happens next," says Gow.

MacAllister leans in to the centre of the table. "Come quietly, or we go after your loved ones."

Gow looks irritated by the interruption. "We know everything about you. Neve, your wonderful daughter Kerry, and your extended family in Coleraine. It's remarkable that they all live so close to one another in this day and age." He stops to give us another of his limp smiles. "And Miro, we know all about your family too. Your aunt Sarah and uncle Donnie, your cousins Fergus and Kirsty."

Uncle. That word pierces me in the gut. I realise they don't know Donnie's dead. They are not all-seeing. They weren't involved. They are what they look like – a bunch of middle-aged, unimpressive men, with only one superpower.

I stare back at Gow. "So if we do what you say, will you leave our families alone? Do we have your word?"

He nods, satisfied.

The others finish their drinks, stand up, put on jackets and scarves, quickly check mobile phones, tuck chairs under the table. We leave as one group, Gow in the lead, the giant at the back, and walk along the alleyway to the right, take another right, and after a few metres stop at a battered door. Gow produces keys, and through we step into a long corridor, which ends at a beautiful oak door, carved and varnished. There is a feeling of passing through layers towards the heart of something hidden.

We step through onto the premises of Sutherland Gow. A light flickers to life, illuminating the lobby. It looks like a lawyer's office. There is a grand mahogany reception desk, and a regal blue sofa and Swiss cheese plant. Two corridors lead off on either side and from where I stand I can see individual offices, one bearing the name plaque for *Gordon MacAllister, Partner, Sutherland Gow*.

The giant frisks us, looking for wallets and mobile phones – but they are safely deposited in lockers at Waverley Station. He looks disappointed. It must be one of his perks.

Gow speaks. "I suppose we should get on with it. Do you want to use the bathroom before going to your room?"

Neve goes first, accompanied by the giant, then it's my turn. In the cramped toilet I pee while the giant shuffles around outside the door. When I emerge he grabs my arm and pushes me back towards the main lobby.

Gow leads us behind the reception desk into a back room with a flight of stairs. We clunk down in single file and go into the same boardroom that Neve and I explored on New Year's Eve 1999. It looks unchanged. I am conscious of the door on the far side of the room and the cell that awaits us. A flutter of my ancient claustrophobia, and it recedes.

The giant pushes me again, and again, propelling me towards the far wall. He grabs Neve's arm as he goes and within seconds he's bundling us in to the cell. A voice calls out behind us: "Sleep tight!"

In the half-light we fumble for our bearings. There is a bucket in the corner but otherwise the room is empty and bare. A whiff of sewage and sick overpowers the faint disinfectant smell. The stink of puke gives me a flashback to how it all began, throwing up on my desk in Singapore. I arrange myself in one corner, Neve opposite me, as far from the bucket as we can get.

"Tradition," she says. "That's a good sign."

I allow myself a laugh. "Yeah. The plan is on track."

CHAPTER 36

We hear them leaving, and the light goes out in the boardroom, plunging us from half-light into darkness. Neve is wearing a wristwatch and the luminous hands are all that I can see. “What time is it?”

“Just after ten.”

I take off my jacket and fold it into a pillow. “Probably ridiculous to think I’ll get any sleep tonight.”

“I hope Kerry is okay at her sleepover.” There is a tremor in Neve’s voice, and I’m secretly glad I don’t have any children. What are our chances tomorrow? Thirty-seventy?

“Maybe we should talk,” she suggests. “Get things out in the open. A confessional of sorts, just in case.”

“What do you mean?”

“The things you’re sorry for. The things you wish you’d done differently.”

I sigh. The darkness encourages honesty. “I regret not spending enough time with my mum when she was dying. I wish I hadn’t spent so much of my life before the Chamber worrying about stuff. It wasn’t worth it. I regret the way I left things with Hannah back in the nineties. If I could change things I wouldn’t have gone to see my father in Leith that night, I didn’t need to know my past. I wish I hadn’t drunk so much in my twenties, it caused so much bad feeling in me and others.”

Silence.

I consider telling her about the red shoelace, how I ripped it off the railing. But no good can come of that. In the dark I say a silent apology to Danny.

I take a breath and continue. "There was a girl I dated in London, a really great girl, and I hurt her badly. I'm sorry about that. I wish I'd seen more of my grandparents before they died. In New York… Dana. I don't regret the way things turned out, she's happy, but I regret the way I left. We can all choose the way we do things. I shouted at someone in the street in Melbourne, this lady bumped into me and I yelled at her and she burst into tears, I should have said sorry on the spot instead of walking off and then looking for her every time I came down the same road for the next six months. I fired someone in Singapore who didn't deserve it. I see all of these people in my dreams. How about you?"

Neve's voice is hoarse. "There are so many things. I don't know where to begin. There was this girl in my class in Coleraine, overweight and shy, and I was brutal to her, just brutal. My first boyfriend, I split up with him without even telling him, just made sure he saw me with someone new. My general behaviour aged eighteen to twenty-five was appalling. I include the way I treated you and Danny. An arrogant little bitch. I regret losing friends through pride. I regret not learning French, never going to Japan, not learning the piano. Part of me regrets not telling Jackson about his daughter."

I notice for the first time how her Ulster accent has been overtaken by east coast Scottish.

She pipes up. "What are you glad for, though? You should also say the things you're grateful about."

"Having a great family. Seeing the world. Making it to age forty-two and experiencing love more than once. The kiss with Hannah two days ago. You?"

"Kerry. Making friends with my sister about thirty years too late. The dogs I had, absolute stars every one. Love. A good glass of red wine."

We stop talking. Alone with our words. Sometimes the darkness is a blessing.

CHAPTER 37

It is the longest night of my life. In the absolute blackness I lie on the stone floor, conscious of every movement from Neve, knowing that she is just as awake as I am; but neither of us wants to talk, or risk any more emotional instability. If the plan is going to work, we need to be focused.

At some point I fall asleep, a shallow unconsciousness where I dream of lying on a stone floor in a basement dungeon, concrete pressing against my bones, and all the time I'm aware that it's not a dream. I am woken by Neve pacing around our cell, stretching up and then leaning down to touch her toes. "Morning trooper," she says.

I sit up, bleary headed. "What time is it?"

"Around eight. They won't be here for a few hours yet."

I need to pee, but the bucket is not an option. I won't let them take my dignity away. Neve gets me to stand up and we do exercises together. After fifteen minutes my head is clear. A grey light leaks in through the porthole window and I peer out onto the boardroom and its sombre formality.

We finally hear footsteps above at noon. Voices. We are ready.

The door swings open and the giant steps in, wielding a pickaxe handle. The cell is too small for me to get out of the way – he stabs it forward, catching me square in the chest. I crumple backwards, head hitting off the wall. As I scramble back to my feet, I am aware of him swinging the stave down on Neve. He backs off, and I am standing there, hunched over, still winded, and Neve is on the floor cradling her upper arm.

"Toilet," says the giant. Just like last night, Neve goes first. The giant locks me back in the cell. When it's my turn, the door opens again and I step out into a busy boardroom. The same faces as last night. I have to suppress my smile. There are no longer thirteen of them. Time and demographics have defeated one aspect of their tradition.

Up close, the giant smells unwashed – sweat, beer, fried food, and something rotten. He jabs me in the back with his stick as we walk to the cubby hole toilet. I take my time – pee, wash my face, drink some water. I unbutton my shirt and see that there is already a blackening bruise next to my heart. I remember how the giant held down Harry Robertson in the chair, and how he carried him away like an old carpet.

The reckoning is coming.

Back in the boardroom they are all dressed for what comes next, each wearing a robe and sheep-skull hat. They are all standing, as if waiting to go to a formal event. Which in a way, they are. The giant pulls back the trapdoor, and the underground smell reaches up to us. They shuffle around me and Neve, walling us in, and hustle us down the steps.

The Devil's Chamber is prepared. Just as we saw it yesterday. Not thirteen chairs lined up, but only eight.

The death throne waiting for us – probably me first. I exchange a glance with Neve. She looks ready; no fear.

The giant grabs me and forces me onto the throne. He lashes my wrists to the armrests one at a time. Gow is standing in front of me, head tilted back a little, as if in some ecstatic reverie. I hear him mutter to nobody: "Bring the claret."

Sutherland peels away towards the corridor with the huge cabinet. I close my eyes and wait for the reaction.

A cry of shock. Another yell, this time summoning the others. The Chamberites follow the noise, and after a few seconds even Gow moves away, leaving just Neve and the giant standing in front of me.

A shout of utter rage, which I think comes from Gow.

I smile.

Yesterday afternoon, before the winter light was squeezed from the sky, I walked along Waterloo Place towards Old Calton Burial Ground. Neve was twenty paces in front, looking a little out of place in the city in her climbing gear. At the gates of the cemetery, our welcoming committee awaited us.

Bob and his eight disciples. They were carrying maps and brass rubbing kits as cover, and half of them certainly looked nerdish enough to pass the test with their rucksacks and cagoules. Bob introduced us.

Four urban explorers, who had heard whispers of the Chamber much like Neve and Danny had all those years ago and had followed the loose ends to Bob's blog. Their names passed over my head and were carried away on the breeze.

Next: a grimly determined-looking freelance journalist and blogger called Barry.

Sandie, a silent short-haired woman, petite, but with the lean frame of a kickboxer. “I used to be homeless,” she said. “I had friends who disappeared.”

Graham. That’s all he said. Judging by his buzzcut haircut and stonewashed jeans he was the cop.

The last one was a forty-something man with spiky grey hair and an equally spiky glare. “Tommy Gallacher,” he said. I realised he was Malky Gallacher’s brother.

As we moved into the graveyard I made a quiet count – four are in it for the thrills, two for a story, and two for revenge. It’s a pretty good ratio.

I led them all up to the back corner of the graveyard and to the Sutherland mausoleum. I stepped forward and dragged back the ancient gate. From my own rucksack I took out my headlamp – purchased that morning at a climbing shop in the New Town – and clicked it on. The beam carved into the darkness and revealed the two plinths covered with a scatter of wood and bone fragments. I tilted my head and saw the wall fall away at the back, the light dissipating into the darkness that led down to the river.

We climbed down the stairs in single file, the dank smell all around us. At the foot of the steps the river flowed sludgily to our left – a relatively dry week meant the water was shallow, easy to wade through. I motioned everyone to follow me and we worked our way steadily through the tunnel. It was exactly as I remembered it – a crude channel, slicked with algae, crumbling brickwork.

The last human presence here had most likely been me all those years ago.

After fifteen minutes we reached the familiar riverbank. One by one we climbed up, careful not to make too much noise. Neve led the way into the corridor. We passed the small room that the giant had used as his den, and it looked the same – a chair, table, crushed beer cans, sandwich containers. Neve exchanged a glance with me, as if to say: *it's still happening*.

We paused at the entrance to the Chamber. Everything was utterly still. The chairs were laid out ready for the following day.

We fanned out, the urban explorers muttering in awe, the others quieter. Neve walked with purpose towards the claret room. I found her standing in front of the cabinet, its shelves still full with bottles, the carved snakes and dragons and screeching birds peering down at us from high above.

"Let's get started," she said.

We called the others through. The smallest of the urban explorers, a lean and wiry Scouser, scampered up to the top level of the grand cabinet and prised open the glass doors. His fellow explorers organised themselves on the lower levels, balancing on the narrow mahogany ledges, and forming a human chain, they passed the bottles down to us where we in turn carried them out into the main chamber until we had emptied the cabinet. It took us more than an hour. The bottles stood in the middle of the floor, maybe a hundred or so, lined up like misshapen bowling pins. Then the next step – we formed another human chain, this time to the river. Neve and I headed up the human snake, responsible for emptying the bottles into the stream. With pocketknives we cut the wax seals, prised out the corks, and held the bottles over the water, the wine glugging out, splashing into the green water and slithering away into the underground darkness. Before long the riverbank stank of spilled wine and something else, a sharp chemical taint that made my eyes water.

And then it was done. All the bottles emptied.

We returned to the Chamber and showed the others the upstairs section – the small balcony, the other rooms. They dumped their stuff, unravelled sleeping bags, made themselves comfortable. The urban explorers were hyperactive, ducking into the labyrinth of corridors, taking photos, whispering to each other in secret code. Neve hushed them.

As Neve and I prepared to leave back through the river tunnel, we found Bob sitting on one of the chairs in the middle of the Chamber. "So this is it," he said.

"You'll keep the others focused?"

He nodded. "Plan A. Project Daylight."

Neve was already trudging back towards the riverbank. We waded upstream in silence, the cold getting into my bones now. By the time we climbed back up through the Sutherland tomb and out into the Edinburgh night it was after nine. Beyond the graveyard, the city glimmered. We weaved back through the headstones and reached the gate. I gave Neve a footie-up and she jumped over. It was harder for me, two attempts, but eventually I scrambled up and over. We got a dirty look from a passing couple but otherwise the street was quiet.

The plan was in motion.

Gow's yell of rage. Other shouts join in. The giant runs towards the noise and after a few seconds something moves in the shadows. It's Bob, emerging towards me with his Swiss Army knife. He cuts the plastic strips that bind me to the chair. More movements in the shadows, and one by one the posse emerges. Gallacher is at the front, holding a bulky metal bar.

Our army is ready.

We prepared it meticulously in the last few days – Bob the archives geek, and me the data nerd.

Step 1: Bob wrote a twenty-page history of the Chamber's activity, the known murders and missing, naming all the known Chamberites with their addresses and personal details, neatly formatted and saved in PDF ready to be sent to fifteen newspapers and available for download on his blog.

Step 2: I called an old friend from New York, a Filipino-American social media whizz-kid called Bernadette Lopez, and briefed her on the project. Once we were ready with our photos and scandalous blurb, she would work her special voodoo to push the content to the forefront of Twitter and Facebook, game the analytics to push the Chamber's secrets to the top of millions of feeds, force the glaring truth down the throat of random Twitter twats and Facebook fuckers for weeks on end. #devilschamber. I transferred two grand to her account as a first instalment.

Step 3: Bob briefed the army on the plan and explained in detail how it would satisfy their curiosity or hunger for revenge. They were all to be ready to square up to the Chamberites, match them in number, and take as many photos as they could of the Chamber and its denizens to share on social media for the benefit of the outside world.

Step 4: The big assumption. We were gambling that in a square go, Chamberites versus Team Daylight, there would be no dead bodies, maybe a scuffle and some blood spilled, but that we would all get out in one piece. Apart from the giant, these were men who knew how to order a killing but would not have the physical presence to harm any of us. They always paid others to kill. So once we'd gathered our content and made our presence felt, we would depart back through the tunnel to hit return on our collective keyboards.

With all of the above, daylight would be let in on magic, and even if the Chamberites used their massive cash reserves to employ contract killers to come after us, the truth would catch up with them before they could respond. Or so we hoped.

Gow is still shouting.

There is a strange moment as we all pause, alone in the main chamber. Bob snaps us out of it and ushers us forward and we move towards the corridor with the grand cabinet.

The Chamberites are all there, standing in front of the massive structure. Empty shelves. Gow is shouting at the giant, who is climbing up onto the first shelf. I see why – we missed one bottle, which peeks out of the emptiness, a black neck jutting upwards like a headless goose. The giant heaves his massive frame up, pauses for breath, and then fumbles for a fingerhold on the second shelf. They scream at him to climb higher. He reaches the second shelf, and Neve's hand closes on my arm.

She has seen it first. A wobble, high up, the entire structure tilting away from the wall, the giant's bulk bringing forth a quiet justice. He reaches up for the third shelf and a loud creak tears through the underground gloom. Some of the Chamberites look up. Sutherland is still yelling at the giant as if he's a racehorse behind the frontrunners.

It is almost graceful when it happens: the giant heaves himself up onto the third shelf and the huge cabinet tips forward, ominous and silent, a tree falling in a forest that nobody knows about. The Chamberites stand as one watching it tilt towards them – Sutherland stops yelling, as if for a brief moment struck dumb, fascinated by the spectacle of what's about to happen. The giant swings outwards and his bulk plummets towards the eight men awaiting their claret.

In one great splintering crash, the cabinet falls on the Chamberites. Wood and glass shatter and scatter; dust ripples upwards in a billowing cloud, unfurling against the walls, spewing debris and shrapnel skittering off the stonework. The noise is astonishing, thunderclap upon thunderclap, the walls trembling.

After the crash – silence. In the aftermath, there is an uneasy quiet, and a fog of dust slowly fading.

Gallacher is the first to speak. “Fuck me.” He drops the metal bar onto the floor.

I walk over to the rubble. At one side, a glistening puddle is leaking out, the trickle of blood running in a steady rivulet along a crack in the floor.

A chunk of stone falls next to me and explodes into fragments.

“Get out!” shouts Neve.

A scatter of cement crumbs sprinkles my head. I turn and run for it. More pieces fall from the ceiling and as I run with the others towards the river the slam and clatter of the falling ceiling shakes the ground under our feet. By the time we reach the river the noise behind us drowns out everything else, a waterfall of tumbling stone obliterating Sutherland and Gow’s secret project forever.

EPILOGUE

White sand at my feet. A clump of seaweed like a discarded wig. The voices move on ahead, but I stay here, staring at my feet. A razorshell juts out, half-buried, and I step on it, enjoying its frail crumpling.

Real sand. I nudge the toe of my Blundstone boot into the fine grain and dig a tiny hole. Real sand, not like the fake beaches of Sentosa in Singapore, where the shores once ran thick with blood of massacred locals, the killing grounds of the occupying Japanese troops converted seventy years later into a holiday resort. I liked Singapore, but that beach never felt right to me. The sand had an oily and gritty feel to it, and the container ships looming on the horizon beyond the palm trees didn't fool anyone.

Now *this* – this is a beach. My gaze moves up from the sand and out to where the North Sea churns and breaks. A trawler bobs on the skyline, and it gets me thinking of fish and chips. Maybe we'll do that later – walk down to the harbour and have a sit-down supper at Giovanni's. Freshly caught haddock doused in excessive salt and malt vinegar.

"Miro! Miro!"

They are all yelling.

Fergus's voice booms out the loudest. "Snap out of it, man!"

My family, standing with their backs to the wind, smiling at me. Aunt Sarah, six months a widow but smiling again; Fergus, dressed in jeans and trainers twenty years too young for him; Kirsty and her partner Stephanie, recently married and back living in Edinburgh. And standing at the edge, my Hannah, and her daughter Chloe.

After that day in the Devil's Chamber, we all emerged back into daylight through the Sutherland tomb, our top halves covered in white dust and our bottom halves drenched from the underground river. Gallacher had a look of quiet satisfaction. The urban explorers could barely contain their excitement.

"This never happened," Bob told us. I hugged Neve and wished her and Kerry well. She told me that I was now free to live my life as I always intended it. I told her that was my plan. I also told her to give Jackson Tillburg a buzz. We all went our separate ways, our underground army dispersing, and I stood outside the cemetery on my own, in shock, struggling to believe that it might finally be over.

The cold finally got me moving. I went down to Waverley and picked up my stuff from left luggage. In the station toilets I washed the worst of the dust off and walked over to the Royal Mile and on towards Dumbiedykes. The Holyrood Tavern was still there, now called Holyrood 9A. Inside, the pub had been gentrified but was recognisable from the 90s version. I sat at the bar and ordered an IPA and a chicken burger. Ravenous after those underground hours, I demolished the burger and racked up another two empty pint glasses. As the afternoon light waned, I held my own private wake for the lost: Danny Gunn, Harry Robertson, Doug and Jeannie Pebbles, and all the hundreds of unknown others over the last two centuries. By the fourth pint the stress had leaked out of me and exhaustion was creeping in. Something else too – a feeling that Edinburgh had been reclaimed. It was a place I could be in again without fear. I caught the train to Fife and watched the dark fields speed by.

The taxi dropped me at the end of the street and I snuck in the back door at Gull View, showered and changed into fresh clothes. I wrote a quick email to Bernadette Lopez telling her to cancel the social media blitz for #devilschamber. I walked out the village onto the coast road towards Hannah's parents' place. It was like she was waiting for me – as I walked up the driveway she opened the door and just stood there, smiling. I told her I had some news. She would see me around a bit more. I was going to move back to Scotland.

I flew back to Singapore. Resigned from the job ("family reasons") and worked out my notice, enjoying those last days sitting on terraces at Boat Quay, eating chilli crab and drinking ice-cold Tiger. I moved back and bought an apartment in Edinburgh in the first week – the first property I'd owned since my Lothian House flat. And since then, for six months, I have dated Hannah step by tentative step. Meals, cinema trips, drinks; then up a level to include Chloe – days out in Edinburgh, then more frequently up to Fife to meet the families. I have not worked in that time, and it's been good to have a break, escape the subterranean lakes of data waiting to be filtered and purified.

I heard from Bob last week. He texted and asked to meet for a beer at The Guildford. A flutter of fear caught in my throat when I walked through the door, but then it was gone again. A regular pub full of regular people, with nothing underneath it anymore. Over a half-pint of pale ale, Bob asked if I'd been following the news in recent months. I shook my head and told him I'd been actively avoiding local news. He passed me his phone. "There are three articles," he said. "Start with this one."

Dated three days after that final trip into the Devil's Chamber, an Evening Times article headlined MY HALLUCINATION HELL, about an Edinburgh Council environmental services worker, who, while testing water quality at a plant on the outskirts of the city inhaled 'chemical fumes' and experienced several hours of wild hallucinations before coming round again face down in the car park. There was speculation about a drug gang dumping their supplies down a nearby drain, and a phone number at the end of the article for anyone with further information.

I toggled to the next session. A Daily Record article about the mysterious disappearance of several Edinburgh businessmen, with a focus on James Sutherland and an interview with his wife, photographed sitting in their 'glamorous townhouse.' She explained that 'James was very private about his business interests' and the article mentioned some tenuous connections between Sutherland and a notorious gangster operating in the city, and hinted that the 'loosely affiliated businessmen' had met their end due to a 'deal gone wrong.'

The final one, another from the Evening News three weeks ago – SINKHOLE TERROR ON EDINBURGH BUILDING SITE. On the site of the nearby St James centre renovation a digger and heavy machinery had plunged ten metres through the ground into what appeared to be an underground tunnel, 'perhaps the workings of a sixteenth-century mine.' Mercifully nobody had been hurt.

"I'm reading the papers every day and that's it," said Bob. "Three articles. Maybe that's the last of it."

We spent a quiet hour peering into our drinks.

The Chamber has gone, but something has replaced it in the darkness. I have not slept well since that last visit underground, and often wake fighting the sheets, imagining I am suffocating under tons of rubble. The thousands of deaths down the decades, and the workings of all that dark money – that knowledge squeezes down on me in the lost hours of night. Those secrets will die with me and a few others. But I have lived with worse for the past twenty years. Now I am with my family, and Hannah. This is a fortress, not easily breached.

The dog sprints towards me over the rippled beach, and weaves away at the last second, then doubles back and bounds past, almost tripping me. I trudge on through the sand – until, to everyone's mocking encouragement I finally catch up, hook my arm around Hannah, and join the group again, walking back to the harbour, back towards home.

A HUMBLE REQUEST

Dear Reader

Thanks for reading The Devil's Chamber. I hope you enjoyed it. You might also like my first novel Amsterdam Rampant, also available on Amazon.

As an indie author I lack the marketing machinery of the giant publishing houses, and knowledge of my book spreads mostly through word of mouth. In order to build a profile, I need online reviews. So if you could please spare a moment, I would really appreciate a review on Amazon and/or Goodreads. Even if you didn't like the book, go ahead and share your views – any review helps me get better next time. I'm in this game for life!

Thanks, and all the best
Neil

PS. I've been blogging about the whole process of epublishing, if you're interested you can read more here: http://ncocker.wordpress.com/

PPS. To find out more about the origins of The Devil's Chamber, go ahead and turn the page…

AUTHOR'S NOTE

Born a mutant. Struck by lightning. Injected with serum, bombarded by gamma rays, bitten by a radioactive spider.

Superheroes have straightforward origin stories.

Novels, not so much.

The idea for The Devil's Chamber had niggled at me for a long time without having any clear form. I lived in Edinburgh for seven years and it's a place that haunts the imagination. Gothic churches, hidden alleyways, basement pubs; tendrils of sea fog slithering around the buildings and blurring out the streetlights; cobbled roads intersecting messily with tarmac, the ancient criss-crossing the modern. A stroll through the city can be a breath-taking exercise in transformation – you can be walking under slate skies past a row of dour tenements and in the gloom the city looks like a sprawling necropolis; then the clouds part, sunlight spills onto the buildings, and Edinburgh sparkles, a granite spaceship flying through azure-blue skies.

The idea of Edinburgh as a schizophrenic city torn between light and dark has preoccupied Scottish writers for centuries. Most famously, Robert Louis Stevenson was inspired by Edinburgh's two faces when writing The Strange Case of Dr Jekyll & Mr Hyde – even though the novel was set in London, the dynamic of a grand old Enlightenment city famed for its scientists and doctors overtaken after dark by the shadows of criminality is a perfect mirror image of Victorian Edinburgh. Even the city's geography has always reflected that duality – in Stevenson's era, the New Town, set out in grids and crescents, represented 'British' Edinburgh, educated and Protestant and law-abiding; on the other side of the city, the Medieval Old Town was 'the Other': tumbledown slums inhabited by poor Catholic Irish and Highlanders, mazy backstreets teeming with pubs and brothels, a warren of sin.

So I knew I wanted to write a dark Edinburgh novel that danced with the supernatural, something that invoked the spirit of Jekyll and Hyde without being cliched. But I didn't know how I would remix those elements of plot, character and setting to conjure up something fresh. Other influences lingered in the shadows: Donna Tartt's weird and wonderful novel The Secret History about Classics students at a New England college accessing a savage Ancient Greek underworld; the modern Scottish Gothic novels of Iain Banks; the snappy dialogue and rollercoaster narratives of the Netflix shows I loved; and all of this mish-mash soundtracked by the alternative Scottish bands seeping into my brain through my earphones – Mogwai, King Creosote, Sluts of Trust, Arab Strap, Frightened Rabbit, Meursault.

In January 2016 I was back in Edinburgh to see family. I had an hour to kill before meeting my brother and dropped into the Guildford Arms for a pint. It's one of many Edinburgh pubs I've always loved, and as I sat there in the afternoon quiet, peering at the sliding door next to the bar which surely led to the cellar, something crystallised. I suddenly saw it – a stairway beneath my feet leading to a cavern lit by a weird luminescence. The Devil's Chamber.

That image provided the spark. Next I had to build a story around that mental picture.

The idea first began to take shape when I thought back on the jobs I'd done at the end of the last century.

During the 90s I worked in a series of dead-end office jobs that took me down Edinburgh side streets into decrepit Edwardian buildings where time seemed to have stood still. To the established staff us office temps were holograms of a kind, there but not there, not really worth getting to know, so we did our data entry and envelope stuffing in silence, then emerged from grey days into the glimmering city thirsty for adventure. And when you're thirsty, what do you do? You drink.

My circle of friends all had this in common – we worked in jobs we didn't like and were overeducated for, we struggled to understand the materialism of the older generations, and we lived in tenement buildings that were invariably cold and unwelcoming outside of the summer months. The city's pubs were warm and cosy and offered excitement and escapism. When you're young and bored, drinking is a daredevil catalyst for change, a way to inject chaos into stagnancy. Back in the 90s, my Edinburgh group's binge drinking brought all manner of chaos and opportunity – love affairs and breakups, street fights and new friendships, injuries and lucky escapes, the fork in the road that can lead to a new way forward or a dark cul-de-sac. For a writer alcohol can be an accelerant for story and character development and in The Devil's Chamber I embraced it. Much like in Robert Burns' famous poem Tam O'Shanter, I wanted alcohol (and the claret) to lead the characters astray and ultimately transform their lives.

Mark Gallacher, one of my beta readers for The Devil's Chamber, correctly pointed out that the characters spend too much time in pubs and drink way too much too quickly. He helped me fix many timing errors (e.g. two pints drunk during around 30 seconds of dialogue, which even for my friends was a bit too much). But I didn't change the backdrop of pubs as a key setting for the novel because I wanted to preserve that dynamic of alcohol-soaked chaos that felt representative of Edinburgh in the late 90s.

So I knew The Devil's Chamber would be a boozy Edinburgh novel, and the city's pubs would provide a multitude of theatre stages. I also knew that it needed to be set in the 90s. One practical reason was that I lived there in the 90s, so my memories of the city are frozen in that time. But I also think that it's a fascinating decade, a hinge in history between a twentieth century of war and heavy industry and consumerism, and a twenty-first century of terrorism and social media and existential dread. My generation lived our formative years with a foot on each ledge.

I wanted to include that underrated moment in history when the internet slowly became 'a thing' – and drip-feed that change into one of those workplaces that hadn't changed for decades. So Miro is starting to find a niche in archives and data that will shape the trajectory of his life; but the internet is like a magic portal only available at specific locations, and meanwhile the old world of rigid working hours and paper memos and jobs-that-last-for-decades dominates.

Miro's backstory developed further. At my high school in Fife, there was usually at least one kid in every class with a Polish surname – the idea of him as the grandson of a Polish paratrooper gave his character a foundation block that I built his family story around. Hundreds of Polish soldiers settled in Scotland after World War Two, unable to return home as the socialist regime in Poland viewed them as traitors. That melancholy and cultural dislocation would prove to be important in shaping Miro's story.

All of this was bubbling in my head but I hadn't started writing yet. I had been studying for a postgraduate degree that took up my weekends, and along with a busy day job, I was struggling for the headspace to make a start. Eventually in October 2016 I submitted my degree project. Around the same time my wife Anna was offered a short-term secondment to New York, and I would join her for three weeks. We left Luxembourg in early November and arrived in a city boiling over with election fever.

I started writing the novel on Anna's first day at work. From the hotel window I could see the silver tip of the Chrysler building; the double glazing couldn't do much to keep out the clamour of traffic and police sirens and construction noises. In the lobby of the hotel there was a huge vat of filter coffee, and I jumped in the lift regularly for a top-up. By the afternoon I'd written two thousand words, and the novel was hatching.

My days formed a pattern – I wrote in the hotel in the mornings, then most days took the short walk to the New York Public Library to write there in the afternoons. The city was in tumult – Trump had just been elected, and protests were erupting all around. When I wasn't writing, I walked around Manhattan, just picked a direction and kept going until I got tired or stumbled across something interesting. In Irish pubs, I sipped IPA and typed notes on my iPhone; in old churches I sat and rested my feet and let my ideas settle. By the time I left New York I had written ten thousand words.

The creative process of writing a novel often reflects a certain period or chapter in a writer's life. The Devil's Chamber began with Trump's election, and I finished the last version of the manuscript just as Biden was sworn in as the 46th president. This period was also bookended by the aftermath of the Brexit vote and the exit of the UK from the European Union, an event which caused me (a British citizen resident in Luxembourg) considerable stress. Writing The Devil's Chamber through these years – the rise of populism and fake news, a sense of being helpless in the face of unchecked power – undoubtedly influenced the novel's villains and their use of dark money to shape the world.

On a personal level, I lived through a difficult time at work and had to cope with serious health issues. No matter what I was dealing with, I dedicated at least two hours every weekend to writing. The wordcount slowly accumulated. We got a rescue dog, Pokémon, who introduced such fun and joy into our lives. We bought a house and undertook a major renovation. I started learning Luxembourgish in order to gain nationality and protect my status as a European citizen. The workload was relentless and overwhelming, but still I kept chipping away. By 2018 I had a first draft.

During our summer holiday I read a printed copy on the terrace at an Air BnB bungalow in Provence, turning the first page in the pale afternoon sunlight and continuing into dusk and the steady song of crickets. I was pleased with the first draft – it hung together – but it was missing something. I farmed it out to my oldest writer buddy, Mat Tate, and he was positive – but he wanted more menace, more intrigue, more conflict. The answers came to me piece-by-piece. Firstly, I realised I had been holding back from the supernatural, 'unrealistic' elements of the storyline. Watching the Netflix show Stranger Things helped me overcome this. In the next draft I had fun writing about the 'spooky' stuff. As part of this, I added something that was obvious in retrospect – Miro and his fellow explorers should drink the claret. This added danger and tension, and their dream trips unlocked a richer, more complex story.

The pieces began to slot into place. We moved into the new house. Work and health stabilised. We got a second rescue dog, Kangaroo. The Covid-19 pandemic took hold. One advantage of lockdown, I thought, would be more time for writing. But I was spending so much time in zoom calls in the day job that I couldn't face the glowing screen outside of work. It took me some time to re-establish the discipline and knuckle down at the weekends again.

I shared the second draft with Mat and Mark, who came back with their customary incisive feedback. My old university friend Jonny Foulkes read it and WhatsApped me his thoughts and ideas. I gave Anna a copy and she returned it with words of praise, but also scribbled notes and big chunks crossed out. Chapters and characters disappeared, lazy language was deleted; eight thousand words lighter, the final draft began to solidify.

As I rewrote the ending of the novel, 2020 – the most turbulent year in living memory – came to an end. A few days after the ceiling fell in on the Chamberites, rioters stormed the US Capitol. My weekends then involved perhaps my favourite stage of the process – shutting myself in the study and reading the novel out loud like a deranged poet. This does two useful things for me: firstly, you immediately notice where the novel's voice works well and where it doesn't; secondly, it taps into the oral tradition of Scottish literature and brings the text to life, like reciting a resurrection spell. So I recited and edited and at the same time I sourced the cover artwork. Suddenly I could see and hear the novel.

And now, I sit by the window in the spring sunshine, looking out at the budding cherry blossom, getting ready to hit the big green PUBLISH button. The process of creating The Devil's Chamber has come to a close, and with it the completion of another chapter in my life. A lot happened over those four years while I typed and rewrote and deleted and reworked. Similar to life itself, novel writing has to be done forwards and understood backwards.

There are many things I'm grateful for.

You need some tough love from your beta readers when you write a novel, and I got it in spades. Thank you, Mark, for highlighting the plot holes and nudging me in the right direction. Thanks to Mat for reading and reviewing both the early version and the late version and providing all those line edits and comments. Mat has now edited and reviewed three of my novels (and I three of his) and it's like he reads my mind sometimes. It's been a while now since we got together in Amsterdam to discuss writing and books and life over curry and pints, and I look forward to the days when that's possible again.

To my wife Anna I owe the most gratitude. Living with a writer isn't easy. Writers get grouchy if distracted from our daydreams, and mope like teenagers when things aren't going to plan. Writers dedicate large chunks of their lives to building imaginary things, which to outsiders may appear to be a kind of mental illness. Anna has always been patient, encouraging, focused on the bigger picture, and a total believer. I have not always been those things. She pulls me back from the edge, pats me on the shoulder, nudges me back on course, and keeps me on the straight and narrow. In my day job I work in the tech sector, where unusual job titles increasingly proliferate. To borrow one, Anna is my Chief Vision Officer. Not just for writing, but for life. Thank you.

Anna is Polish, so was also able to sense check my creation of Miro's backstory. Much like the ancestors of my Fife schoolmates, her great uncle parachuted into

Arnhem and survived the maelstrom. I wrote the paratrooper scene in part as a tribute to all those young men who jumped into darkness and left old lives behind.

Unlike poor Miro, I have been blessed with great parents who have always been there for me throughout my life. Miro's family story of grief and loss and sadness is not my story – this author made it all up. Immersing yourself in someone else's pain is educational and made me count my blessings.

What's next?

First, I'll take a break from writing for a little while. That mad urge to tell stories needs to grow back organically. There is already an idea that's following me around, snapping at my heels – and it came out of my garage.

The previous owner of our house explained that the lower part of the structure was originally a farm building, and in 1944 it was sequestered to barrack U.S. soldiers following the liberation of Luxembourg. Sometimes, in the shadows of my garage, I'll lean on the rough stone wall and imagine those dozen or so young men here, cursing the discomfort, smoking, playing cards, writing letters, thinking maybe that they were through the worst of it. Not knowing that within two months they will be sucked into the nightmare of the Battle of the Bulge, fighting hand to hand combat in snowy forests. Many of them no doubt did not survive.

Their ghosts are calling to me, and maybe I will start writing their story sooner rather than later.

But first I need to walk the dogs.

Printed in Great Britain
by Amazon

82825617R00190